TRUE
COURAGE

*Also by Dee Henderson
in Large Print:*

True Devotion
True Valor
Danger in the Shadows
The Negotiator (Published in Spanish as
    el Negociador)
The Guardian

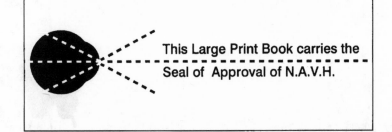

Book Four in the
Uncommon Heroes Series

TRUE
COURAGE

Dee Henderson

Walker Large Print • Waterville, Maine

Published in 2005 by arrangement with Multnomah Publishers, Inc.

The text of this Large Print edition is unabridged. Other aspects of the book may vary from the original edition.

Set in 16 pt. Plantin by Minnie B. Raven.

Printed in the United States on permanent paper.

The Library of Congress has cataloged the Thorndike Press® edition as follows:

Henderson, Dee.
    True courage / by Dee Henderson.
       p. cm. — (Uncommon heroes series ; bk. 4)
(Thorndike Press large print Christian fiction)
    ISBN 0-7862-7432-8 (lg. print : hc : alk. paper)
    ISBN 1-59415-079-6 (lg. print : sc : alk. paper)
    1. Government investigators — Fiction.   2. Kidnapping — Fiction.   3. Large type books.   I. Title.   II. Thorndike Press large print Christian fiction series.
PS3558.E4829T777 2005
813'.54—dc22   2004031059

moved out of earshot. "I'm working a murder case. Life is a bit hectic today."

"I'll be glad to save you a place if you need to go make some calls."

"They can wait." Luke looked tired. It wasn't in his posture or expression but in his eyes.

She found her own nervousness disappearing and in its place a comfortable concern starting to bloom. They would see each other for decades to come at family gatherings; he was safe to treat as family. "Then you must come over to the restaurant. It will be quieter, and you can have something more substantial to eat for dinner than cake."

"I'll do that. It was a beautiful wedding, Caroline. You did a nice job."

She felt a blush start and hated the fast warmth. "Thanks, I enjoyed helping Sharon put it together."

He just smiled at her demur. Someone had been telling him details she thought were private. Sharon had needed to work more hours on call at the hospital in order to get time off for the honeymoon, and Caroline had been able to stagger her summer job hours so she could help with wedding preparations. Making it a perfect day had been her gift to her sister. She spend much time with them either treated her eight-year-old nephew as if he were half that age or expected him to behave with the maturity of a young adult.

"You would make a great lawman one day," she concurred, brushing Benjamin's honey brown hair back from his forehead with a quick swipe and dislodging the confetti. "I'm afraid your mom needs us for a few more pictures in the chapel."

"More? They already took a hundred."

"Just a few more. Then she said you could lose the coat and tie."

"About time."

Mark laughed and held out his hand. "Come on, buddy. We'll go help your mom look beautiful."

Caroline risked meeting Luke's gaze. The man was still watching, a slight smile playing around his mouth. "You're welcome to join us. We'll be moving over to the restaurant after the pictures are complete, and I think —"

His pager went off, interrupting her. "My apologies." He glanced at the number but didn't make a move to return the call. "You were saying?"

"Just that it will be a bit less chaotic." She nodded to the pager. "Trouble?"

He looked to make sure Benjamin had

"Every one then who hears these words of mine and does them will be like a wise man who built his house upon the rock; and the rain fell, and the floods came, and the winds blew and beat upon that house, but it did not fall, because it had been founded on the rock."

Matthew 7:24–25

As the Founder/CEO of NAVH, the only national health agency solely devoted to those who, although not totally blind, have an eye disease which could lead to serious visual impairment, I am pleased to recognize Thorndike Press* as one of the leading publishers in the large print field.

Founded in 1954 in San Francisco to prepare large print textbooks for partially seeing children, NAVH became the pioneer and standard setting agency in the preparation of large type.

Today, those publishers who meet our standards carry the prestigious "Seal of Approval" indicating high quality large print. We are delighted that Thorndike Press is one of the publishers whose titles meet these standards. We are also pleased to recognize the significant contribution Thorndike Press is making in this important and growing field.

Lorraine H. Marchi, L.H.D.
Founder/CEO
NAVH

* Thorndike Press encompasses the following imprints: Thorndike, Wheeler, Walker and Large Print Press.

Prologue

Wedding guests crowded the reception hall, and the accumulated noise made it hard to carry on a conversation. Caroline shielded her sister's wedding dress sleeve from a guest turning abruptly with a piece of chocolate cake. She wished she could convince Sharon to find a place to sit for a minute instead of circling the room greeting every guest again. Caroline leaned in toward Sharon. "Who's the man talking with Mark?"

Her sister looked around people to see who her new husband was speaking with. "The good-looking guy in the tux and black tie? Mark's cousin, Luke Falcon."

Caroline's interest was piqued. Luke stood taller than most around him, watching the gathering, even as he held a glass and gestured occasionally as he spoke. Twice in the last ten minutes he had made a point of turning to keep track of where

7

she and Sharon were in the crowd. He was probably keeping track of Sharon rather than herself, but it was still disconcerting.

Even from across the room she was aware the scrutiny came with neither a smile nor a frown; he just studied. It reminded her of the first days of a school term as wary students scoped out their new teacher.

"The cousin who's an FBI agent?" Caroline asked. If Luke had gray eyes to go with that thick black hair, curling just a bit around his temples, and a pleasant voice to listen to, she knew what she would decide about him. She already liked what she knew about him by reputation.

"Yes. Luke arrived about twenty minutes before the ceremony; I heard his flight got delayed by bad weather." Sharon picked up a piece of wedding cake from the refreshment table. Caroline gratefully accepted an offered cup of punch, her throat dry from the nonstop exchange of greetings.

"The photographer wants a few more wedding pictures in the chapel before we move over to the restaurant for the evening," Sharon said. "Could you find Benjamin for me?"

"I can try." Her nephew was incredibly proud of the fact he'd been allowed to stand up with Sharon and Mark and hold the rings for them. He wasn't so thrilled at the realization that he had to wear the suit and tie even after the ceremony. Caroline wouldn't be surprised to find Benjamin had made an escape to less confining surroundings once his duties were done.

She left Sharon at the refreshment table with the minister's wife and started the search. Small boys were not easy to locate in a sea of adults. Benjamin had slipped behind some chairs to join Mark and Luke, his tie still on but tugged loose, and what looked like a stack of baseball cards in his hand.

Relieved to spot him, Caroline headed across the room. Mark saw her coming and leaned down to say something to Benjamin. Moments later her nephew came to meet her, parting the adults in his way like a general going into battle. "I'm to rescue you."

"Good, I need rescuing." She let him catch her hand and tug her toward the guys.

"Mr. Luke, this is my aunt Carol."

She wasn't ready for the instant introduction, but she smiled and offered her hand. "Caroline Lane."

"Hello, Caroline. Luke Falcon," he re-

9

plied, shifting his glass to free his hand.

Baritone — a really nice baritone that had a mellow smoothness and matched his nice smile. She liked it instantly. She held his gaze as he took her hand and she liked what she saw: realistic, grounded. He must have seen too much in his job to have the eyes of a dreamer. Luke was taller than she had realized and not quite as handsome as she first thought. Too much living showed on his face.

When he released her hand, she wrapped both of hers around her glass of punch and realized it was time to take a breath. He looked good in the tux, relaxed. No one should be that comfortable in a tux. He was studying her again, but in a casual way, having apparently made up his mind about her.

She glanced at Mark, quickly smiled, and looked down at her nephew, much more at ease with someone a third of Luke's age.

Benjamin slid a badge bigger than his hand into his suit pocket so it rested shield out. "Aunt Carol, I'm going to be a lawman too."

"It looks great." And it looked real. She silently gave Luke credit for being comfortable around kids. Adults who didn't hadn't realized others would hear about her efforts though.

"Mark's happy. It's nice to see," Luke said.

"So is Sharon."

"Benjamin mentioned he gets to spend the next week with you?"

Caroline nodded. "We're going on day trips to a nearby ranch to ride horses."

"An ideal vacation for a young man." Luke set down his glass and tugged a pen from his pocket. He wrote a number on his napkin and offered it to her. "If you need anything in the next week, call me. I'll be back at my Sandy Hill home for the foreseeable future. Just in case Benjamin tumbles off one of those mighty steeds as he does battle with imaginary dragons. Mark and Sharon will be more than a few hours away."

"I appreciate it." She memorized the number as she folded the napkin in her hand. "Benjamin is serious about the badge and the idea of being a lawman. I'm sure he'll be asking you some questions over dinner."

"He already asked if I would teach him to shoot."

"And what did you say?"

He smiled. "Ask Sharon."

Caroline ran her tongue around her teeth. "Smart man. I need to go get my picture taken."

"Hmm. I'd like one."

"A wedding picture?"

"That too. If you keep blushing like that, the photographer will get a wonderful photo."

"You're not supposed to notice."

"That would be a shame."

She smiled back at him, unable to resist his subtle flirting. "You can comment then."

He offered his arm. "Let me see you safely to the chapel."

She rested her hand on his jacket sleeve. Her long dress made walking with a natural stride impossible, but he adjusted to the constraint from the first step. The crowd parted for them. At the door to the chapel, Luke's pager went off again. Caroline slid her hand from his arm. "They'll just keep trying to get your attention. You might as well make your calls. I'll make sure we wait for you."

He looked at the number on the pager. "Unfortunately true. Go finish your work of the day while I finish mine, and then come keep me company tonight so we can talk without distractions."

She wasn't used to someone so swiftly claiming her time, but she laughed, appreciating it and him. "I'll do that." She smiled as she walked into the chapel, wondering just how much of her own life was about to change as a result of this wedding day. She wasn't one for taking great adventures, but occasionally — a little diving into the deep end of life might get interesting, and she was in a mood tonight to find out.

"Would you like to walk awhile?" Luke leaned down to be heard as he paused behind her chair at the restaurant table.

The bride and groom were away, and the guests were dispersing. Caroline nodded. She needed to stretch her legs and get some fresh air before she called it an evening. It was either accept the invitation or admit to herself she was too flustered by his attention to do so.

He held her chair for her, caught up his jacket from the back of his chair, and said good night for them both. The hotel where she was staying adjoined the restaurant, and Luke escorted her through the restaurant to the garden path connecting the two buildings.

He'd waited for her in the hotel lobby

earlier while she went up and changed from her wedding finery to something more comfortable for the evening meal. He had left his tie in the car and turned up the sleeves of his white shirt to his elbows and relaxed, while she had just lost her bravery.

"I learned a lot about Sharon and Benjamin at dinner. Now tell me about Caroline Lane."

Caroline wasn't sure how to answer. "There's not much to tell. I grew up in Benton, went away to college to get my teaching degree, and returned to Benton when I graduated. I've been teaching fifth grade at a private Christian school ever since."

She caught his smile at how she summarized her life. "You love to teach."

She glanced away to inspect the flowers along the garden path. "Yes. I grew up thinking of myself as a teacher, the same way my sister wanted to be a doctor." He didn't ask another question, and she tried again to get him to talk about himself. So far this evening he'd smoothly turned aside questions by other guests at dinner. "Did you always want to be in law enforcement?"

"I like making the world a safer place." His smile reminded her of Mark's — self-knowing, touched with humor. "That makes being an FBI agent sound grander than it is, but the job suits me. There aren't a lot of gray areas to crime." He gestured to the bench up ahead, and she moved that direction, taking a seat.

She noted that while he said the job suited him, he hadn't added that he enjoyed it. She knew it couldn't be that pleasant, the way his days unfolded. He'd come to the wedding with a murder investigation underway, and even through dinner he'd received two more pages. It was obvious that when he was quiet, his thoughts hadn't been on the conversations around him but rather on the details of a case that left him looking grim. "It's nice to have this day over; it's been long."

"Very. Do you think Sharon and Mark getting married was a good idea?"

She turned startled eyes toward him. "Don't you?"

"It's just a question, Caroline." He stretched out his legs and folded his hands across his chest, relaxing as he had earlier when talking with Benjamin, like a load was shifting off his shoulders.

"It took Sharon a long time to get over the death of her first husband, and as time passed, I wondered if she'd ever want to move on. Mark — he made her laugh again like I hadn't heard in a long time. Sharon enjoys being married, being a wife. So yes, I think it will be a good marriage. They love each other a lot."

"My cousin has been career focused since college. He waited so long to marry, I admit I was surprised when I got his call. I understood once I met Sharon. Mark already loves Benjamin like his own."

Maybe it was the day and the direction of her thoughts today, but Luke sounded wistful. Caroline hesitated but asked the burning question anyway. "Have you ever been married?"

She knew so little about Luke Falcon. While Mark had mentioned him often and spoke highly of the man, his remarks hadn't included many hard facts.

"No. I came close back in college, but the timing never seemed to work out. Jenny and I dated through high school and college, but I ended up going to one coast and her to another for graduate work." His expression cleared. "I'm glad now in a way; it would have been hard on her. Some people have a life that can be shared more easily than others. My partner is married. Jackie's got two boys and a husband who adore her. I watch them and often wonder

18

how they've made it work."

"You've got a job that's hard to leave behind at the end of the day."

Luke nodded. "The day they invented the pager and mobile phone was the day police work fundamentally changed for the worse. The job's changed me," he admitted. "Didn't someone once say something about the sadness of innocence lost? A few years at this job took away a lot of good assumptions I had about people."

He shook his head. "How did we get on such a morbid topic as work? Are you and Sharon big into holiday traditions?"

"The important things about blending families." She nudged off one shoe and drew her leg up under her, smiling as she considered his question. The traditional days to celebrate mattered a lot to her, if only because they provided excuses to stop and reconnect with friends and family. If she had her wish, every one of them would be a big deal.

"The very important things," he agreed. "What should I know first?"

"We're a close family." Because she thought he was alone too much in his life, she searched her memory for all the events that would clue him in on how that was about to change. She smiled. "Next time he sees you, you're sure to get a Benjamin welcoming hug. He's into establishing his circle of important people right now, and getting a dad and an 'uncle' in a matter of a day is a big deal for him. This wedding anniversary will be more than just a day for Mark and Sharon to remember."

She pushed her hair behind her ear. "I like Christmas best. Snow, the smell of fresh-cut pine, and hot cider. I start piling gifts away in October, and around the second week of December the tree goes up. Benjamin likes to try to guess the gifts."

"Would it be a bit scrooge of me to mention I often choose to work the Christmas Day shift? By the end of December I've had about as much Christmas as I want for the year."

"It does get a bit overwhelming when Christmas music starts in November. We're more traditional about birthdays — there's always a favorite meal and a cake, and depending on what seems most important, either a trip somewhere or one significant gift. It's always been kind of like a wish-come-true day for us."

"I like that idea."

"You do celebrate birthdays, don't you?" Caroline teased.

"I take the day off if possible — leave the

20

pager at work — and find somewhere off the beaten path to explore."

"Time being the most precious gift of all, given the demands in your year?" Caroline asked.

"Yes."

"Where have you explored?"

"Caves, forests, underwater reefs, shipwrecks. I went skydiving one year, and about ended up with permanent vertigo."

"Do you have plans for this year?"

"I'm getting old. I'm leaning toward horseback riding for the day followed by a steak grilled over the fire. No more walking."

She laughed, suspecting he could probably do a ten-mile hike on a bad day without breaking a sweat. "That sounds like a nice day to look forward to."

"Have you settled on plans for your News Year's Eve yet?"

"No."

"Spend it with me. Those two days I will have off, and I'd enjoy sharing the celebration with you."

"Thank you, Luke, but you don't need to save me from being sad. I won't have Sharon and Benjamin with me for the holidays this year, but it won't be so bad."

"I'm asking purely for selfish reasons."

"It's over two months away. You might change your mind."

"I won't."

"I admit, you're puzzling me. It seems like an odd request, asked so far in advance."

"Not from where I sit."

She didn't quite know what to say. She slowly nodded. "Okay. I'll block off New Year's Eve and day as taken."

"Thank you." He leaned back to study the hotel. "What time did Karla say she was bringing Benjamin back to the room?"

She glanced at her watch. "I've got another twenty minutes before the pool closes. Benjamin will stay in the water until the last minute and ask to swim again first thing in the morning."

"Then there's time for coffee." Luke rose and offered her his hand. "You prefer the flavored kind I noticed."

She let him pull her to her feet and balanced against him while she slipped back on her shoes. "A touch of French vanilla makes coffee so much more memorable." Like this evening had turned out to be memorable. She was glad she had joined him.

ONE

ONE YEAR LATER

Mark Falcon knew success and enjoyed it. As the late afternoon sun came in the floor-to-ceiling windows of his office, it reflected off the architecture awards on the side table, a rainbow painting the wall. His son made the shadow of a barking dog in the blue and purple bands. Mark judged the distance and made a bear appear, which moved in to gobble up the dog.

Benjamin laughed. "Your hands are huge, Dad."

The boy's wonder combined with the name *Dad* — he had done a few things very right in his life, and marrying Sharon and adopting her son last year were near the top of the list. "Yours will one day be as big." He made the shadow of a tree house. "The tree house blueprints should be done printing. Why don't you go see?"

Benjamin dashed from the office to the

open drafting room. Mark followed at a more relaxed pace. Nine now, with a touch of McGyver in his unquenchable curiosity, his son seemed to be thriving under his attention. Mark was trying to rearrange his life to provide that time, but he had worried about the transition.

He was confident now that keeping the family in Benton, Georgia, an hour and twenty minutes outside Atlanta, had been the right decision. The schools were good, the hospital and medical clinic where Sharon continued to work top-notch, and the town still had open land and woods around it. Mark didn't mind the occasional commute to Atlanta when business required it; the pace in Benton better fit what he wanted for his family.

He watched his son carefully tear the blueprint from the wide printer. "It's perfect."

Mark picked up an empty carrying tube. "I'm glad you like it. We'd better stop by the lumber mill this weekend to order our supplies. By the end of October you'll be inviting your friends over."

"You'll teach me to use the saw?"

"I will. You can even make the trim if you like; we'll finish this tree house right. A good architect always finishes the finer details." He offered Ben a pen and an official label for the blueprint tube. "What do you say we pick up your mom and get dinner? I'm starved."

Sharon tried to keep her last patient appointment to no later than five on Wednesday nights so they could have a family night. The last couple of weeks their dates had been hot dogs from a street vendor and rented inline skates at the park. For a practical doctor, Sharon didn't always act much older than her son.

"Can we invite Aunt Carol?"

"If she's free." Mark had a soft spot in his heart with Caroline's name on it. She had introduced him to Sharon. "Call her and see."

They ended up at the mall after eating at the pizza buffet. It was Benjamin's idea of the perfect evening and Mark would agree. He walked with his wife window-shopping while Caroline and Benjamin invaded stores to compare toys and laugh at silly things like fish wind chimes and talking doorbells.

He paused with Sharon at the upper floor courtyard, waiting for Benjamin and Caroline to catch up, and couldn't resist leaning over to kiss his wife. A year since their honeymoon and she could still make him forget his name.

Mark reluctantly ended the kiss. "Tell me you don't have early rounds tomorrow."

She smiled slowly. "Nine o'clock."

Mark rubbed his thumb on Sharon's shoulder blade, appreciating the answer, and even more the promise in her smile. A guy didn't deserve to be this happy. He couldn't resist reaching up to touch her face and trace her smile and the perfect little dimple next to it. "I'll take the morning off and drive you in to work, then take Benjamin to school." His words were simple enough, but the huskiness in his voice conveyed a return promise for tonight. He hoped Benjamin would find a book and volunteer to turn in early with his Snoopy desk light on. It was time to go home. Mark slid his hand down to grasp Sharon's, looked around, and didn't see Benjamin.

"He's across the way at the pet store scoping out the puppies," Caroline offered. She was leaning against the railing overlooking the lower level, her attention focused across the walkway at his son.

The faint blush coloring her cheek and the back of her neck made Mark squeeze

Sharon's hand, move to the railing, and lean forward to see Caroline's expression. "Sorry."

She smiled even as her blush deepened. "Don't be." Caroline watched Sharon join Benjamin at the pet store window and laugh with him as one of the puppies rose to plant his feet on the glass. "My sister deserves to be happy."

"So do you."

"I am happy."

"Hmm." Mark thought she was, to the extent she didn't know what she was missing in life. "Would you like a date next week? I know a nice guy who's interested."

"You know I'm seeing Luke."

"My cousin could use some competition. He's cancelled on you too often due to work."

"He's been busy."

"No disrespect to Luke, but he's had a year to get his priorities sorted out. Work followed him to the wedding, and it's still following him. I'd say that's enough time to reevaluate things. Besides, you would really like this guy, Caroline. Let me at least introduce you."

"Is he an architect or in construction?"

"He owns a furniture business."

She turned to rest her back against the

railing. "He sounds more interesting than your financial advisor."

"Who thought you were adorable and was crushed when you politely declined a second date. Come on. You'll enjoy yourself. You ought to take me up on an introduction at least once a year."

She answered his verbal nudge with a smile. "Next week —" She shook her head. "Sorry, school extracurricular events are just getting started, and I'll be tied up with registration and scheduling."

"And the following week you'll be busy grading papers."

"What can I say? A fifth grade teacher's time is in high demand." She patted his arm. "I'm comfortable being single and still looking. Marriage is work."

"But the compensation is high." How Caroline ended up shy when her sister was an extrovert was a mystery, but he thought it rather a nice one. He was going to help her find a relationship that worked; he had set his mind on it. She was just going to take someone special. He thought it was Luke, but that wasn't coming to pass as he'd hoped, much to his disappointment. Mark leaned down to pick up the new package resting near her feet. "I see Benjamin found his kite."

"It will need a lot of string and running room to launch it."

"Those are the best kind." He slipped the receipt in his billfold, then tugged out the money to repay Caroline, and tucked it along with an extra twenty in the side pocket of her purse. "Go to a movie on me."

"Thanks, Mark."

"You're welcome, and please rub off on your nephew a bit more. I had to tug the fact he wanted a kite out of him." He added the sack to those he carried. Benjamin was just beginning to accept that it was okay to ask him for something. "He's frugal to the point of making me feel like the kid and he the adult."

"He'll grow out of it by the time he gets a driver's license and wants to borrow the car and twenty bucks."

"I hope so. Ben's making me feel guilty about being rich. It's been a while since that emotion was around."

Caroline laughed and he smiled back. She had long ago given him the gift of liking him regardless of what he owned.

He remembered what he meant to ask earlier, and Mark's smile faded. "Any more hang-up phone calls?"

Caroline's smile disappeared too. She shook her head.

Someone had developed the habit of calling her at six a.m. and hanging up when she answered. "You'll tell me if they start again?"

"Yes."

He searched her face, looking for any indication she was merely being polite. If he thought trouble was blowing in again, he'd mention it to Luke. Hang-up phone calls had started the trouble for her last year, and Mark wasn't going to let it flare up again without reacting early.

Luke and Caroline had gone several tense rounds last fall over what to do. Luke tried to protect her against an unidentified person on the edge of stalking her, and Caroline found Luke's concern smothering. Mark didn't want to open that can of worms again now that they were finally getting their relationship back on track, but if trouble had returned, ignoring it wouldn't help. Mark understood the edgy concern Luke felt — a few of the "gifts" involved had been sent to Sharon to be delivered to Caroline.

"You've got that look again. That protective, in-your-domain, determined look," Caroline remarked.

"You *are* in my domain," Mark replied, keeping it low-key, still feeling out the boundaries she'd accept.

"I appreciate it, but let this be."

If she was denying getting calls, he didn't have much choice. "I'll let this be."

She smiled her thanks. A guy could get lost in that smile. It was time he reminded Luke a year had passed. If the man wasn't so busy with work, he would have long ago realized just how special Caroline was and made their relationship permanent. "Are you going to join us for Labor Day weekend in Atlanta?"

"I'll have to bring some work along, but Benjamin insists I come see his Atlanta Braves in person."

"I'm glad." He'd known if he set Benjamin to the task he'd get a yes. "Plan to come Friday and stay through Monday evening."

"We'll talk about it."

Sharon and Benjamin joined them, and Mark squeezed her hand and let the matter drop. He stepped forward to offer the sack holding the kite to his son. "Let's go home, buddy. I want a rematch on the video game."

Caroline slowed her sedan and lifted a hand to acknowledge Benjamin's wave as Mark pulled into his driveway. It wound

31

back to the home he had designed and built with a family in mind. An evening at the mall had been a nice time. She appreciated the fact Mark went out of his way to include her occasionally in their family nights.

She clicked her headlights to high beam as she entered the heavier woods, glad the country road was rarely traveled except for residents who lived in the area. Down an incline, around a forty-degree curve to the left, she slowed and made a sharp turn into the gravel driveway to her house. The headlights bounced off trees and hanging branches and cast moving shadows along both sides of her car.

She pulled into the garage and parked, the darkness total as she shut off the car. Her keys held as weapons between her knuckles, she walked to the farmhouse, opened the kitchen door, and flipped lights on inside. The kitchen counters were clear, the spider fern turning slowly in the movement of air, a faint steady click and then the icemaker dumped ice. She was alone.

She shut off the alarm system and walked over to touch the new message button on the answering machine. The single message was the library confirming that a requested book was in. Whoever had been calling her had moved on. The troubles last fall had been more than enough for both Luke and herself: phone calls, unexplained small gifts, that last frightening bouquet of roses. The matter was behind her now, and she wanted it to stay buried.

Caroline moved toward the hallway, stepping out of her shoes and tossing them toward the steps. When Sharon and Benjamin had lived with her, the living room was often strewn with toys and the cupboards filled with the basics that little boys loved. The house was too quiet now, and the holes on the shelves where Sharon's knickknacks had been were still waiting to be filled.

Caroline sorted the mail she'd picked up at the roadside mailbox after school and took the two magazines with her to the back patio. She turned on the outside lights and looked around the backyard and woods before settling into a chair. The backyard was her special domain, the terraced flower beds and winding walkways her creation.

She flipped through the first magazine. What would she do with a garlic press? She turned down the corner of the catalog page, marking it as a good illustration to use during her chef elective. Somebody in the class could find an Italian recipe that called for the use of this special gadget. Pungent foods tended to get the boys interested in at least trying cooking for themselves.

Caroline thought again about Mark's offer to set up a date and knew she would eventually say yes, if only to sidestep the friendly pressure. Mark was right; Luke had been busy lately, and she had been content to let their relationship drift and not press the issue. She longed for a deeper relationship with Luke. She wanted more, but it hadn't happened over the last year. Maybe it was time to let go of that hope and move on.

I'm not sure what to do, Lord. Luke is not the kind of guy you push. I'd like to be more than casually dating him, but I don't know how to get that to change. I can't compete with his work, and I'm smart enough not to try. I just don't think he's ready to settle down.

It was so easy to love Sharon and Benjamin. During the last several years since Sharon's first husband had passed away, Caroline had poured her time and love into helping her sister with Benjamin. It had been a joy to do so. Loving her students was easy too, for she could find ways to help them enjoy school.

But figuring out how to love Luke — he was nearly as much a mystery after a year as he had been the day of her sister's wedding. She admired what she saw in him and thought loving him would be richly worth it, but she didn't know how to get inside his head. He wasn't a man who easily shared much of himself.

The phone rang. Caroline waited for the answering machine to kick in, not willing to answer any calls without first screening them. She hoped there never was another heavy breathing phone call while Luke was around. The man was a bit frightening when he shifted into work mode.

The phone stopped ringing.

Caroline closed the magazine. Uneasy now with the night around her, she rose. She stepped back inside the house and shut the patio door behind her. No one was out there. No one. But she didn't like the feeling on the back of her neck, wondering if someone was watching again . . .

He watched her rise from the chair through the zoom lens and took one last photo. He'd rattled her with the phone call. He didn't like it when her smile disappeared and those worry lines reappeared, but at least the call had gotten her to look up so he could get the silhouette photo he wanted.

Going by touch, he slowly advanced the film to minimize the clicking sounds. He'd need to develop the photo with care given the backlighting from her house, but he thought all the photos from tonight would turn out.

Leaves tickled his face as he turned to follow lights coming through the trees. A car slowed through the turn in the road and then drove past Caroline's driveway.

Months of watching Caroline had shown she rarely had company after sundown. Her routine was stable — relax on the back patio, go inside and fix dinner, move into the family room to review lesson plans while she watched some TV. If only Caroline could see herself as he did, she'd understand why he had come back.

He was smarter now on how to approach her. He had photos of Benjamin, and he had just about finished his photos of Sharon. He slid the camera into his bag. Easing from the log on which he sat, he moved deeper into the woods.

He would fit into Caroline's life this time, not intrude. Luke would be out of her life soon and Caroline would be all alone again — and his.

TWO

Luke Falcon followed his partner's directions taking I-20 to exit 154, listening to the police scanner and watching Labor Day weekend traffic build. It was coming up on two p.m. Friday, and traffic would only get heavier until it peaked around ten o'clock, as people streamed out of Atlanta to vacation destinations across the state.

Luke touched his brakes to slow and pulled onto the exit ramp. Out of habit he reached over to the dashboard and picked up his sunglasses. He didn't need them to shade his vision, but he did like the fact the dark glasses concealed his expression. Lying, anger, fear — Luke could read a record of someone's emotions in their eyes. He preferred not to have someone read his. Even Caroline who, like his partner Jackie, sometimes saw too much for comfort.

The Sunrise Motel sign rose high over

the highway. The building itself had a white pasty plaster exterior, twenty-four rooms, and an office with a solitary tree outside the door and a sign advertising VACANCY. It qualified as cheap accommodations for travelers who didn't mind a motorcycle revving in the parking lot and a semi-truck and trailer blocking numerous parking spaces.

Luke parked behind one of the cop cars crowding the lot.

Jackie Milner stood by the open doorway to room 15, talking with Taylor Marsh, a detective from the state homicide division, flipping pages in her notebook as she wrote down what he said. A body was coming out of the room in a black bag on a stretcher, moved by two men from the coroner's office.

Frank Hardin had a preference for interstate interchanges, and this hotel fit the sort of place he might choose to stay. Luke picked up the folder of photos and got out of the car. He walked across the white gravel lot to join them. "Sorry to be late, I got held up by a call as I was walking out the door. Hello, Marsh."

"Falcon." Taylor offered his hand. "Nothing breaks for a year on this case, and now we're deep into it again. I hope you didn't have plans for the weekend."

"Frank exists to mess up my dating life." Luke's plans to get away early and meet Caroline for dinner were fading. Life kept intruding on his well-laid plans. "What do we have?"

"I agree it's probably Karen," Jackie said. "Time of death is less than twenty-four hours ago; housekeeping found her. If she was our unnamed caller to the tip line, looking to cash in on the reward, Frank must have found out."

Luke walked over to the body bag. An officer unzipped it and Luke didn't let himself react to the smell. The woman's neck was snapped. The photo on file was not very flattering, but it was enough to confirm visual ID. "Karen Iles, last known girlfriend of Frank Hardin. There are fingerprints in the file," he agreed, passing over the folder to Taylor.

Luke waited until the body was loaded into the coroner's van before walking to the motel room to look at the crime scene.

The room was like many he had stayed in over the years. A queen-sized bed, an age-worn dresser, two wall lamps, and a color TV clamped to the dresser. The heat and air-conditioning unit under the

39

window was still on, the aged compressor rumbling. The room looked lived in with the old bedspread pushed to the floor, sacks of fast food piled by the overflowing trash can, spare change on the dresser, damp towels on the bathroom rack. "Talk me through what we know."

Jackie pointed with her pen. "She was found on the floor beside the bed, resting on her side, no visible injuries beyond the broken neck."

"No sign of defensive wounds?"

Jackie shook her head.

Luke looked at the makeup open on the dresser, the uncapped perfume bottle, a single high heel resting on the bed. He'd seen neat lipstick on her mouth. Karen must have been getting ready to go out for the evening when Frank snapped her neck and left her on the floor.

"The room was signed for under her name," Jackie went on. "The car she listed is still in the lot — the blue Pontiac by the dumpster. Her purse is here but the wallet and credit cards are missing. The coroner's guys are guessing time of death tentatively between six and nine last night; they'll get it narrowed down for us."

Luke stepped out of the room to let the crime scene technicians going through

Karen's belongings finish their work. "What else?"

"The clerk picked out Frank's photo as the man with Karen," Jackie said. "They arrived together on the afternoon of August seventeenth. No room-to-room calls, no indication they knew anyone else staying at the motel. No one heard loud voices or saw others coming or going from the room." Jackie broke the seal on a bottle of cold water and took a long drink. "The last time anyone saw Frank around the motel was just after ten p.m. yesterday. One of the guests reported seeing him get into the passenger side of a van."

She pointed to the end of the parking lot. "The van was parked down by the dumpster next to the Pontiac; the guest remembers its slot because he would have thrown away some empty liquor bottles but for having to pass by Frank. He says the van was light colored, white, maybe beige, a cargo or panel type without windows. He's certain there were no logos or writing on the side."

"So someone picked Frank up. Do we know anyone in his circle of family or friends who drives a white van?" Luke asked.

Jackie flipped through her notes. "A

41

friend has a black SUV, and there's a pickup truck registered to his father," she said. "Nothing close to a light-colored van. Officers are interviewing the other guests to see if anyone else saw the van arrive or leave."

Luke looked at Taylor. "Anything useful you can add about the van?"

"Statewide, none have been reported stolen in the last two weeks. I'm hoping the driver filled up at one of the gas stations at this interchange or the next ones along these interstates. There are only so many places to stop if he stayed on major roads. I've got officers getting whatever security tapes are available, but it may take a while. We'll have a lot of white vans to eliminate."

Luke looked around the parking lot. "Frank knows that we keep track of his friends; he's been staying out of state for the last several months. He came back now for a reason. If he was on his way into Atlanta, why stay this far out of town for over a week?"

"He needs cash to stay on the run . . . he's hired muscle . . . he came back for a job in this area?" Jackie proposed.

"It fits his profile," Luke agreed. "If he's been here over a week, there's a chance he's been out canvassing the location of his next job. A newspaper, a fast-food receipt — maybe he left us some marker so we can figure out which town he's been visiting along these interstates. We've got a lot of ground to cover."

"I'm just surprised he didn't leave our phone number written on the mirror for the arriving cops like he did last time."

"So am I. And I'm tired of being taunted by this guy." Luke pulled out his keys. "I'll get the call center spun up and information out to the media on the van, Frank's and Karen's photos, and reminders about the existing reward. Half of the state is traveling this weekend. We need someone to spot him. If he's still in the area, he's got to be sleeping somewhere."

Luke was tired of standing over Frank Hardin's victims. The man had to be stopped, and this time they might have a chance to catch him. It would mean Luke's weekend off would be spent working, but it couldn't be helped. The leads were hot and they had to be run to ground before Frank disappeared again.

Caroline was getting shortchanged again, and Benjamin would be disappointed when he missed the Braves game. Both reactions were coming and both were deserved; work's toll on his personal life was getting steep. But some cases had to be solved, no matter what the personal cost. This was one of them.

School would be dismissing early for the holiday weekend, and Caroline didn't even try to teach for the last half period. She needed a break as much as her students did. The crossword puzzle sketched on the board at the front of the classroom had the easy questions answered. "How about five down? Does anyone have an idea?" Caroline stepped back to study the list of questions. This was a hard puzzle.

Lynn raised her hand. "Maybe . . . *temperature?*"

Caroline counted the letters. "Beautiful job." She filled in the letters. It was the first time Lynn had volunteered an answer today. She was a quiet student, but today was unusual. Something was bothering her, and Caroline still hadn't figured out what it was. Papers rustled behind her as students filled in five down on their copies of the puzzle.

The last bell of the day rang.

"Whoever finishes the puzzle gets an extra ten minutes of art time. Enjoy your long weekend."

Her kids were already moving, backpacks straining with books, assignment folders, and gym shoes. The boy in the third row, fourth seat, didn't move with the others. Caroline set a three-by-five card on his desk and softly said, "fifty times." He tugged out a piece of paper and pen without debating the point. Detention had become almost routine for both Kevin and herself.

Caroline followed her students to the door. Lockers lined the hall, and the sixth graders from the next room dominated the hallway so that her kids disappeared into the crush of bodies. She smiled greetings to kids from last year and saw from the milling parents in the hallway that the third grade class was not yet back from their half-day field trip.

Benjamin had told her all about the trip while he waited in her classroom this morning for the bus that would take them to the museum. He'd be back soon, overflowing with news of what he had seen.

Caroline turned back into her classroom, out of habit advancing the calendar page by the door, then switched the blue cards that gave the lunch choices to next week's menu. She straightened desks. In this small private Christian school she served as janitor for her own classroom.

She started updating the schedule on the sideboard that would run the class Tuesday. She assigned Lynn as the teacher's assistant so they would have a few minutes to talk.

Kevin slid out of his chair and brought her his paper. "I'm done."

She took it and scanned the repeated sentence: *I'm a better man than I acted today.* "Your penmanship is improving."

Kevin shrugged. "I need a new pen."

"I can probably handle that for you. Do you have a ride, or can I give you a lift home?"

"I'm okay; football practice is this afternoon. Can I go now?"

"I want a story from you. Ten pages, as extra credit to make up for the science project you had problems with."

He shifted on his feet. She knew his daddy would be on him about the science project and Kevin did too. Saving face still mattered. "Five pages," Kevin countered.

"Seven."

"Any story?"

"As long as it's written for me as the audience and involves some science fact you had to look up."

He nodded and turned to get his backpack. "I'll bring it next week, Miss Carol."

She smiled as he disappeared through the doorway, his backpack rubbing the floor. He liked creative writing, even if he was reluctant to admit it.

She looked around the empty desks, names and faces coming easily to mind, reviewing how the day had gone for each one of them. Her students were doing fine, even those like Kevin who forgot to pay attention when he should. *They've worked hard this week, Lord. Bring them safely back to school on Tuesday ready to learn.*

She shut off the lights and locked her classroom, as relieved as her kids to be out at two for the Labor Day break. Driving into Atlanta to see the Braves' game Saturday had blossomed into a full weekend schedule. Caroline joined the flow of parents heading to the parking lot to meet the arriving bus.

She set her briefcase on the bench and leaned against the light pole taped with flyers for the upcoming school band concert. Benjamin finally appeared at the top of the bus steps. He flew off the bus and ran toward her, his school uniform of black jeans and blue shirt looking broken in with dirt and sweat, his feet still in the black gym shoes he loved and had conveniently "forgotten" to change this morning. A frayed backpack strap fluttered behind him, the heavy canvas blue backpack already showing some wear.

Caroline straightened and he collided with her in one of his super hugs — his hands on her shoulders and his shoes stepping up on hers as she balanced for them both. They had been full hugs when he was younger, now the super hugs were more a teasing greeting so he wouldn't be embarrassed when his friends saw, but she loved them just the same.

"We're going?" Benjamin asked, catching the loop of his backpack to lug it in one hand.

"I'll drop you off at the clinic so you can ride home with your mom and help her finish packing, then you'll be on your way to Atlanta." She smiled at his whoop of joy. "Your daddy will drive in when he finishes a house inspection. I'm going in early so I can get my schoolwork done before the fun starts. I told your mom we should find a movie for tonight."

Benjamin walked backward on the sidewalk. "Animated?"

"Sure."

Caroline parked beside her sister's car at the medical clinic and followed Benjamin inside. Sharon's office at the back of the clinic was a comfortable place to come and talk; the conversations here were as helpful to Sharon's patients as what went on in the exam rooms.

Caroline paused at the side table dominated by a huge bouquet of roses and carefully tipped one of the perfect blooms to smell the rich fragrance. Three dozen bright red roses among a bed of greenery — Mark was spoiling her sister.

The newspaper on the coffee table was folded back to the movies showing this weekend. Caroline picked it up and scanned their options, glancing up to smile as Sharon came through the door slipping a prescription pad into the pocket of her white lab coat. "Busy day?"

"Never-ending."

Caroline set down the newspaper and nodded to the receptionist area. "Ben spotted the new video game in the waiting room. The receptionist promised to keep an eye on him."

"I'm running a few minutes late, so that's perfect. Thanks for bringing him over. You have keys to the condo?"

"Mark gave me a set." Caroline opened her purse to double-check.

Sharon leaned against her desk. "I talked

to Luke last night. He said he was joining us this weekend."

Caroline's hand slowed as she searched for her keys. She glanced up. "He's going to try. Just don't push, Sharon." Luke had been distant the last evening they had shared together, not wanting to talk about the work that occupied his thoughts, and she'd learned she didn't handle being shut out well. They needed time to reconnect, not dodge leading questions from family. "I'll start dinner when I get to town, something that will stay hot so we can eat when everyone arrives."

"I promise not to meddle, at least not too much. Drive careful."

"I will." Sharon's phone rang. Caroline waved good-bye and walked through the clinic, relieved to be away, pausing briefly in the waiting room to say farewell to Benjamin. She walked out to her car.

What was she going to say when she saw Luke? *I miss you.* The honest words would only hurt him, so something a little less direct. *I'm glad you were able to get free.* No, it would sound like she was nagging about the hours he worked. It wasn't like they were engaged; she had no claims on him and his time. Caroline adjusted the rearview mirror. She wanted him to be different than he was, and that wasn't fair to ask of anyone.

Caroline followed signs to the highway and headed to Atlanta, relieved she had the drive to think about what to say to Luke. This weekend was becoming a turning point in her mind — either she figured out how to get things on track with him, or she accepted reality and gracefully let the relationship go. There was nothing wrong with being just friends. It would be a disappointing outcome, but she'd survived disappointing outcomes before.

If only you were focused on me, Luke. She glanced toward the sky and the storm forming on the horizon.

Lord, it would help if Luke made a decision on where he wanted this relationship to go. One way or another, just get us to a decision point.

Frank Hardin studied his injured hand as the blood washed away. He had scraped the back of his right knuckles on the framing in the hidden room, and the soap stung as he washed his hands at the kitchen sink. It would pass for the after-effects of a bare knuckles fight. He nudged the water off with his elbow and picked up a towel.

The automatic garage door opened. Frank glanced through the dining room windows to see a white van pull into the driveway. It disappeared into the spacious garage.

"I told you he would be back right on time."

Ronald rose from the table at the bay window.

"Billy's a liability. He talks too much."

"He's young, eager."

Frank glared at his friend. "He'll have to be dealt with." He wasn't going back to jail because some guy hired to drive liked to talk too much.

Ronald hesitated, but reluctantly nodded.

Frank tapped out his cigarette. He scanned the list on the counter. Months of planning had come down to today. Someone else might be paying his fee, but this job was personal. He wanted more than just to hurt Luke Falcon; he wanted the man afraid.

If he couldn't shake the man hunting him, he could make Falcon permanently regret it. "Let's get this underway."

Ronald picked up the box with a roll of duct tape and three ski masks. Frank followed him to the garage.

THREE

Sharon had married into money. Caroline knew it, but rarely experienced it to the degree she was today. She slipped a grilled cheese sandwich onto her plate and shut off the burner. Cooking in this kitchen with its black marble countertops and shining appliances made her nervous.

Mark Falcon's condominium in Atlanta, which took the entire eighth floor of a brownstone building, was much like an upscale hotel. Carpets were plush, furniture new, and the kitchen well stocked. He had lived here before marrying Sharon and still had a housekeeper come in three times a week to keep it ready on a moment's notice for guests. Caroline wished there was something out of place so her arrival would feel less disruptive.

The phone rang and Caroline turned in a full circle to isolate the sound. She found the cordless phone in the side cabinet beside the refrigerator. "Falcon residence."

"Good, you're there. Did you by any chance see my baseball glove at your place?" Benjamin sounded a little panicked.

Caroline poured her soda over ice. "Remember the church baseball game Sunday afternoon? You put your glove in the trunk of your mom's car beside your shoebox of spare baseball cards."

"Oh, that's right. Thanks."

"Where are you, Benjamin?"

"We're finally leaving the clinic. Mom says we have to stop by the house to —" A clatter cut off his sentence.

"Benjamin?"

Caroline heard a jumble of sounds and static before it finally cleared. "Sorry. Some van cut Mom off. I dropped the phone."

"You're okay?"

"She owes the glass jar two quarters for swearing."

Benjamin sounded impressed. Caroline smiled. "Tell your mom to drive safe."

"Mom, she says to drive more carefully."

Caroline took her plate into the dining room where the table was set for six. She moved aside good china to set her plate down.

"We're going to stop by the house so Mom can finish packing, then we'll be on the way. An hour and a half and we'll be there."

"More like two hours," Caroline replied, thinking about the traffic already building, "but soon. I'll start dinner and have it waiting for you."

"What are you going to fix?"

"Your favorite, Italian Beef."

"Awesome! I'm already starved. See you soon."

"Love ya, Benjamin."

Caroline glanced at the time as she set down the cordless phone. Three-fifty. Sharon and Benjamin should easily be here before six. Mark was out at a construction site for a new home he had designed and promised to be here by seven.

Caroline bowed her head before beginning her meal. *Jesus, You understand what I'm feeling in this place, not quite belonging, just a little out of my element. Thank You for sending Sharon a wonderful husband and Benjamin a great father. Please handle the details of this weekend so I can look back on this time and be glad I came.* She lifted her head.

Caroline picked up her sandwich. She'd enjoy the weekend for all the uncertainty. She would smile at Luke and wait for him to start the conversation. It worked every time.

After eating, Caroline settled in the living room and turned her attention to her schoolwork. Teaching at a Christian school allowed her to have a Bible class, and it was one of her favorite subjects.

She started the school year by giving her students a week to answer an essay question, one that tried to make the Bible personal to each student. Last year the essay question had been: *God loves you unconditionally. How does that impact your life?*

Caroline drew circles on the page as she thought about this year's essay question:

Jesus taught that a firm foundation based on living what He taught would allow a person to survive great trouble in life. What did you learn from the Sermon on the Mount that will change how you live?

Before the weekend was over, she would take up pen and paper and write her own answer to the essay question, for tradition dictated she share her own perspective with the class.

She picked up her Bible from the floor, the cover worn and the pages stuffed with notes she used in her class. She found the summary passage for the Sermon on the Mount in Matthew 7:24–29 and read it again.

"Every one then who hears these words of mine and does them will be like a wise man who built his house upon the rock; and the rain fell, and the floods came, and the winds blew and beat upon that house, but it did not fall, because it had been founded on the rock. And every one who hears these words of mine and does not do them will be like a foolish man who built his house upon the sand; and the rain fell, and the floods came, and the winds blew and beat against that house, and it fell; and great was the fall of it."

She had chosen the essay question partly because of the events she had lived through last fall — the phone calls, notes, and flowers from an unknown sender. They had arrived as a sudden storm of trouble and had rocked her life hard. She'd come through the experience with a damaged sense of her own security. God was still her rock; unfortunately she'd just made the mistake of putting some of her trust in things that had shown themselves to be sand. Hopefully she'd learned that lesson.

The timer in the kitchen sounded, interrupting her work. Caroline set aside her notebook and headed to the kitchen, pausing only long enough to turn on the TV and increase the volume so she could catch the start of the local evening news.

As she stirred the Italian Beef, the news headlined a murder investigation. *That poor lady.* The motel and interchange mentioned — she'd passed it on her drive into town. She leaned around to see the TV. She studied the photo of the murder suspect.

She added more water to the crock-pot and, since dinner was close to done, turned the temperature to low. She looked at the clock: 6:05. Getting packed and on the road must have presented a few unexpected challenges for Sharon.

The salad was ready. The buns were set out to steam. Caroline looked through options for dessert and got out the tapioca. Mark loved it more than a homemade pie. It was a small thing, but it would be appreciated, and she wanted to say thanks for his invitation to join them.

She fixed tapioca, listening to the rest of the news. Traffic sounded heavy but there were no unexpected delays on the highways, no reported car accidents.

At 6:40, the tapioca set aside to cool, Caroline picked up the phone and walked back into the living room. She tried Sharon's car phone and gave up after it rang ten times. She hated to page her, for if Sharon wasn't in her car, she probably had been called back to an emergency at the hospital. She wouldn't be late over something trivial. Caroline compromised and called Sharon's private number at the clinic, reaching Sharon's head nurse. "Amy, do you know if Sharon got called back to the hospital or the clinic to see a patient?"

"Not that I've heard, but it wouldn't surprise me. Hold on a sec." Amy went away and came back a minute later. "Kim hasn't paged her, and for what it's worth, her car isn't in her reserved parking space."

"Thanks, Amy." Caroline set the phone on the side table. *Car trouble?* Forty minutes late was not unusual, but the silence was. If they had returned to the house or the hospital, Benjamin would have called. *Where are they?*

Caroline got out the English tests she needed to grade and tried to focus on them while she listened for the door to

open or the phone to ring.
Come on, Sharon, call.

Luke pushed back his headphones, tired of listening to a lot of gossip, recipes, and soap opera discussions. "This is a dead end." They already had wiretaps on Frank's family and some of his friends. If Frank Hardin's aunt had seen him, had heard anything about him returning to town, she wasn't telling even her best friend. "If Frank had any plans to get in touch with family or friends for cash or help, he would have done it by now."

Jackie hung up her phone and marked another hotel on the blown-up map with a red dot. "I don't think he moved hotels. Most are already booked for the holiday weekend. It's not easy to walk in and get a room."

"He has to sleep somewhere." Luke shifted his left foot to rest atop a packed box. The Bureau was relocating their offices to larger quarters over Labor Day weekend; the move couldn't be happening at a more inconvenient time. "What did Frank come back to Georgia to do?"

"He could have already done it. Since ten last night he's been missing, and a dead girlfriend suggests he wasn't planning to stay around much longer."

"Good point." Luke paged down the database of calls being logged at the call center, looking for leads. "We know he likes murder."

"Armed robbery, maybe a bank heist, a jewelry store — I can see him going for a lot of cash."

"I wonder who he's traveling with. That would help answer the question. What time was Marsh going on TV?"

Jackie looked at the clock. "He'll be live on the local newscasts at ten. If someone has seen Hardin, they'll be reminded it's a very profitable phone call."

"Someone has seen him. The question is, will they take the risk of reporting him?"

Jackie shrugged.

The last one to call in a tip on Frank was now dead. It wasn't encouraging. Luke sighed and kept scrolling through the call-in reports.

FOUR

Caroline listened to the clock tick through seven-thirty and got up from the couch. Three-and-a-half hours to pack and make an hour-and-twenty-minute drive — Sharon was moving beyond late to troublingly late. Caroline punched in Sharon's car phone number again, listening to it ring as she walked through the condominium. Surely if the phone were dead it would be a fast busy signal instead of this constant ringing.

Caroline pulled out the chair and sat at Mark's desk. She looked at names on the pad of paper. She'd started writing the list an hour ago as a way to control her worry. She couldn't wait and wonder any longer; she had to know.

She dialed Mark's car phone again, and finally hung up after twenty rings. He wasn't near his car phone, and his cellular phone was either out of range or the battery was dead. Mark would walk through that door any minute and he'd know what was best to do. He probably assumed Sharon and Benjamin were already here. He had no reason to suspect otherwise and was himself only half an hour late from his tentative arrival time.

Caroline knew she tended to see a problem where there was none; ample personal history testified to that. But this late — it was trouble. She took a deep breath and dialed the Benton sheriff's office, hoping Linda was working tonight. She had taught the lady's two girls last year.

She asked for the dispatcher and was forwarded. "Linda, I'm so glad you're working tonight. Sharon and Benjamin are late, and I'm a bit worried about them. They were driving into Atlanta tonight. Have there been any reported car accidents on I-20?"

"Nothing but an overheated engine, and it was a tourist from Kansas. Sharon hasn't called?"

"No. And the hospital hasn't received an answer to their page to her either."

"That is odd. I know Lewis is on patrol along I-20 between Benton and Sandy Hill. Sharon is driving her car?"

"Yes."

"I'll punch up the DMV records for the license plate info and have Lewis keep a look out for her car."

"Thanks, Linda. I'm at Mark's condo if you hear anything. I really appreciate it."

Caroline hung up and looked again at her list. No matter what scenario she scripted, it didn't end in silence. There had to be a way to somehow get in touch with Mark. His Benton office automatically transferred to an answering machine with a message about being closed for Labor Day.

Feeling like she was prying into private matters, she opened drawers in Mark's desk until she found a personal address book. She started turning pages, looking for the home phone number of one of his partners.

"Mr. Jenson, it's Caroline Lane. I'm looking for Mark Falcon. Do you know what house he was looking at tonight, or how I might be able to reach him?"

"He's not in Atlanta?"

"No, and I can't raise him on the phone. It's pretty urgent."

"He left the house about five-thirty after we figured out a problem with the skylight. He mentioned he wanted to stop by the bank before closing and then needed to buy gas, but that should have taken only twenty minutes or so. He was in a hurry to get to Atlanta."

"Do I have his phone numbers right?" She read them off her list.

"Yes. Let me try them from here. If I can't raise him, I'll make the drive back to the house and see if he had car trouble or something."

"I'm sorry to interrupt your evening, but I really appreciate it."

"It's no problem."

Caroline looked at her list again. She was running out of options. Sharon and Benjamin were somewhere unreachable. Mark couldn't be found.

She taught fifth graders. She knew that Murphy's Law often happened. Their phone had been accidentally left on and the batteries were dead . . . they had remembered something left behind and went back to the house . . . there had been car trouble . . .

Mark could have easily been delayed by a conversation at the bank over a construction project. Or maybe Sharon and Mark had talked and changed their plans, intending to come into Atlanta together. Every scenario Caroline drew had someone calling to say they would be here late. She could start calling hospitals.

Jesus, what do I do? Where are they?

Caroline looked around Mark's expensive home. She was so far out of her league
in this place, for this problem. It wa:
family. She couldn't let it sit. *I'm scarec
now.*

"This is going to be another dead end."
Luke shifted his hand on the steering
wheel to hit the turn signal, taking the exi1
to get them off the highway and out of the
bumper-to-bumper holiday traffic. The gas
station off of I-20 had cars at every pump
and two cars waiting in line.

"One of the leads will pan out eventually." Jackie shuffled her paperwork and
called to confirm their arrival with the coordinator assigning the leads.

"Marsh beat us here." The state cop car
was parked to the east of the gas station office, taking the space between the adver-
tisement for tire rotations and the flashing
sign for cold sodas. Luke parked beside
him and waited until Jackie got out of the
car, then locked the doors. He walked past
a long display of windshield washer fluid
on sale this Labor Day weekend, breathing
in gas fumes and stale coffee.

Jackie held the door for him. "Come
on."

"I'm relishing the fact this is about the thousandth gas station we've invaded in our lives and they all look remarkably the same, down to the gum you managed to step on and are now leaving in strings behind you as you walk."

Jackie looked down and studied the bottom of her right shoe. "Great. Why can't people just take two more steps and toss the stuff in a trash can to begin with?" She scraped what she could off on the concrete step.

Luke took hold of the door from her. "Ice. You can buy a fountain drink, pour it out because it's going to taste horrible anyway, and use the ice to freeze that gum fragment off your shoe."

"Don't smile like that, Falcon. I could have gone off duty a while ago and saved my favorite pair of shoes, you know."

"You could have," Luke agreed easily, knowing it was an idle threat. Getting Jackie off this search for some reason other than her kids' soccer game or the fact her family was out of clean laundry wouldn't happen. Jackie was married and loved it, but perish the criminal who thought that would give him a little breathing room.

"I'm thinking you should just keep more

shoes at the office now that you'll have a huge new office to clutter with stuff and won't have to put your extra pair in my un-used bottom desk drawer."

"You never actually put something in your desk; you just stack it on top. How you keep your house spotless and yet keep a desk like you do . . ." Jackie headed in-side to find Taylor Marsh and the manager who had phoned in the tip.

Luke picked up a Tootsie Roll as he passed the candy display, offering the clerk a buck and tearing the paper as he waited for his change. Taylor was deep in debate with someone who looked like the store manager, a video punched up on the secu-rity monitor. There wasn't enough room behind that counter for the manager and three cops unless they turned the clerk into a Popsicle. He'd let Taylor and Jackie sort out the first impressions.

"How's business been tonight?" Luke asked the clerk.

"Stick around a few more hours, and maybe I won't get some flipped-out idiot trying to rip me off tonight."

"That good, huh? You've worked this corner a while."

"Six years."

Luke tugged a couple photos from his

pocket. "Have you seen either of these people before?"

The clerk slid the photos over the counter to see them better. "The lady goes for two packs of cigarettes and a pint of ice cream; the guy must be pumping the gas because I would certainly remember a scowl like that. She's part of the one to two a.m. crowd. A regular. But I haven't seen her in the last couple days."

The odds they had a photo of Frank on that security tape had just gone up considerably. Luke pocketed the photos. "Thanks."

He walked down to where Jackie and Taylor were studying the security monitor. Buying gas at the same place was a habit even criminals had. Luke leaned against the counter to see over their shoulders. The videotape had been used so many times it was worn over and ghost images appeared in the static, but it was better than some he'd seen.

"I'm satisfied," Taylor said, stepping back. "That's Frank."

It wasn't a clear image, but the man shoving over his cash and impatiently running his left hand back and forth on the edge of the counter could be Frank Hardin, a tight haircut and an additional ten pounds since the last picture they had notwithstanding.

Jackie sorted security tapes for the outside cameras and popped another tape into the player. She fast-forwarded to the time index in question. "Here's another shot of him."

The camera, which had been focused on the far bay of pumps, showed Frank walking to a compact car, circling the rear of the vehicle, and getting into the driver's seat. The image kept flickering in and out of focus as the camera kept blooming the exposure, its control chip dying. "There." Jackie paused the video while the image was stable. "What's that license number? KV7 . . . it's fuzzy. Maybe the video guys can clean it up and get us a full plate number."

"Maybe KN7 . . ." Taylor suggested. "A Toyota?"

"Yes, with some kind of luggage rack."

"I wonder what happened to the van." Luke looked at the time stamp, then checked the current video against his watch to make sure the camera clock was accurate. It was. "Frank was here at 6:19 tonight. He's got a full tank of gas. If we assume he's hitting the road to get out of this publicity, he won't stop again until he's at least a state away. If he's an hour plus ahead of us . . . he's still within a hundred miles of here." Luke looked at Taylor.

"We'll saturate the interstates with patrols. If he's on side roads, we'll still need some luck."

"Frank will likely stay on the interstate to meld into traffic," Luke said. "Let's get this car and partial plate added to the APB while we walk the tape through the lab to get a full plate number and find out who Frank's traveling with now. Tell your guys to be careful; with two outstanding murders already to his credit, Hardin would kill a cop before he'd think about surrendering."

"I'll pass the word that caution really means caution," Taylor agreed. "Give me a minute to talk with dispatch. Do you want to shift manpower off the call-in leads to add coverage in this area?"

It was a hard choice. Luke shook his head. "Not yet. We need another confirmed sighting to know which direction Frank is heading. That is more critical. Jackie, make a couple calls and find out which lab can give us the fastest turn on analyzing that tape, state or federal. I'll fill up the car while we're here so we can cruise the highways for a while without stopping."

"Will do."

Luke dug out his car keys as he walked outside. *I'm coming for you, Hardin. This time you're not going to slip away.*

He moved the car to a free pump and selected high octane. His phone rang as he removed the gas cap. Luke tugged out his phone and accepted the call as he started pumping gas. "Luke Falcon."

"Luke, it's Caroline."

She paused but he remained silent. Her tone sounded desperate. If he said anything, she wouldn't have enough breath to get out her next words.

"Sharon and Benjamin, Mark — they're all very late. And I can't find them."

FIVE

As Luke paid for the gas, Jackie joined him at the counter. "What's wrong?"

Luke smoothed out his frown. "Caroline called."

"Trouble?"

He instinctively shook his head. "No. Sharon and Mark are running late in this traffic and Caroline can't reach them." Caroline got jumpy. After dealing with his extra careful sense of security for the last year, he couldn't blame her. If she overreacted occasionally now, it was as much his fault as hers. They were late, but —

He glanced over his shoulder at the highway. This traffic could disrupt well-laid plans in any number of ways. "I need to swing by and see her later."

"They want the tape at the state lab, and Taylor can drop me off there. Go see Caroline while I walk this through the lab.

When we have results in, I'll give you a call and you can pick me up there."

"Thanks, Jackie."

"No problem." She rested her hand on his arm to pause him. "I'll have some time to kill while they work on this. If Sharon and Mark are this late — do you want me to call hospitals for you? Just to make sure nothing bad did happen?"

"I'm sure it's just traffic or car problems."

"I'm sure it is too, but I could rule it out for you."

Luke hesitated, then nodded. "It would be easier than Caroline listening to me make those calls an hour from now."

"Consider the calls made. Tell Caroline hello for me."

Nine o'clock. Caroline stirred the Italian Beef since the burner had been shut off for the last hour. Wherever Sharon and Benjamin were, her nephew was probably very tired by now. The icemaker dumped ice. The sound broke the silence, startling her, and she dropped the lid against the counter.

I just want my family to walk through that door. I don't want a real-life example to illustrate what life is like in a storm, Lord. Just keep them safe and bring them here.

A very bad car accident topped her list of maybes now. She couldn't come up with good explanations at this point. Not for both Sharon and Mark being late.

Luke would know what to do. He had sounded just like he always did, as if the conversation was about everyday matters rather than her sister, her nephew, and his cousin being hours late and unreachable. She hated that calmness even as she depended on that steadiness.

Knuckles rapped against the front door. She hurried down the hall to unlock it. *Please be Sharon or Mark.*

"Luke —" her hand tightened on the knob — "thank you for coming." He leaned against the doorjamb with one hand, the edge of a frown on his brow. She stood straighter.

"Still no word?" The words were oddly gentle for him.

She shook her head. "I would have called you back. You couldn't get through to them either?"

"No." He stepped into the condo and closed the door behind him. "You're dripping something, Caroline."

She looked down and saw the spoon in her hand. "Oh! I was fixing dinner. Or rather I fixed dinner earlier." She flushed and hurried back to the kitchen. She dumped the spoon in the sink, grabbed a wet rag to wipe the spots on the kitchen floor, then went to see about the hallway carpet.

Luke stepped out of Caroline's way. Her color was high and her knuckles white on the rag, her movements a bit jerky. She was attacking the carpet as if it were a grape juice stain rather than a drip. *Don't make a trivial remark next time,* he reminded himself, watching her. She finally finished and he didn't give her a chance to see another spot. He took the rag from her, stepped to the kitchen doorway, and tossed it toward the sink. "Let's go sit down."

He didn't give her much option, walking her into the living room. He wanted to hug her, but there was so much emotion flowing off her at the moment his instincts warned him to go the other direction. Caroline sank onto the brown leather couch Mark had bought three years ago and practically got swallowed by the plush cushions.

"You can't help me if you don't calm down."

"I *am* calm."

"Lean back, close your eyes, take several

deep breaths, and just sit there." He'd never imagined a scenario where he'd be telling Caroline the same prescription he gave victims and witnesses. She took the order well, considering. He covered her hand with his and held it while he tugged out his phone with his other hand.

Caroline cracked open one eye to see him, but Luke merely looked back at her as he dialed his partner. "Jackie, I'm here and they aren't. Do you have anything?"

"Nothing so far. I'm calling the hospitals from Benton to Atlanta. Give me another twenty minutes, and I'll have them covered. As a precaution, I went ahead and put the description and plates for both of their vehicles out to the state patrols."

"Thanks. I'll call you back in twenty minutes." He hung up.

"I didn't panic," Caroline whispered.

She'd calmed down enough the involuntary twitch beside her right eye had stopped. "You were just getting close," Luke said kindly. "I'm sorry I wasn't here earlier. Talk me through the plans for this weekend."

She ran both her hands through her blond hair. "I talked to Benjamin when he and Sharon were leaving the clinic, just before four p.m. They were going home to finish packing before driving in. Mark was checking a house under construction and then driving from there. One of his partners said Mark left the house about five-thirty. I've got notes of the calls I made."

"Go get them please."

Luke watched her leave the room. She'd have a list; she liked to be organized about problems and decisions. He glanced around the room for the first time and realized she had the room transformed into a bit of an office, stacks of papers neatly arranged on the table, school books turned so she could read the titles on the spines.

Caroline returned with a spiral-bound notebook and handed it to him. "I was using the second phone line for the calls so I wouldn't block this number."

"Good thinking." There were two pages of small print: Friends. Family. Work. Hospitals. Police. As he read the neat handwriting he saw she'd covered most of the bases. "Benjamin and Sharon left the clinic about 3:50; Al Jenson talked with Mark at 5:30. It's now 9:18. You've found no one who saw or spoke to them between those times?"

Caroline shook her head.

"Mark would have called if he was going to be this late. You know Sharon. I assume

78

the same would be true for her?"

"She'd call me."

"Therefore, they aren't in a place where they can call or the call can't get through. A cell tower near Benton having problems might explain it. There may be a problem dialing into this building. Have you had any incoming calls tonight?"

"No."

Luke opened his phone, called Jackie, and asked her to call Mark's main number. The phone rang. "Okay, that's not the problem."

"They must have been in accidents. They could have driven here twice over by now." Caroline crossed her arms and rubbed at her forearms. "I've been calling the hospitals . . ."

"It's possible, but the cops would have seen an accident. Maybe Mark on a back road could be missed, but not Sharon coming in on the interstate. Jackie's getting nothing talking to hospitals either." He looked at her list. "You called the Benton sheriff."

"He had an officer drive by their house and confirm that Sharon and Benjamin appeared to have left. He checked my place too since it was on the way. His patrols haven't seen either car."

"The clinic doesn't get an answer when they page Sharon?"

"No." Caroline started rocking ever so slightly on the couch. "Something has happened to them."

"Something didn't go as planned." Luke reached out to touch her knee and stop her movements. He was worried about Sharon and Mark, but it was a work-the-problem worry; Caroline concerned him more. He'd be managing her as much as the search. She wasn't accustomed to a crisis like this, and only a cynic would want to push someone out of her sheltered life to learn the coping skills this would require. "Relax, that's an order."

Her gaze touched his for a moment and immediately shifted away as a blush chased the pallor from her cheeks. A year of dating her and he still had the bad habit of embarrassing her.

He quietly sighed and moderated his voice. "It's going to be okay, Caroline. If Sharon and Ben coming in first had car trouble, Mark would have seen their car and stopped to help. I'm betting they're together. And I'm willing to bet on a Labor Day weekend it is possible to go over three hours hassling with the system to get a tow truck and a phone that works."

He checked her list one last time and made a couple decisions. "I want you to get a folder or sack and walk through the house here, collect any address books, calendars, day planners, church phone directories, or work phone sheets you can find. If it has a phone number on it, bring it.

"Everyone is a creature of habit: he'll call a garage he used in the past, a rental car company, even a credit card company that provides roadside service. We'll find what we need somewhere in those numbers. After that, get your purse and shoes. We'll drive the interstate back to Benton."

She squeezed his hand. "Thanks. I'm glad you're here. Give me a couple minutes." She got up to head to Mark's study.

Luke waited until Caroline left the room. He called Jackie back. "I need someone to sit here and listen for the phone who can watch a couple movies and stay awake. Someone who doesn't panic if there's bad news to relay. Does a name suggest itself?"

"Try Mary Treemont. She works night shifts for the dispatch center. She's off this weekend and would do it for baby-sitting money if you throw in a bonus for the last-minute call. I use her as backup all the time. Hold on, I'll find her number."

Luke closed his eyes and squeezed the

bridge of his nose. His family was missing. *At least Caroline has the smarts to look as scared as she feels.* He'd freeze up like she was doing if he let himself feel it.

Jackie read the number off to him and he added it to Caroline's list. "We're heading back to Benton. Odds are still good that this is car trouble, but if that changes, can you be ready to run the search from here? I'll leave a packet on the counter," he said calmly, knowing what he was saying. A missing persons case for an entire family would require dozens of law enforcement officers, hundreds of searchers, thousands of flyers.

"Luke, you know that's a yes. As soon as you feel you need to escalate this, call me."

"It's appreciated, Jackie." He selected pictures from the shelves and removed the backs to retrieve the photos. He put together a spread of individual and family photos into a folder. "Give me a couple hours and let's see what we find in Benton." The script for a missing persons case was one they had both run in the past. This wouldn't get that far, not if he could help it. "Change of subject: If there's a solid hit on Frank, call me. I'd like to know that situation is dealt with tonight too."

"I will."

Luke heard Caroline move from the study to look in the kitchen drawers by the phone. "Let me call you at the bottom of the hour from the interstate." Luke hung up and then used Caroline's list and dialed one more number.

"Benton sheriff's office. May I help you?"

"This is FBI Special Agent Luke Falcon. I need to speak with the sheriff. It's urgent."

SIX

Luke kept the car air conditioner on to make it easier to stay alert. Caroline leaned forward in the passenger seat, the shoulder seat belt pulled tight, scanning the opposite lanes of traffic going back into Atlanta. "If they are off the road, it's hard to see across the lanes."

"We'll go as far as Sandy Hill, turn around and drive back toward Atlanta in those lanes as they would have done," Luke replied. The speeds were picking up and the hour was growing late. It would only take one driver with a bit too much to drink to cause a horrific accident. "If we don't find something between Sandy Hill and Atlanta, we'll search the stretch from Sandy Hill to Benton."

"I should have called you hours before. In the dark, this is impossible."

"We'll stop at pull offs and show the photos around. Benjamin is not going to make an hour-plus journey at the start of his vacation without one stop for a soda, a restroom break, and an ice cream cone."

He didn't add that staff at rest stops had probably changed shifts, that a mom with a young boy was the norm, that Benjamin had likely changed from the clothes Caroline remembered from school before leaving home. Finding them on this road was a long shot; it was just better odds than the next option on his mental list.

"What do you think happened?"

Luke glanced at the dashboard clock. 10:05. Caroline had waited longer than he expected before asking the question. He didn't plan to tell her what he thought. She was definitely in the civilian side of the world, and the law enforcement answers would just turn her pallor a deeper gray. "I don't know, Caroline. Right now we have too few precious facts."

She went quiet for too long for his comfort. He glanced her way. "Tell me about this month," he asked.

"What do you want to know?"

He just wanted her talking rather than brooding. "Start somewhere and catch me up on what's been going on with everyone this last month. Has anything unusual happened?"

"Not like last fall, if that's what you're really asking."

Her fast reaction told him a lot about how last fall still stung in her memories. "As I said at the time — the only reputation you've got with me is that you notice things. And frankly, right now I'm hoping you've got a really good memory as well."

She shifted in the seat. "Sharon had her first patient who gave birth to triplets. She's carrying photos around like she was the one to deliver them. I think Mark was in Atlanta a couple times to meet with his partners, but otherwise he was working out of the Benton office. Benjamin has been talking about the tree house Mark is helping him design and anticipating seeing the Braves game this weekend."

"Anyone new around their place? A handyman, a landscaper?"

"No. Mark and Sharon have been talking about starting work on the pool they want to add to the house, but they haven't done more than Mark developing the blueprint for it. Mark hired a couple new people at his office, and I think Sharon hired another nurse."

Luke glanced over at Caroline. She'd about circled the top of her Styrofoam cup with fingernail marks, and the cup was going back around for a second circle of impressions. "You've got a good memory for details; it helps."

"I don't know how. I don't know where they are."

He didn't know how to explain it, but he listened to her words and relaxed. She reacted to trouble as if she had an antenna tuned to it, and nothing in her memories concerned him. "Trouble tends to advertise itself. A normal routine is good news. If you'd said one of them had recently had a flat tire while the car was in a parking lot, or someone tried to break into one of their offices, I'd be worried."

"I'm scared, Luke." He covered her hand and just held it. She finally sighed. "I don't do trouble very well."

"We'll find them." Luke reached for his cell phone in his pocket and handed it to her. "Why don't you call Mary Treemont and see if there have been any calls at the condominium. Check if she's been able to figure out that hundred button remote control sufficiently to get her movie to play."

Caroline accepted the phone. She looked relieved to have something to do. She punched in the numbers.

Luke watched the lanes of oncoming

traffic flow by, listening to Caroline. She was trying so hard to stay hopeful and positive as she dealt with this, but it was like watching someone standing on a ladder realizing the rungs below them were breaking. She was scared.

And so was he.

It was wearing him out keeping the conversation going, to not let himself slip into the silence he preferred that would fill this car if Jackie were beside him and not Caroline. *What do I think happened to them? I think they're in real trouble.* Two vehicles with a common destination did not disappear without a trace. However this ended, it was not going to be all good news.

I hope I'm simply being morbid without cause. Caroline would regather her hope this would work out soon and positively; he was already bracing himself to hear the worst. And the realization that he'd likely be the one breaking the terrible news to her was not something he wanted to dwell on.

Failure is not an option, Lord. I've spent my life trying to avoid a big failure, and it's going to hit in my personal life and happen to my family — the one thing that the rest of my life hinges on. Seconds right now are clicking by painfully like the impact of a thousand fine cuts. I can handle a few shocks; I can't handle a catastrophe.

He glanced at Caroline. *And neither can she.*

They stopped at each interchange along I-20, showing photos in the fast-food and sit-down restaurants. Luke made a point of showing each waitress a photo of Mark Falcon. His cousin made an impression with his good looks, and this was one evening Luke didn't mind exploiting that fact.

He got two maybes and one proposition that if he was related she'd love to have his card. He gave the waitress his card and his partner's number.

"It's after eleven, where do we try next?" Caroline joined him back at the car, her hands around a super-size soda. She'd come back with candy bars and ice cream cones and big drinks.

Luke had figured out after the third stop that she felt compelled to buy something in exchange for a look at the photo. She'd go broke as a cop. But she had gotten one sympathetic manager to run back his security tape and show them the one car he remembered that matched Mark's. It hadn't been his, but it had been a hopeful moment in an otherwise too quiet night.

"I was thinking we'd show their pictures at the stops between Benton and Sandy Hill, but I think it might be better just to go to Mark and Sharon's house and let you get a look around and maybe figure out what Benjamin is wearing."

"It's okay with me. What did you buy?"

He looked at the package in his hand and the seam he was wearing in the plastic. "Baseball cards. For Benjamin."

Her smile made the seventy-nine cents plus tax worth a few more pennies.

"Let's go to Sharon and Mark's," she agreed.

SEVEN

Luke turned on his high-beams as he drove into the stretch of woods outside Benton near Mark and Sharon's home. The country road was narrow. It was an accident waiting to happen as he passed yet another driveway he didn't see until he was right on top of the roadside mailbox. "Benjamin knows these woods."

"Like the back of his hand. Why?"

Luke slowed further, looking for the drive. "It just strikes me as an interesting place to hide and a great place to build that tree house. What do you remember about your conversation with Benjamin this afternoon?" He turned into Sharon and Mark's driveway.

"He was worried about his baseball glove. He couldn't remember where he had left it, and I told him I thought it was in the trunk of Sharon's car. Benjamin said they were leaving the hospital, thought they would be an hour and a half. I said two hours was more likely . . ." Her voice trailed off.

Luke looked over at her shadowed profile. "What?"

"Benjamin dropped the phone. One of those mid-sentence cutoffs. A van had cut his mom off and he dropped the phone. I told him to tell his mom to drive carefully," she whispered.

A van. For a moment Luke let himself be paranoid and hoped it hadn't been a white van. He reached over and squeezed Caroline's hand, to reassure her but also to comfort himself. All he needed was Frank Hardin somehow mixed up in what so far still looked like a difficult missing persons case. Caroline's hand was cold, and he left his hand on hers for a moment to warm it.

He made the last curve in the driveway and the house appeared in the headlights. It was a spacious two story designed to accommodate friends and family for barbeques now and someday swim parties for the kids. It was a physical statement of permanence promised to both Sharon and Benjamin. Mark had cast the Falcon name around them.

The house was dark, not even a security

light marked the perimeter. Luke knew it was misleading and that security here was solid. He pulled around to the back of the house and parked in the empty driveway. "Stay in the car while I glance around."

He got out without waiting for a reply, knowing Caroline would do as he asked. A touch of the switch on the side of the garage and ground lights clicked on along the path of stepping stones to the house.

Luke walked to the dark house, opened the screen door, and unlocked the back door. Inside the house he studied the alarm system, typed in his own middle name, and the alarm system disarmed. He hadn't expected Mark to read the manual and actually change the administrator code.

He stood motionless in the doorway listening, hearing nothing but the hum of the refrigerator and the faint click of the wall clock. He walked into the kitchen, his steps echoing on the hardwood floors and his hand touching the edge of the counter to orient himself. Sharon had left a stack of linen napkins on the table, and resting against the wall was Benjamin's plastic bat.

Luke headed to the right, walking the hallway past Mark's office, Sharon's sitting room, a downstairs guest suite, and the living room. No signs of trouble, foul play, or burglary here . . . He hadn't expected to see any. He went back the way he had come, turned on lights in the kitchen, and walked outside to get Caroline.

"What do you think, Luke?"

"That they came home, packed, and then left as planned for Atlanta." He pushed his hands into the back pockets of his jeans, enjoying the comfortable night air and wishing it wasn't hiding tragedy. "When you get inside, I just want you to walk through the rooms and look around. In particular Benjamin's. Tell me if you can what he's now wearing. The same for Sharon, see what she packed."

"I'll try."

Luke let her walk ahead of him, not wanting to interfere with what she might notice. He entered the study to check the answering machine. No messages. Papers were neat on the desk, what appeared to be yesterday's mail from the postmarks was opened and sorted in the in-box. He didn't see today's mail. Sharon's touch had placed a bowl of mints on the desk, fresh flowers, and a framed sketch of one of Mark's best house designs.

Mark or Sharon would have left a message on this home machine for the other one if they were not together, for the messages could be retrieved remotely. He continued to hope they were together.

They had both been planning to travel I-20 to Atlanta. If Sharon got in trouble and Mark saw it and stopped to help her — it had to be that sequence since they knew Sharon had left first.

Come on, Mark, you're good. You were already concerned about Sharon after last fall's coincidences regarding Caroline, and you've always been alert to your own surroundings. You wouldn't get taken by surprise easily. What happened? Where? He heard Caroline coming and relaxed with his hands in his back pockets again as he turned.

"Benjamin changed clothes when he got home. The shirt he wore to school, the pants, were beside his bed. The books and folders on the bed look like they came out of his backpack. I think his Braves shirt is gone, and I don't see the display book of baseball cards he loves. I can't tell what shoes he has on, and I think he may have taken a cap, but I'm at a loss for what he's wearing."

"Knowing he changed after school helps. What about Sharon?"

"She went shopping last week for this weekend, and I can guess at least two of

95

the dinner outfits she took along. But she has too many clothes; I can't suggest what she might be wearing now."

"It was a long shot. There's no sign of anything here that delayed them. I want you to log on to their computer and see what time the last e-mail was downloaded. They might have checked messages just before they left."

She pulled out the chair at the desk. "I had hoped somehow there would be something here to suggest what might have changed their plans."

"We're going to find them, Caroline. Trust me on that."

He didn't have much to give her beyond his word, but she nodded, accepting it. She'd dig deep and find the stability she would need for this crisis. He was confident her faith would hold her together while they endured this night.

He wished his own faith had that same strength. There had been too many hard events over the years, too many times when he was like Peter walking on water, halfway across to Jesus on faith when a glance at reality made him sink. It was hard to trust God on a night like this, when he was all too aware of what might have happened. Caroline was going to weather this better than he would. She might be shaky at the start, but she'd finish in better shape.

Luke walked through the house to the kitchen and put on a pot of coffee. The clock clicked past midnight.

Too many dead people, Jesus. If I doubt during the next hours, please be merciful and remember You made me of dust, not steel. I was prepared for a holiday this weekend, not a storm. And this one is going to be vicious. I wasn't ready.

When Caroline joined him, the coffee was almost ready, and he poured her the first cup. She sat at the kitchen table and swiped her hands across her eyes. "The last time they were on-line was this morning about 7:20. What are we going to do, Luke?"

He squeezed her shoulder. "Call in even more help. Pray."

Her hand covered his and what nails she had left made an impression before she released his hand. Scared. He understood that emotion. He rubbed his thumb on her cheek, then gently tugged the braid she'd put in her hair. "Drink the coffee, we'll be leaving shortly." He stepped outside to make his calls.

Luke stopped pacing to lean against his

car fender. "Jackie, we're at Sharon and Mark's house now. It looks like Sharon and Benjamin came home, Benjamin changed out of school clothes, they packed, and they left. There's no sign of trouble. And no word from Mark."

"I could understand one of their cars disappearing, but both?"

Luke sighed. "This was planned. Well planned." And with that part of his hope died — that this would have a swift ending, that it would turn out okay, that somehow he'd be able to be Caroline's white knight and solve this. Really bad news was coming. Luke adjusted, because he had to.

"I left the packet of photos with your name on it on the counter by the phone at the condo. Start calling in every favor you think either one of us is owed. Get the photos ready to hit the early morning newscasts. I want Benton, Sandy Hill, and Atlanta saturated with news and flyers by dawn. You can start running a tab against my personal credit cards; they should hold out until dawn when I can call and bump up the credit lines. If you have an idea that you think will work, don't ask, just run with it."

"I'll get it started. Do you want me to handle the media interviews?"

"Please. Caroline can't handle it, and I don't have the patience for it. I'll call security at Mark's condo and let them know anyone you want to bring up — cops or television crews — are to be cleared in. Sharon's too trusting; someone could have gotten to her. And if they then went after Mark . . ."

"You're jumping to worst case," Jackie said softly.

"Worst case, they are already dead. I can work with anything better than that. The cops haven't been able to find either car. I'll need helicopters ready to go up at first light with heat detection gear. The woods around here are thick. Find me a good profiler who can look this over."

"Headquarters is going to appoint another agent to run the case."

"I know. Get Henry James in the loop. He's the best in the division for missing persons cases. The Atlanta SAC owes me; he'll let Henry take it." Luke tried to think through threads they could work. "The last call Caroline had with Benjamin, he dropped the phone. He said someone in a van cut off his mom as she left the clinic parking lot. Get security to pull all the tapes for the hospital's and the clinic's parking lots. There's a chance Sharon was tailed. Mark was going to the bank and to fill up the car with gas. There should be security tapes at both places."

"Luke, this will get worked as a possible kidnapping."

"I can only hope it's a move for money." If this was someone thinking a person's life and a sum of money could equate, Luke might get them back. "Tell Henry to put taps and recorders on all the family phone lines, including my home phone and Caroline's. I'll keep my second phone line free if you need to forward a call."

He looked at his watch. They needed to check the clinic tonight, which meant waking someone up. "Change of subject: Has there been anything on Frank Hardin?"

"A decent lead by a trucker had him heading west."

"He did whatever job he came to do."

"It looks that way."

"Any more bodies show up?" Luke shoved a hand through his hair. "No, don't answer that. I'm pushing the edge of morbid tonight. I'll call at the bottom of the hour. I'm taking Caroline by the medical clinic and Mark's office. We'll be back at her place before the first newscasts announce that family is missing. I want Caroline to have a few minutes in familiar surroundings before that hits her."

"Hang in there, Luke. We'll find them."

"I just hope it's soon."

Luke hung up the phone.

How many of them have I already lost, Lord? One? Two? All three? It's been seven hours. The odds are already against us. Why did this have to touch the entire family? Benjamin's just a boy.

Of all people to end up in trouble, it shouldn't be Mark, Sharon, and Benjamin. Trouble should have come after him. Had someone who wanted to get to him come crashing through his family to make a point? Luke did his best to keep public knowledge about his family to a minimum, but it was out there.

The back door opened. Caroline backed out of the door, balancing two mugs in her hands and using her foot to ease the screen door closed. She saw he was off the phone and gave a fast smile that came and went as she walked over to join him. She offered him one of the mugs of coffee. "Black."

"Thanks." He was grateful for the warmth.

"What now, Luke?"

"I want you to show me around where Sharon works, where you dropped off

Benjamin, what you know of her routine when she normally leaves to drive home. They appear to have gotten to the house, but if someone followed them — I want to figure out how hard that might be to do."

Caroline took the words better than he expected, her attention shifting to the night sky and then back to him. They wouldn't find her family tonight. "It's going to be okay," he said softly, not sure how he could back up that promise but feeling it had to be given, for his own sake as much as hers.

"Benjamin hates sleeping without a nightlight."

He felt his throat choke up. "He's a tough kid, Caroline."

He finished the coffee, then squeezed her shoulder and nodded toward the car. "I'll lock up the house and set the alarm. Give me a minute."

EIGHT

The building manager unlocked the doors to the medical clinic. "I gave the security tapes to the sheriff's deputy; I hope that was okay."

"It's fine," Luke reassured him. "They're reviewing the tapes now. I appreciate your meeting us here this time of night."

"The idea that something happened to the doctor —" The man shook his head. He turned on lights for the reception area. "Building security walked through the clinic with the deputy. They found nothing out of place. As far as we can determine, Dr. Falcon left the premises around four p.m., and nothing indicates she returned."

"Does the receptionist keep a call log?"

"Yes."

"We need to see phone logs, outgoing calls, anything to indicate who Dr. Falcon spoke with today."

"You'll have it. Give me twenty minutes. Her office is at the back of the corridor on the right."

"I know the way," Caroline said, heading down the hall.

Luke nodded to the building manager and followed her. She paused in the office doorway and turned on the lights.

"What do you notice, Caroline?"

She shook her head and stepped inside. "It looks the same as it did this afternoon."

Luke walked over to the desk and opened the calendar. He pulled out his notepad and picked up a pen. "See if you can find today's mail, any clue regarding a last-minute errand Sharon might have decided to make." He wrote down the notations Sharon had made on her calendar during the last week. A stop at the dry-cleaners and post office were noted for today.

"The newspaper is gone; I was reading the movie times earlier when I dropped off Benjamin."

"Did you see a dry-cleaner's bag when you were by earlier?" Luke asked.

"No, but it could have been hanging on the back of the door and I wouldn't have seen it."

"We'll check if she picked up the order."

He closed the calendar. "Anything in the mail?"

"Just her notation on the hospital bulletin to remember to bring in cookies next week for the retirement party for the hospital administrative secretary."

Luke studied the papers left on the desk. Sharon was neat in her filing, if overworked. This had the feel of a dead end. He looked around the room. "The roses are new."

"Mark sent them."

Luke walked over to the table where the vase sat and fingered the perfect blooms. "There's no card. Did Sharon say Mark sent them?"

Caroline didn't answer him. Luke looked over at her. She sank down on the couch. "No . . . I assumed it."

"We'll find the florist who delivered them."

"It's the same bouquet, the same unique vase," she whispered. "I should have realized it. The guy who stalked me last fall just sent the same bouquet of roses to my sister that he sent to me. That's what you're wondering."

He was, but the confirmation of it was beyond what she could bear. He crossed the room and reached for her hand. "Stop,

Caroline. The roses are just one of the things that happened today, like a van cutting them off as she pulled out of the lot. Nothing means anything beyond what it is. We'll rule out the roses easily enough. Mark may have sent them and she took the card with her."

"Luke, last fall, roses were what he used when he said he wanted to meet me . . ." Caroline bolted up from the couch and disappeared into the hall.

"Caroline!" Luke slammed the office door shut behind him and headed after her. He should have just checked out the roses without asking her about them.

Caroline shoved open the door to the clinic and surged outside, seeking the darkness to hide her tears. She didn't want Luke telling her what he was starting to wonder. *O God, where are they? What happened to my family?*

She shoved her hands into her jacket pockets, searching for a Kleenex left over from the packet she had been using in the car. Her throat burned so bad she couldn't swallow. Not finding any tissues, she paced over to the car and opened the door, searching through the glove box to get the napkins she had stuffed in there. She wanted to drown in these tears.

Luke stopped beside her, breathing hard. "This isn't going to be a stalking. Not with Mark's disappearance too."

She looked over at him, fighting the urge to swear at him because he was around and this was beyond anything she could bear. She needed and yet hated the fact that he was treating this like a case to work.

"I need you to be prepared to get a ransom call."

She reached toward the car to steady herself. *A ransom call.* The words cut like a sharp knife. "That is what you've been organizing while taking me around," she whispered.

"Yes."

She struggled to stand without leaning against the car, feeling like she had to find the strength from somewhere even as she died inside. She walked shakily toward the medical clinic before turning back to stare at Luke. "Ransom calls . . . accidents . . . worse. You just reel them off. Don't you *feel* anything? It's your family missing too!"

The muscles in his jaw tensed. "Don't, Caroline. We've been down this road before; let's not go there again. I can't help Mark if I let emotions overwhelm my ability to do my job. You've got enough emotion for both of us."

"Well I'm sorry I'm upset!"

He took two steps back and leaned against the side of his car.

"What's the matter, did I touch a nerve? You do have them, don't you?" He stood there, arms folded, watching her. Always just watching her. She spun away. "There are times I hate you."

"I know."

She lowered her head toward her knees. To think she had wondered about loving this man. She closed her eyes and took a deep breath.

The events of the last hours replayed in her head from the first suspicion about Sharon and Benjamin being late to the last decision she had made when the fear hit — calling Luke. She had trusted him to be able to do something to help her. And now she was angry that he was doing his job. "I'm sorry, that was uncalled for."

"I'm going to find them, Caroline. All of them."

She stood up. "What are we going to do now? I know you've got a plan."

"We'll go back to the house. You're going to eat something, and we'll talk through what to say if a call comes in. Jackie has technicians setting up phone taps now. In a few hours, flyers with Sharon, Benjamin, and Mark's photos will be flooding the news, and we'll have command centers organized in both Benton and Atlanta to run a full search with local police and volunteers. Sharon, Mark, and Benjamin are somewhere and we will find them."

"Alive?"

"What do you want me to say, Caroline? It's killing me that —" His voice broke. He cleared it. "Speculation is not going to help either one of us get through this night."

"I can't lose my family, Luke. They are everything I've got."

"You've got me."

She looked at him. She couldn't handle who he was. Whatever happened this weekend, the job he did, and the control he kept — they couldn't work this out. She walked around the car to the passenger door. "Let's go to the house."

The back door to Mark and Sharon's home opened before Caroline got the car door open.

Luke's partner met her partway across the driveway with a hug. "Caroline, I'm so sorry. So very, very sorry."

Caroline tried to smile when Jackie stepped back. "Thank you for coming to help. Luke says you've been busy."

"The guys here — Luke tapped the best in the Bureau to help. Come on, let me introduce you."

Caroline left her notebook on the kitchen table and went with Jackie to meet the people using the dining room as their work area. Jackie introduced her to four men and two women. "Let me get you a seat, Caroline, and I'll show you what we're arranging."

The thought was too overwhelming. Caroline took a step backward, and Luke's hand settled on her shoulder. She wanted so badly to lean against him and just let the tears keep falling. She shook her head. "In a bit. Let me find us something to eat while you two talk. I need a minute first."

Luke rubbed his thumb on her shoulder blade. "Something with pickles for me."

She tried to smile. "Sure. Excuse me." She made her escape.

Jackie and Luke were good together. Jackie was the kind of lady he needed to find for his personal life too: Someone who didn't crumble when hard days came. Caroline just wanted to burst into tears, go hide, anything to get away from the horrible fact that there was nothing she could do to help her family right now. Others had to find them.

"She'll be okay, Luke."

He turned from watching Caroline retreat to the kitchen to look at his partner. "Yes." He rubbed his burning eyes, wishing he wasn't letting Caroline down so badly. As support for her tonight, he was failing miserably. "What do we know?"

"Mark did not send the roses."

Luke dropped his hand to focus on Jackie.

"I tracked down the florist as soon as you called me. The woman who took the phoned-in order said it wasn't Mark, that he didn't want a card, and that it was thanks for Sharon being a wonderful doctor. She said he paid by cash, that —"

"That bouquet wasn't from a grateful patient," Luke said with certainty.

"You think Caroline's stalker from last fall transferred his attention to Sharon?"

"It was the same bouquet, Jackie, and as a thank-you —" He shook his head. "It feels very wrong, especially given its timing. Yes, I think it's a distinct possibility the man just transferred his focus. This time he skipped the preliminaries and just grabbed what he wanted."

"What about Mark? That might explain what happened to Sharon, but not your cousin."

"I don't know. But if this is not a kidnapping, it's going to be something extreme. We need a way to eliminate stalking as a possibility."

"We'll figure it out." Jackie nodded to the kitchen where Caroline disappeared. "How prepared is she to get a ransom call?"

"She's not. But she'll get there. Are we ready here?"

"Any line they might conceivably call is tapped."

Waiting for the phone to ring qualified as slow torture. Caroline stopped her pacing at the doorway to the dining room. Too many people; too much confusion; she couldn't think. And the words she had been coached to say were echoing around in her mind like a broken record. *I'll give you the money. But I need to know they are alive.* "I want to go home, Jackie. They could call my house."

"The phones are being covered."

"Still, I want to go home."

Luke put down the papers he held. "I'll take you."

She nodded and abruptly turned to head outside. She could walk home faster than waiting on him to drive her, but tonight she wouldn't get out of here without him.

"Luke, stay over there with her. Stretch out on the couch and get a couple hours of sleep. You're running on fumes. There is a very long Saturday ahead of us. Any call that comes in here, we can route to her place."

Caroline didn't hear Luke's reply to Jackie as the door swung closed behind her. Her vote would be no. She had no desire to have company. But not much of today had gone her way.

"He's not coming."

"He'll come," Frank replied, lighting another cigarette. The shadows of the church bell tower danced across the hood of their car. Silence returned, thick and heavy.

Ronald looked again at his watch. "We need to cut our losses and get out of here."

"Not until I get my money."

"Frank, it's almost one a.m. There isn't going to be a ransom paid. Let's put a bullet in her head, dump her in the woods, and move on. We were hired by an idiot who turned out to have a very bad plan."

"No. I'm going to get paid one way or another." Frank crushed his cigarette. "But the price just went up."

NINE

Luke's car headlights passed over the terraced grounds at the side of Caroline's house. Back when this had been an active farm, any bit of flat land had been kept for crops and cattle. The terraces created flat stretches of land for flower beds and water breaks to keep rain from rushing against the back patio. She'd inherited the place from her parents, and he'd always thought the home was perfect for her.

Luke shut off the car and the silence around them was complete. "Let's go in."

She didn't move immediately, then pushed at the car door and got out. She dug in her purse for her keys.

Unlocking the side door of her house, she pushed it open, shut off the alarm, and stepped into her kitchen. Luke followed her. The ceiling fan turned on with the light. The room was warm and smelled faintly of cinnamon rolls. "Do you have a flashlight? I'd like to look around outside."

She retrieved it for him. "I'm making myself some tea. Would you like some?"

"Please." He needed to send her to bed for a few hours, but while she was this tense — it wouldn't be a restful sleep.

He stepped outside and clicked on the light. He walked the driveway toward the roadside mailbox, searching the woods on either side for signs of a disturbance. The mailbox was freshly painted red with white daisies. He opened the latched door slowly and shone his light inside. No note. Most kidnappers preferred phone calls. So why didn't they call?

He walked back to the house, listening to the woods. He hated the outdoors on nights like this, hated having to fight the darkness of nature as well as the darkness of the soul in the man he feared might be out there, watching. The perimeter seemed quiet. He paused to wipe his feet before entering. He skirted around Caroline and put the flashlight away under the sink. "I'll go wash up."

Photos lined the hallway, several of Ben and Sharon, numerous casual photos of Caroline's students. There was a new photo of Caroline, her arms draped around

116

Ben's shoulders, the boy laughing as he held up a big turtle. Luke wished he'd been there to see that scene.

He stepped into the small bathroom off the hall. His eyes were dry and gritty, and he could almost taste the traffic fumes still lingering on his shirt. He splashed cold water on his face to ease the fatigue and picked up the soap to wash his hands. Caroline used this small bathroom regularly. A Post-it note on the mirror counted down the days until Christmas, the numbers crossed off and shrinking fast. He smiled at the reminder of how much Caroline liked the holidays. She'd framed a note written in her handwriting and hung it above the towels.

HOW TO BE A GREAT TEACHER

Know your students.
Know your subject.
Make it relevant.
Teach in an organized place, in an organized way.
Encourage curiosity.
Ask the questions: Who? What? When? Where? Why? How?
Time is priceless.
Care.

The list sounded so like her. Caroline loved teaching fifth grade. Luke touched the small chimes hanging on the wall, sending them into motion and then turned off the light. He walked through the house. He wasn't looking for anything in particular, simply signs that there had been unwanted attention also focusing on Caroline.

He couldn't discount the fact that by leaving early for Atlanta, Caroline had unknowingly saved herself from being part of whatever had happened. If someone had grabbed Sharon and Ben and also Mark, had they intended to grab Caroline too?

Luke took a seat on the stairs and rubbed the center of his left palm with his right thumb seeing the lines smooth out and re-form. *Caroline part of this . . . when had she made that decision to leave early for Atlanta?*

Had someone been tailing her too and she hadn't realized it? Or maybe she lost them in traffic? Someone had come after the Falcons in Benton and taken three of them. It wouldn't be much of a stretch to see them also plucking Caroline from her travels. His hand tightened over the other to stop the tremor. This hadn't been accidental — the hours since they had last been seen made that improbable — and that left intentional. *Who are you? Why did you do this? What do you want?*

He pushed hands through his hair and looked for a moment at the ceiling. If he came apart tonight, so would Caroline. She'd pulled herself together but she was still on that fragile line of panic. He suppressed the overwhelming emotions he felt. He could do little for his family tonight, but he could still do something for Caroline. As much as she hated his calmness, it was still for her benefit.

He was doing the biggest snow job in the world right now, implying he was okay. *I am so scared, Lord. All I can see is finding their bloody corpses. You might as well kill me with a heart attack first; it would be more merciful.*

He took a deep breath, stood up, and walked back through the house. He reentered the kitchen from the other direction. "I still think you have a great home. It's got character."

"I like it."

Old-fashioned glass jars with stick candy in a variety of flavors lined the counter. Luke took an orange stick and walked to the patio door to check the dead bolt.

Caroline brought the tea over to the

table, and a plate of sandwiches. "Come and sit. You barely touched what I fixed earlier; you have to eat something. Would you say grace for us?"

"Sure." He pulled out a chair and waited for her to settle in her chair before reaching for her hand. "Jesus, please bring Sharon, Benjamin, and Mark home to share the next meal around this table." Her hand cut off the circulation in his. "Please keep them safe." He ended the prayer before it overwhelmed her. She looked like she wanted to lay her head down on her hands and bawl.

He picked up the sandwich he would have to wrestle to swallow. A glance at the clock showed it was 2:23 a.m. "If you eat, you'll rest better."

She nodded and ate a few bites of the sandwich. He needed more things from Caroline: lists of friends and neighbors and answers to a dozen other questions about who might have reason to hurt the family, but he couldn't bring himself to ask them right now. The team already had their hands full getting ready for the six a.m. newscasts. A couple hour's delay for those names wouldn't materially affect how fast they could be investigated.

Caroline pushed aside her plate and

rested her chin on her palm. "They aren't going to be found alive, are they?"

He flinched. He looked at her and couldn't answer her. Not given what he'd seen on the job the last few years. He couldn't offer much hope that he could give her back all three of them safe and unhurt. He might be able to give her back some of them alive. Sometimes he hated his job that made anything better than death good news.

She looked away, toward the night outside the patio doors. "Tell me what comes next, Luke. If we don't get a ransom call."

"We'll talk after you get some sleep." He took the dishes to the sink, rinsed them, and stacked them in the dishwasher.

"I'm scared to sleep. They're out there somewhere, needing help, and I'm sleeping."

"Finish the tea." A marathon was coming, and she was still thinking sprint. "With the coming of dawn, the world will be at your doorstep, all wanting to help. You'll need your voice to answer all the questions."

She turned her glass around. "I want to stay with you later today, wherever you go."

"You'd survive better if you stayed a step

away from the investigation."

"If we don't find them, what does it matter? There will be only me. Without family, who cares how neatly I survive this?"

He sighed. That made two of them. Without Mark around, what was his life going to be worth? He rested his hand on her shoulder. They'd been tossed out of the same boat and both expected to swim. "Go sleep while you can. We're in this together, Caroline, for as long as God allows this storm to last."

She covered his hand briefly with her own, and maybe that was the one encouraging point in the night — they were in it together. They weren't exactly in sync with each other, but they were in the same storm. "I'll wake you at six. Try not to dream."

She tried to smile. "No problem. Life is enough of a nightmare right now. Get some sleep too, Luke. You look awful."

He rubbed his face. "Yeah. I feel it too."

Her eyes met his, and the emotion in them — She reached over and hugged him hard, then abruptly left the room.

For the first time since the suspicion that something was wrong had set in yesterday afternoon, Caroline had nothing else to distract her from her thoughts. If only the images and fears would go away. Only the faint sounds of wood creaking as the cool night air contracted floorboards broke the silence. Tonight she only wished that footsteps of weary family members making it back home were on the stairs to wake her up.

Caroline's bedroom was at the end of the hall, the room she had used since she was a child, decorated now in soft white walls, with colorful pillows and throws for splashes of impact. The room was simple, but hers, and comforting.

She tugged back the blankets and moved the pillows to her preferred pile on her right. She set the alarm clock for 5:40 a.m. She could be ready to join Luke at 6 o'clock. She picked up the hairbrush from the bedside table but didn't have the energy to use it.

Something horrible happened to them; there was no other explanation. *Jesus, I just want to curl up and retreat from life, from this gaping wound and unbearable pain. We have to find them. I need to be out there looking, even though I know experts are already searching.*

She got to her feet, left the hairbrush,

and headed out into the hall. Her parents' bedroom had been turned into a guest room and sitting room years before. Her sister had used the bedroom across the hall from hers, and Benjamin had his own room near the front of the house where the dormer angled out from the wall. Caroline walked down to Benjamin's room and sat on the slender bed.

He'd left a book on the bedside table. She opened it to the bookmark he'd made from a thin blue strip of colored paper glued to a piece of cardboard. He penciled on the bookmark his own bar graph to record how many books he read this year. Caroline smiled and set the book back down.

She picked up his pillow and hugged it. So many memories were in this room. Days of tucking him in and reading him a last story. Nights when he had whispered questions like: Could he be in her fifth grade class one day? Would she help him make his mom a bracelet for her birthday? Was Mark really going to be his new father? She was his aunt, and he trusted her to back up what his mom said, to tell her his thoughts and dreams. He liked to try ideas out on her before testing them on his mom.

It had been several weeks since Ben last spent a night under this roof on a sleepover. He was still getting comfortable with the security of his new home, and Caroline understood his subconscious desire not to be away from Sharon and Mark for long. Benjamin hero-worshipped his new dad, and it was still sinking in that *permanent* really meant forever.

Caroline curled up on Benjamin's bed and pulled over a second thin pillow. *Hang tough, Benjamin. Luke will find all of you.*

Sharon was a strong woman. She had made it through medical school while married with a son. She had survived the shock of her husband Zachary's unexpected death. She had picked up and come back to Benton to build a good life for herself and her son. She'd had the courage to say yes when Mark proposed.

Sharon, I'm going to be lost without you. If you're hurt, if someone grabbed you, if you're protecting Benjamin — please, figure out a way to get word to us. I've always counted on you to figure out what to do.

Caroline wiped at the tears flowing onto the pillow. She wasn't sure how Luke was getting through this night. It was his family too. If she could guess at what might have happened, Luke had firsthand experience on which to base his suspicions. As much as she hated his silence and distance, deep in her heart she knew he was staying silent because he likely did know what had happened, and it would be news too hard for her to hear.

Jesus, I'm just so scared.

Caroline closed her eyes and wished for the night to be over.

Luke turned on the couch, tossing off pillows and trying to get comfortable, needing to be downstairs rather than in the guest room to hear if something was disturbed outside.

What was he dealing with? Who? Why Mark and Sharon and Benjamin? The boy was a good kid; he would do the Falcon name proud for the next generation. Luke sighed. He should have paid better attention to the details of the suspicious events occurring around Caroline last fall and what they suggested about the stalker's behavior. How much of what was happening today was rooted in those days?

He watched moonlight shadows drift across the wall. Mark might survive a fight, Sharon would try to negotiate an out, but Benjamin had no defenses. He was resourceful, not as likely to realize the extent of the personal danger he was in, but defenseless to the emotional hit if he saw someone hurt his mom. Luke closed his eyes at that image. He couldn't even imagine where the three of them might be found.

Just let it be something I can deal with, Lord. Even if it's a snatch and a ransom — something for which there's at least hope they will be found alive.

Life already had a before and after quality to it. He would gladly trade his own life for any of theirs. His worst fear was that he wouldn't have the chance.

TEN

Caroline got up quietly after two hours, her sleep too filled with nightmarish images to close her eyes again. She pulled on sweats and heavy socks. Not wanting to wake Luke by going downstairs, she settled in the sitting room, which had once been her parents' room, curling up on the rocking chair with a blanket across her lap to keep warm.

Her attention drifted across the photos and the books, the display shelves with mementos from family trips. So many memories here . . .

Unable to help herself, she reached for the photo album on the bottom shelf of the table beside the rocking chair and set it in her lap. The old album needed retaping to hold the spine together and saved programs and ribbons moved to a more secure box, but it was a project still waiting to be done. Her family had documented every-

She let herself remember that night, wanting to be back in those happier times.

A carnival was not how Caroline had expected Luke to want to bring in the new year, but she was willing to admit it was growing on her.

She laughed at the strange balloon animal he handed her. "I'm not going to ask."

"Think giraffe meets ostrich; it's nothing but a very long neck and very thin legs."

"I suppose it can be construed that way."

He handed a bill to the balloon vender and then reached for her hand. "You asked for as many gifts as possible that were basically made of air, and you have to admit, I'm excelling at the challenge."

"The cotton candy was delicious too."

"For pure air volume, the blown glass figurine beat it in spades. Are you up to another ride?"

She studied the Ferris wheel ahead of them, the colorful lights twinkling in the dark sky. "I admit to being overwhelmed with movement. We'd better just plan to sit awhile."

"The twirly seats did you in."

"I think it was the spinning barrel where the floor dropped away."

The carnival crowd had grown as midnight approached, and finding a table at one of the food spots turned out to be a challenge. Luke cleared away trays at a small table for two and created them a place. "Would you like more coffee or something to eat?"

"Get us some chips to share? Salt sounds good right now."

"Be right back."

Her arms had filled with packages during the evening, and she settled the sacks around her. When he returned, she shifted aside her pad of paper and helped him set down the tray. "Your idea of something to share is a meal."

"Bigger is always the better value."

She didn't laugh although her lips twitched. She picked up a tortilla chip and tried the salsa. She liked his taste in food. He turned her pad of paper toward him.

"It's tradition on New Year's Eve to look back at the year and try to decide how life will improve."

"You just like lists," Luke replied, grinning at her.

"I'm good at them."

"Buy new car. Take Benjamin to see a musical. Get graduate course catalog for masters program. Sleep more." He slid her list back

around. "Those last two sound mutually exclusive."

"Getting the course catalog is not the same as signing up for classes, Luke."

"It's one of those long long-term goals."

"Exactly."

He ate a chip. "You forgot a couple important ones."

"Such as?"

"Buy more candy sticks."

"You liked those, did you?"

"Benjamin and I have good taste. Those old-fashioned candy jars you keep on the counter are unique; I like that."

She wrote it down.

"Add one specifically for me: *Date Luke*."

Her pen missed the paper. "You just got done telling me you don't date."

"When did I say that?"

"On the log ride — which, let me point out, had water much colder than you predicted."

"It's going to be January in a couple hours; it's supposed to be cold water. I said I don't date because of my job, as in *make a habit of it*. For you, I'll make an exception."

She bit her lip.

"Write it down," he offered helpfully.

She wrote it down. "I don't understand you."

"I'm not that hard to figure out. I don't have enough free time to make elaborate what should be simple decisions."

"You met me at the wedding over three months ago and invited me to tonight. Now you're asking about the next year."

"If I don't ask, how are you going to say yes?"

Caroline laughed. "I suppose there is some logic to that."

"When you have to compress a relationship into the time available, and it's agonizingly short, it gets easier to focus on the things that matter." He ate another chip.

"You planned this evening, Luke."

"Just the when and where. The thing that mattered most was your being here."

"It's going to take me a while to get used to the non-work side of you. You're not nearly as serious about life as Mark is."

He smiled. "Mark planned Christmas Day, did he?"

"Mark wanted their first Christmas to be enjoyed by everyone. It was nice. We even went for a sleigh ride."

"I don't get that detailed. And my job is serious enough; there's no reason to let my occasional day away stay serious."

"My schedule is a bit of a challenge during the school year. And you live an hour away from Benton."

"We'll figure it out. What would you like to do next?"

"We need a picture to memorialize tonight."

"We do?"

She nodded. "For my scrapbook."

"I'm not big into pictures."

"Tough."

He laughed. "I suppose I could go along with this, just as long as I get a copy of it."

"Admit it; you keep photos around. I know you picked out a couple from the wedding photos. Sharon told me."

"I liked how you blushed. Which you're doing again by the way."

"Don't remind me." She slipped from her chair. "I'm going to go find a mirror. Watch the packages?"

"I'll even save you the last chip," he promised.

She knew he watched as she joined the crowd. Luke Falcon was not what she expected, not even close. And it made her smile.

Luke left Caroline in the rocker, knowing the sleep mattered more than the comfort of a bed. If they got the bad news he feared, she would be struggling to get that sleep in the days ahead. People who had lost loved ones often ended up working nights so they could sleep days. The hours after dark and the memories they brought were so heavy as to make sleep impossible.

Her house had floorboards that creaked, but he moved slow enough to keep the sounds to a minimum. He didn't look at a clock. He picked up the quilt he had set aside on the couch and stretched out again.

If Caroline lost her family, Luke knew he was going to lose her too. There were not enough good memories built up between them to overcome the weight of this weekend. This day would be the raw memory she could never get past. He wiped his eyes and closed them, longing to find the escape of sleep.

ELEVEN

Luke woke to the sound of a phone ringing. He pushed himself up on the couch, his left arm numb, his back aching at the twisted way he had slept. He grabbed for his phone on the side table. "Luke Falcon."

"They found Mark," Jackie said.

So close to a nightmare, so pushed without sleep, Luke heard Jackie's words, and his first instinct was to see blood. "Where?" he choked out.

"He's alive. A country road near the home he designed, a farmer's pond. The car is wrecked and in the water. Mark extricated himself from the car and out of the water before he collapsed. The paramedics haven't even reached him yet. I'm giving you what the sheriff called into the dispatcher less than a minute ago."

He saw the clock. 5:10 a.m. His cousin had dumped his car into water a good twelve hours ago. "Is he conscious?"

"It doesn't sound like it. An air ambulance is on the way to the scene. Hold on, dispatch is working to get me a radio link with the sheriff." Jackie dropped off the line. Luke reached for his shoes and tugged them on with one hand. Jackie came back. "It sounds like Mark has serious chest injuries. Luke, if you want to see him before he's airlifted to the hospital, you've got to go now. You might just be able to get there in time."

Luke pulled over the pad of paper. "Give me the directions."

She listed country road turns. "As bad as this is, it's still good news."

"He's alive. But it leaves a lot of confusion. If Mark simply had an accident . . ." Luke was still sorting out the implications of it. "I really hoped they were all together. Anything at all on Sharon and Ben?"

"No. We've got full media coverage ready to go with the six a.m. newscast. The command centers in Benton and Atlanta will be operational shortly thereafter."

"I'll call you back from the site."

Luke tore off the page of directions and bolted for the stairs to wake Caroline. "Caroline."

He heard a sound to his right and

turned, spotting her in Benjamin's room just stirring on the bed. She had moved to sleep in Benjamin's room. The sight broke his heart.

"What is . . . ?"

"They found Mark."

He caught her as she fell, her feet catching in the blanket pulled from the bed with her. "Easy. Mark had a car accident. He's hurt but alive. We still don't know anything more about Sharon and Ben."

"Where is he? How is he?"

"We're going to go see him. I've got directions to the scene. Find something warm; it's cold this morning."

"Get the car. I'll be right behind you."

Luke paused the car at the top of the hillside where the accident had happened so he could see the full scene. Had he been alone, he would have been tempted to swear at what he saw. Mark's car had missed a turn, slammed through a fence line, and gone down a manmade embankment to crash into the water. It was a wonder the car hadn't rolled and left his cousin dead.

"Mark would never have gone so fast on a country road as to lose control like this without cause," Caroline said softly.

Luke reached over and squeezed her hand. "I know." Something really bad had led to this wreck. Luke drove down the hill and parked on the roadside behind the cop cars. He opened the car door. The air ambulance in the north pasture ascended gracefully a few feet from the earth and turned south, lifting away with a loud beat of blades against the cold morning air. They were too late to see Mark.

Caroline pushed her arms into her jacket. "He's alive. If he had the strength to get through a night outside with his injuries, he'll make it from here."

Luke swallowed against the bitter taste in his mouth and the fear that he might not see his cousin alive again. "He's a fighter." Luke forced himself to look from the departing helicopter to the accident scene. "It could have been a blown tire," he offered, feeling out what might make this an accident rather than foul play. So much of how they handled the search today depended on their conclusions at this scene.

Caroline handed over the jacket she pulled from the backseat for him. "Let's go see."

The steep embankment had been torn into by the rescue equipment. Luke offered Caroline a hand, and they half slid down the steepest stretch.

"Stand back in case this winch snaps!" The man on the tow truck called to the deputies trying to shift brush debris from the pond where the car had gone in. Only the back fender of Mark's vehicle was visible, the car's nose in the water. The tow truck operator started the power winch, and metal strained against the weight of the water.

The sheriff came to meet them. He offered his hand to Luke. "I'm so sorry. I wish I had better news."

"He's alive."

The sheriff nodded. "His vitals are strong, and the doctor on the air flight was hopeful the chest injuries didn't result in massive internal bleeding. We think the air bag deployed before the car reached the water, saving Mark's life."

The car began to inch out of the water, metal chains grinding. The car appeared, covered with pond moss and mud and disgorging water. The driver side rear tire had practically disappeared into the crumpled metal of the wheel frame.

"What in the world did he hit?" Luke asked.

"I doubt that damage is from hitting the water," the sheriff said. "Not at a back tire." As the car came to a rest, the sheriff picked his way through the mud to get a closer look.

"Mark could have hit a tree or a fence post," Luke said, not wanting to put a second vehicle into this accident just yet. Several had been torn away during the descent, some of them still embedded in the bank of the pond.

"This tire still has good air pressure even under this crumpled frame. What about the others?" the sheriff asked.

"They look fine. He didn't blow a tire," his deputy called.

The engine block had been shoved back from the abrupt impact with the water and ground. Luke looked at the car and turned to study the road. Had someone hit his cousin's car and sent it careening off the road? If they had, then why wasn't more of the car showing damage? The back door and the trunk area were barely dented. Another vehicle striking Mark's car at the back wheel area should have crumbled the entire area.

"If this doesn't have anything to do with Sharon and Benjamin disappearing . . . then it's one incredible coincidence in timing," the sheriff said. "Maybe someone wanted Mark out of the way? Causing an accident is a good way to make that happen."

"If you want him out of the way, then let him go to Atlanta as originally planned. He's over an hour away when he realizes something is wrong." Luke walked over to the stretch of ground where Mark had managed to pull himself before he collapsed; the medical supplies used still marked the area. Dried blood stained the grass. "His thrashing to get out of the water to this spot would have occurred in the minutes immediately after the wreck. Someone simply idling their vehicle on the road would have known Mark survived. So they weren't intent on killing him. And setting out to injure him — it isn't logical."

"You said the damage could be from the car hitting a tree or a fence post," Caroline interjected.

Luke turned to look at Caroline. "I think it could."

"What if Mark got a call saying Sharon and Benjamin had been grabbed, and that Mark had to withdraw the ransom money before the bank closed? Mark's attention would be caught by the horrific call and he drove off the road."

Luke looked from the road to the pond and saw a straight line. A huge tangled knot had just been sliced and made simple. His stomach roiled.

"Sometimes the truth is simply what is in front of you. He drove off the road and into the water," Caroline said.

Luke tugged on his gloves and climbed up on the tow bar to get a look inside the car. The phone handset had been pulled from its cradle and now dangled on its cord wrapped over the top of the steering wheel, pinned between the wheel and the inflated air bag. "He was using the phone when this accident happened." Luke turned, searching for the paramedic. "Did he say anything when he was found?"

"He was never lucid enough to speak."

Had a ransom demand been made? Was a clock ticking on delivering money to save Sharon and Benjamin's lives? The only person who knew for certain was flying away from here, heading toward hours of surgery. Luke knew a surge of panic like nothing he had experienced before. "Someone get on a radio to the hospital and clue them in to what's going on before they sedate Mark! We've got to know who he was talking to on the phone."

"I'm on it." One of the deputies sprinted toward his car radio.

"Unless he can be awakened, we're not

going to have much to work with. Jackie was working on phone records last night. Was she getting the car phone logs too?" the sheriff asked.

"She should have them soon." Luke stepped away from the car. "Walk through the timeline. Sharon and Benjamin leave the hospital before four, then drive to the house and pack. They head to Atlanta about four-thirty. We know Mark left the house being built sometime around five-thirty. That puts him here about ten minutes or so later? A call to Mark around six . . . Sharon and Benjamin could have been grabbed near the end of their journey."

"What about at the condominium itself?" Caroline asked. "It has a private parking garage. I didn't raise a concern until after seven, and that was with the sheriff for the Benton area. Jackie was the one who got the Atlanta PD involved hours later."

The sheriff looked between the two of them. "If it's a kidnapping for ransom and it becomes public knowledge, they may kill them and run to cut their losses."

"If Mark was to deliver a ransom last night or early this morning, then we're already too late," Luke countered. "The kidnappers won't know what happened to him, just that he didn't show with their money. The best thing we can do right now is get word all over the media that Mark is unconscious. We might get a second call."

Luke looked to the sky where the helicopter had disappeared. If only Mark had been able to confirm one way or another if this was indeed a kidnapping gone bad. "We've got to figure out where Sharon and Benjamin got into trouble. I doubt they'd be snatched on a highway. We need to make searching the roads near Mark and Sharon's home in Benton and getting officers to walk the areas around the condominium a priority. We do the one thing we can." Luke looked at the ground fog beginning to dissipate. "We search."

Sharon hit her head when she tried to stand, for the room ceiling was low. She stumbled as her feet stepped on tangled blankets and the black pillowcase that had been over her head caught on her one remaining shoe. She ripped at the tape on her mouth, got it off and would have screamed, but her headache swam so bad she couldn't risk the sound putting her in a curled-up ball of pain.

How long had she lain there, how long?

An hour? Six? Twelve? There was no sense of time, no windows, only a small light clipped on the headboard, and her watch was gone. The duct tape binding her hands had been half cut and left for her to work off, the pillowcase tugged off her face for her. A concussion put someone down for a long time, and touching her aching temple and fighting the double vision, she knew she was badly concussed.

In her terror the room was registering. A place designed for someone. A bed. Shelves. She reached for the lamp she saw and whimpered at the glare. Everywhere color, and not what an adult would find appealing. Posters on the walls. The room barely five feet high. Half crouched, trying to stay on her feet, she read labels on the big plastic bins on the shelves: movies, puzzles, books, junk food. What *was* this place?

She sat back on the only thing resembling furniture in the room — the short bed with Mickey Mouse sheets. Directly across and touching her knees was the television with a page taped there with blue block letters.

You were kidnapped. The next time the door opens, you'll be on your way back to your parents. It will just take a few days to work out the details. There is food and drinks, new clothes, television. Think of it as camping out. The scary part is over.

They had designed the room to hold her son. The shock broke her. Her anger crumbled into tears. *Benjamin, oh Benjamin, please keep running . . .*

TWELVE

The Benton community building, turned into a temporary command center, could hold 150 people when full. Caroline judged 80 people had already come in to pick up maps and flyers and join the search. "Caroline, we need more flyers." Lynn joined her at the table; one of dozens of her students who had come to help.

"We've got more," Caroline reassured her. Jackie had managed to get thirty thousand flyers printed overnight. She retrieved another box of a thousand. "How are the packets coming?"

"We're making them up as fast as they can highlight the street maps."

Caroline started another pot of coffee, trying to keep busy and stay out of the way. The team Jackie had sent to coordinate this center knew what they were doing. Volunteers continued to flow in, get briefed, get assigned territories, and head out. Teams were already working the interstates, stationed at each restaurant and gas station to give out flyers. Atlanta and Sandy Hill had similar centers up and running. Surely someone would report seeing something soon . . .

Caroline looked at the clock and reached for her cellular phone, which Luke finally convinced her to buy. She pushed through a side door and stepped outside. The head surgical nurse took her call.

"Mark's still stable, Caroline, if a bit thready on the pulse."

Caroline noted the vital sign on her notepad. "How's the bleeding?"

"The surgeon is hopeful. I know how critical it is to find out what Mark knows," Trish sympathized, "but it's going to be another two hours before he's out of surgery and far enough out of the anesthetic to be able to talk. Hang in there, Caroline. Has there been any news there?"

"No. I'm coming to the hospital shortly to sit with Mark when he wakes."

Caroline hung up the phone. Four hours since Mark had been airlifted from the car crash. *Mark, we need to know what you know.* If only the phone records would tell them something.

Luke had left the command post over an hour ago to join the sheriff searching the roads around Sharon and Mark's home. She joined the deputy inside who was co-ordinating the searchers on a big map of the area. She'd lived here all her life and never realized the extent to which the vast woods and waters stretched around Benton and Milo and Sandy Hill outside of town.

"Where is Luke now?"

"They've closed two miles of the road that runs in front of Mark and Sharon's house and are walking it," the deputy said. "Air assets are coming into the area to search the woods."

"I'd like to get out there too." She wanted to hug her sister and tickle her nephew and hear "Aunt Carol . . ." in Benjamin's voice. She had to do something more than staff a table here. *We search.* Luke had said it all in that simple statement.

"I'll get someone to take you," the deputy offered.

Luke folded his map and slid it back into his pocket. Fellow searchers rustled in the underbrush on either side of him, sometimes only visible even ten feet away by the bright yellow vests they wore. Only four families had a reason to travel the two-mile stretch of road that passed in front of Mark and Sharon's home, and all four said an immediate yes to the inconvenience of the road being closed. Searchers were walking the road thirty feet out on either side of it for the duration of the two miles. They were not going to miss anything that could be found.

He looked at his watch. Ten-thirty a.m. They had started shortly after seven, and if his group had covered more than a third of a mile he would be surprised. The terrain was a challenge. He looked up as a helicopter crossed overhead, relieved to see it working this area.

"Luke, you're needed back at the road."

He was near the far end of the line of searchers. He let the officer delivering the message take his place, and Luke walked back toward the road. The heavy underbrush had to be shoved through; he was at the ditch by the road before he realized it was near. He saw Caroline approaching, walking in the middle of the fine oil-graveled road.

"Can I walk with you for a bit?"

"Sure." He joined her on the asphalt and opened his water bottle. "How's it going at the command center?"

"Over a hundred people had already been in when I left. There is a heavy media presence. It's impressive, if only it weren't being done for Sharon and Benjamin. How far are we walking?"

"Through this grove of trees, up to the bend. Another team is working back to that point."

Luke kept them on the road rather than ask her to struggle with the terrain. "You need to wear a hat and sunglasses to keep that headache from getting worse."

"I'll survive. I'm glad it's not raining and washing away whatever clues might be found."

Luke passed over the water bottle. "Drink more than you think you need. Sharon had her drive planned. At what point along that route did Sharon's plan derail? If it's a stranger coming at her, there are natural vulnerable points at the house, an empty road like this, a stop at a restaurant or gas station, when they arrived at the condominium. If we can eliminate one or two, it simplifies the rest of the search."

"I've been reading a copy of the handbook they use to guide the command center," Caroline said. "The odds suggest this was done by someone Sharon or Mark knows."

"Statistically that's true. The special agent running this for the FBI is Henry James. He won't miss anything. They're doing background checks of Sharon's coworkers, the list of friends' names you gave me, Sharon's patient list. If they were snatched, we're looking for someone who needs money and knew where they would be."

"I've been thinking about last fall."

Luke nodded. "So have I. Does any of this raise a glimmer of a connection?"

"No."

"We dug out the file on your unwanted company. The sheriff is looking at who bought those roses, to see if he can trace him."

"A stalker isn't going to ask for a ransom," Caroline said.

"I know. We need those phone records."

A helicopter passed low overhead.

Luke watched Caroline shove back her hair for the third time, wiping the inside of her wrist across her forehead to push off sweat. "Drink more."

"And have to hike half a mile back to the house? I've finished one water bottle; it's enough."

"We'll have shade soon, that will help."

"Yeah. I wish I were one of those soaring hawks. They can see whatever is around here to find."

"I'm guessing the air search would have spotted a vehicle off the road, and at least around here there are no ponds for the car to end up in. But you could run a car off the road into these woods and not see it."

"Luke." The call came over the radio as they were nearing the grove of trees.

Luke keyed his radio. "Go ahead, Sheriff."

"The searchers found something a mile east of Sharon's drive, around the curve of the road."

"We're on our way."

Caroline broke into a trot and Luke matched his stride to hers. "Take it easy; this isn't going to change if we get there in two minutes or four."

She just looked at him and kept her pace.

As they arrived officers were blocking off the area with yellow-and-black crime tape. Luke put a hand on Caroline's shoulder and steered her to the left, around the area.

The sheriff came to meet them. "There are a few pieces of clear rigid plastic, possibly from a broken headlight. We've got signs a car went off the side of the road. Farther down, there appear to be muddy car tracks as a vehicle backed up."

"Stay here, Caroline." Luke stepped under the tape. A deputy set down an evidence marker beside a jagged triangle of plastic and several shards. Rigid plastic from a headlight? Cars had bumped. It wasn't much, but it was a place to begin.

Luke knelt and scanned the area in a full circle, looking for the sight of gathering flies, the darker stains of blood. He braced to see it, for even a drop or two of blood would attract insects. Only a few gnats came to buzz near his ear. *That's a gift. No blood.*

He rose and glanced toward Caroline. She stood with arms wrapped across her chest, rocking up on her toes and then back on her heels. He wanted to warn her to temper the hope he could see in her face but couldn't say the words. They would work concentric circles out from this point of impact and hope to find something.

"Over here!"

Luke turned to see a searcher raise his hand on the opposite side of the road a good fifteen yards toward the woods.

"I've got snagged fabric on these brambles."

A straight line for someone taking off to the woods. The fabric could be old, from horseback riders who occasionally came this way, hikers or birdwatchers, or it could also be evidence of something that had happened yesterday.

"And I've got small-print tennis shoe tracks," a searcher five yards closer to the woods stopped and called.

"Everyone hold where you are," the sheriff ordered. "Clint, back that security tape another two hundred yards both directions. What do you think, Luke?"

"Sharon's car is forced to stop here by another vehicle; assume at least two people are in it since both cars were driven away from here. One person goes for Sharon, the other for Benjamin. Sharon yells for Benjamin to run and he sprints toward the woods . . ."

"The dogs are working near the pond where Mark was found. They can be here in twenty minutes."

Luke felt an enormous sense of hope swell. "Clear the searchers out of this entire area. We don't need them disturbing the scent." He turned to Caroline. "I need something Benjamin wore recently."

She just about came out of her tennis shoes as she leapt on the request. "The shirt he wore to school Friday?"

"Perfect. Get it."

Caroline sprinted toward the house.

THIRTEEN

The bloodhounds bayed as they clambered from the back of a van accompanied by their trackers. Luke took the shirt Caroline had brought over to the trackers. "Benjamin's nine years old and he knows these woods. He's been out there overnight."

"The ground is perfect to track. If he's in there, our dogs will find him."

The three dogs tangled their leads as they strained to go. They practically tasted the shirt as they absorbed the scent. "Let's go, boys."

The dogs began to prowl back and forth, working the road in an excited wandering. The lead dog bayed and peeled off into the woods. Within seconds, the other two dogs joined the track, tugging their handlers to keep up. The dogs crashed through the thick brush.

"Benjamin was running," Luke said softly.

"Let's follow them."

Luke stopped her. "No, just listen to the dogs. They'll tell you what they find by their baying."

"If he only ran a short way and was caught, brought back . . . would the dogs circle back?"

"Yes." Luke knew the odds that a boy could outrun a man coming after him were at best fifty-fifty. And given the options, seeing the dogs come back might not be so bad. He worried more about the boy being shot, or being somewhere out there with a broken leg.

"If Benjamin ran away, why didn't he make it to a neighbor's house to call for help by now?"

Benjamin had been out there at least sixteen hours and he knew the woods. He couldn't have easily gotten lost when there were eventually roads in each direction. Under most circumstances, he would have made it to help by now.

"Don't borrow trouble, Caroline. We'll know what happened soon enough."

The sounds began to fade as the dogs moved deeper into the woods. Luke turned up his radio, listening to the trackers.

"The boy crashed through brush, running hard, not turning to move onto what foot trails he does cross. I've got fragments of cloth and several spots where it appears he fell. If there's someone running after him . . . We're crossing muddy ground and I'm only seeing small shoeprints."

"He's still heading due east?"

"Yes."

The sheriff came over carrying a map and showed the path the trackers were reporting. "Benjamin looks like he deliberately headed into the deepest stretch of the woods. Does he play there often? Would he know where he's going?"

Caroline bit her lip. "Snake-hunting trips, overnight camping . . . Benjamin knows this stretch of woods pretty well, but if he got off the trails he normally used — he'll get disoriented. And I doubt he has a destination in mind. He's probably just running."

"Assume he's very scared. Will he hole up and hide?"

"Maybe. But first he'll keep going until he can't run anymore."

The sheriff looked at the map and then at Luke. "If he managed to run a mile or two into the woods, wore out, and then sat down to rest and hike out . . . the far side of these woods opens onto the pastureland Wilson uses for his cattle. If Benjamin is staying on this course, he could still be in there trying to walk his way out. We can get a team of searchers working in from the road bordering the pastureland."

"Let's do it."

The sheriff nodded and started assigning searchers.

"You want to move over that way or stay here?" Luke asked Caroline, willing to leave it up to her.

She studied the map and where the dogs were at now. "Let's move to the half-way point between here and the pasture road."

Caroline leaned against the fender of the deputy's car, feeling like time was crawling. Beside her Luke didn't show anxiety, his arms crossed over his chest, the volume on the radio turned up so they could both listen. Benjamin was out there somewhere. He had to be so scared. "They'll find him?" she asked again.

"The dogs are good. They'll find him." Luke tossed the twig he was stripping of leaves. "This is every kid's nightmare, being chased in the woods at night with a bad man after him. He was running, so he's probably not badly hurt, and he's scared but alive. I'll take that outcome."

"Sharon would have told him to run and not stop."

"I am very glad Benjamin listens to his mom." Luke turned, hearing a vehicle. "The ambulance is just insurance; you know that."

"I know." Caroline stared, debating how her shoes would handle a hike through the woods.

"No, we're not going in there. When they find something, we'll just cost ourselves time having to double back to get to where they are."

She looked over and Luke smiled at her. "Your face is an open book." He held out his notebook. "Work some more on the list of names of those Sharon and Mark had over to their open house last month."

She found the page she had begun work on earlier and leaned against the car, using the hood as a makeshift desk. "About all I remember from the open house is getting caught by kids in a water gun fight."

"So list the kids' names, and we'll assume their parents were there."

She wrote them down. "How rich is Mark, really?" She looked over, hoping Luke wouldn't be offended by the question.

"Rich enough. The business is well

known in Atlanta and his two partners are a little more flashy with their income than Mark is. Someone looking for a target would know he was doing quite well."

"No offense meant, but is it new money? You're not rich."

"Mark put his inheritance from our grandfather into his business; mine sits in treasury bills. I've found the only thing that happens with really good cars is they get stolen and stripped for parts, and I've got all the house I want."

A voice broke through the radio static. "Sheriff, I've spotted a baseball cap. It's caught on a limb going down a ravine. I'm sending it out with the deputy."

Caroline surged back onto the road to pace. "He's hurt, Luke! He took a tumble in the dark of night."

"They found a baseball cap, not Benjamin wearing it. Don't jump to conclusions."

"Let's go."

"Not yet."

Twenty minutes passed before the deputy appeared from the woods farther down the road. Caroline broke into a trot to meet him. Luke easily kept up with her, and he paused her before she could reach for the cap. "Just look; it needs to be checked for any possible evidence."

"Those are Benjamin's initials on the brim."

"We found it here." The deputy marked a location on Luke's terrain map. "The ravine is pretty steep, but if he slid down it intentionally, Benjamin could have been using it as a safe place to escape. There's a dry creek down there, and walking it is a lot easier than pushing through the underbrush up here."

Luke traced the riverbed. "He's got to be somewhere inside this mile square — between this road, the pastureland, the river, and where we found his cap."

"Why isn't he answering the trackers' calls?" Caroline asked Luke as additional people arrived and clipped on yellow vests to join the search.

"Let's find him and answer that question." Luke handed her one of the yellow vests. "Just promise you'll stay with me."

FOURTEEN

"Over here! We've got him over here."

"Benjamin!" Caroline missed her footing and crashed down the embankment, sliding on her left side. Luke winced at the impact to her elbow and back as he followed her down. Caroline shoved a half-slipped-off tennis shoe back on and kept running, heading down the riverbed toward the whistle being blown to mark the recovery location.

Luke came alongside her, shoving aside the branches in their way. They turned a bend in the path.

Caroline took the impact of a nine-year-old boy moving at full speed head on and about lost her footing again. "Benjamin." She laughed as he melded into her. Luke wrapped an arm around her waist to steady her. Caroline leaned down, her head near Benjamin's. "Hey, buddy. I'm so glad to see you."

"They took Mom."

Luke knelt beside the boy. "Who did, Benjamin?" he asked gently, for the boy's words were tripping over each other. Benjamin turned toward him. The look in Benjamin's eyes was not something Luke wanted to ever see within his family. Desperate panic in the eyes of a nine-year-old jarred any sense of justice in the world.

"Two men. They wore ski caps. Mom told me to run, and I did."

Luke rested his hand on Benjamin's shoulder and soothed the tense muscles while he inspected the boy. A swollen cheek and black eye showed clearly, as did tear traces, but Luke saw no bloodstains on his jeans or shirt, only thorn scrapes and insect bites on Benjamin's arms. If he'd been grabbed during his struggle to flee there didn't appear to be bruises marking the event. Luke would take small favors where he could get them. "The dogs showed us the path you took. You did an excellent job running at night."

"Is Mom okay?"

Caroline wrapped her arms tighter around Benjamin. "We don't know, honey; we're still looking for her."

The boy's lower lip started to quiver.

Luke used his shirtsleeve to wipe away his tears.

"They hit our car hard — there wasn't anything she could do." Benjamin choked on the words.

"I know. We found the impact site." Luke waited until Benjamin took a deep breath and then another, trying not to cry. Sixteen hours of running — no matter what he said Luke doubted it would be worse than what Benjamin had already wondered. "Your dad had a car accident last night too, and they took him to the hospital; otherwise he'd be right here leading the search."

"He's hurt bad?" Benjamin whispered.

"Mark's like you, tough. He'll be okay. I'll take you to the hospital so you can see for yourself. And I'll find your mom, Ben."

They looked at each other, and the boy nodded. They were both Falcons; they both loved her. They would find her.

"I wanted to help her, but I couldn't."

Luke understood the shame under those simple words. "Benjamin, you're here to tell us what happened. That's the best help you could do for your mom. My word on that."

"I want to help find her."

"Then you can. I'll ask you lots of questions, and you can tell me what you re-member. But we'll do that back at your aunt's house over a big breakfast."

"I want to see Dad."

"He's in Atlanta, Ben, and it's a long drive. Let's eat and clean up first, then we'll see him."

Benjamin gave a sigh and nodded. He leaned his head back to look up at Caroline. "French toast? I dreamed about French toast and I am *so* hungry."

"I can do that. And as long as you don't tell your mom . . ." Caroline tugged out a plethora of candy bars stuffed in her pockets for him to choose from. "Why didn't you answer our calls?"

"One of them was back in the woods this morning, trying to find me. He called my name. So I hid. And then I guess I went to sleep." Benjamin tugged the wrapper off a Payday and stuffed the paper in his pocket.

Luke stood. Someone coming back to look for the boy . . . He looked at Caroline and didn't like the fear he saw reflected in her face. Luke looked at Benjamin. "When did you hear the guy that came back?"

"Right after dawn. I saw him a couple times. He wasn't wearing a ski mask, but he had his jacket collar up, and his hat was tugged down. I wanted to get closer to see

169

what he looked like, but I didn't want him to hear me."

"A wise decision. Was he a big man, a small man?"

"Kind of like our neighbor Jim, tall but skinny, and I think this guy knew the woods. He would stand quiet and listen, and he didn't slip much even when he moved up and down ravines. He had this tall walking stick."

Comfortable with the woods, so probably not a guy out of Atlanta. "Do you think he was one of the same two men from the day before?"

"He wasn't the one who chased me last night, and this guy followed my trail like he knew exactly where I had run. He even crossed the creek where I did. He was here a long time. I think he left when the helicopters came this way. I'm sorry I didn't come out sooner."

"You did just fine," Caroline assured him. "The sheriff's going to look around and see if they can locate where this guy went. What do you say we go home?"

"Are we like miles from home?"

"A little ways. You want a lift out of here?" Luke offered.

"I'm too big."

Luke smiled. "Maybe next year you'll be

too big. Come on." He turned and knelt and Benjamin climbed on his back. Luke easily lifted him. "You did good, Ben, real good." Luke skirted around the dogs now pacing around them, Caroline close behind with her hand touching Benjamin's arm.

"These dogs are really here just to track me?"

They loped around them, occasionally jumping to sniff the boy's tennis shoes.

"Yep."

"I wish I'd let them find my sleeping place. I came down the hill to meet them and they slobbered all over me and sat on my feet."

"Tell you what, after this is over I'll take you to see where the dogs train, and maybe you can be their handler for a day."

"I want to be the hidee again, and this time they can sit on my stomach like I'm some dog rug."

Luke laughed at the image. "Do I gather you would like a dog someday?"

"I saw these really cute puppies at the mall. Dad said we can get one once school is out and I have time to train it."

He ducked so Benjamin could avoid a tree limb. "I had this really great dog when I was your age. I lived up north, and he loved the snow. You should get something really big that likes to take your mom's shoes, and shed on the carpet, and come sleep on your bed and crush the mattress."

"Mom would spend days chasing it out of her white carpet room. I could name it something cool like Samson."

"Mention dog training classes; you can use that as leverage." Luke paused to let Caroline go through a narrow section of the trail first. She was crying, but he figured it would do her good as long as she didn't miss her footing and go down for a third time. He smiled at her, and she smiled back as she passed.

Two found, one to go, and then he was definitely going to take Caroline out for a very calm quiet dinner somewhere and try to ease those tears. "When we get back to the house, Ben, do you think you can remember what your mom was wearing yesterday?"

Luke set down his fork and picked up his pen. Caroline slid another piece of French toast on Benjamin's plate and another two on his. Luke smiled his thanks. He turned another page in his notebook. "What time did you leave the house, Ben?"

"Questions can wait two minutes. Eat

while it's hot," Caroline suggested.

Luke reached out a hand, caught her wrist, and tugged her down into her own chair. He slid one of the pieces of French toast onto her plate and handed her a fork. "You, too."

Benjamin giggled.

"She's like this short order cook who has no stop button. She keeps forgetting to eat." He picked up an orange and his knife to peel and segment it. "We're eating." Luke passed orange slices to Benjamin, as fast as the boy could wolf them down. "Last one."

Benjamin ate it, then reached for the maple syrup.

"Tell me some more about how they hit your mom's car," Luke asked.

Benjamin drew a tick-tac-toe board on his French toast with the syrup. "I was sorting out my Braves baseball cards and wasn't paying much attention until Mom suddenly swerved. I looked up to see this van passing us. It suddenly pulled into Mom's path so she had to swerve again into the ditch. Our car stalled and she couldn't get it started again.

"A guy got out of the van's passenger door and tried to open Mom's door. You should have seen her. Mom shoved her door open and hit him under the chin and then slammed it closed on his fingers. Then when she saw the man coming around the car to my door, she got the car to roll forward so he had to scramble out of the way. She told me to run, and I didn't want to leave, but she insisted. I thought if one of them came after me to the woods, she might be able to take the other guy."

"Do you remember what the van looked like?"

"White, kind of plain, like a square box with wheels. It didn't have a sliding door on the side but two doors that swung open."

Luke felt an awful knot forming in the bottom of his stomach. "Any logo or words?"

"Just white and pretty clean, like it had been washed recently. I didn't see the license plates." Benjamin shook his head. "I wish I had."

"Do you remember anyone else passing you, another car on the road?"

"Just the postman going the other direction. We passed him when we left the house because Mom paused to let me get the mail from the roadside box."

"Yesterday's mail was in the car?"

"In the backseat." Benjamin covered a yawn. "Can we go see Dad now?"

"You've got time for a shower and a change of clothes and then we'll go," Caroline said. "I laid out one of your favorite shirts and a clean pair of jeans, and fluffy towels are on the bathroom counter. Use the lotion I set out on your bug bites. It will stop the itch."

"I feel like I slept outdoors."

She laughed and ruffled his hair, then leaned over to sniff his shirt. "Smells like it too, buddy. Don't forget the soap. Just remember to use your kind of shampoo; mine will make you smell like strawberries."

"Girl smells. They should make better girl shampoos." Benjamin headed upstairs.

Caroline leaned back and listened to his footsteps overhead. Luke watched her. He could almost see the emotional weight from the search for Benjamin lift. She looked over at him. "Thanks."

"You're very welcome." He leaned over and gently worked free a leaf still caught in her hair. "You took a bit of a tumble. Benjamin handled himself with a great deal of common sense."

"Benjamin is a pretty practical kid." She looked up as water came on upstairs. "He's

175

going to be up there as long as my hot water holds out." Caroline rose from her chair and took Benjamin's plate to the sink. "Finish that toast, Luke, and I'll make you more. Or an omelet? Some bacon? Maybe a grilled cheese?"

"Why don't you make up half a dozen peanut butter and jelly sandwiches? I'll have one, and Benjamin will be hungry again soon. He'll sleep during the trip to Atlanta and then wake and probably go through three or four sandwiches like he was inhaling them."

She nodded and got out the bread and the peanut butter. "Why did you tense when he described the van?"

Luke didn't want to answer that question, but he didn't know how to avoid sharing what she would soon realize for herself. "Back in the hours before you called me to say they were late, Jackie and I were looking for a white van."

Her eyes widened when she remembered. "The lady who was murdered at the motel; I saw it on the news. That white van? You think it's the same one?"

"After the last day, I'm willing to say anything could be a coincidence, but this one — it's a tough coincidence to accept. I know there were two men in the van

176

Thursday night; I know one of them was seen driving a Toyota Friday night at 6:19, alone, heading west. He was in this area for over a week. He headed out Friday night after we know Mark went off the road. The distances fit what's possible."

"A guy who killed the lady in the motel might have been involved in grabbing Sharon?" She pushed back her chair. "Luke —"

He reached over and covered her hand. "Don't, please don't assume the worst. If this guy was involved — his name is Frank Hardin — he would have been hired to do a job. He's a violent man, but he's not into killing strangers for the thrill of it."

Luke wished he could figure out good news in any of this. "We know now someone intended to grab both Sharon and the boy. This was planned. If we know the vehicle and one of the men involved, we're an enormous step closer to solving this. Frank is not going to go down alone."

"You said he was seen heading west?"

"Yes. And he wasn't driving the white van. I'm betting it's been abandoned and probably somewhere near here. Two men, a white van, and from what Benjamin said, at least one of the men very comfortable with this area and thus probably local."

"If this was the stalker, and he had help making the grab . . ."

Luke shook his head. "A stalker isn't the type to work with company."

"So why haven't they called with another ransom demand?"

"It's likely going to be soon." Luke squeezed her hand and stood. "Why don't you go pack what you and Benjamin will need for the next couple days. We'll take him to see his dad and spend the night in Atlanta. Whoever has Sharon is going to be in touch. She's findable, Caroline, and she was alive when last seen. Hold on to that."

FIFTEEN

Luke parked in the hospital lot reserved for doctors. Security arranged it so they could bypass the media staking out the hospital as word got around that Mark Falcon was recovering here.

"They want his story," Caroline said.

"Yes." They all wanted interviews with the man at the center of this case — missing for twelve hours, found hurt, his son escaped from the kidnappers, his wife still missing. "Let me come around for Benjamin." Luke circled the car. Caroline opened the car door. The sleepy boy stirred as Luke picked him up. "Come on, buddy. Let's go see your dad."

Benjamin wrapped his arms around Luke's neck and laid his head against Luke's shoulder. For a moment he felt all the protective instincts of a real father, and he breathed deeply as he returned the hug.

"He's really okay?" Benjamin asked again.

Luke rested his hand against the boy's back, feeling the heat from the sunburn he had acquired. "He's really okay."

They walked into the hospital. Caroline held the elevator door for him. "Eighth floor," Luke said.

She pushed the button.

"I'd like to say hello to Trish, the surgical nurse who's been giving us updates on Mark."

"Why don't you and Benjamin both do that while I have a brief word with Mark first?"

Caroline looked at him, then nodded. "That might be best."

The officer stationed by the ICU ward held the glass doors for them. "Jackie's on her way up," he told Luke.

"Thanks."

Luke stopped at the nurses' station and lowered Benjamin to his feet. Kneeling, he brushed back the boy's hair from his eyes and studied his face. "I need to talk with your dad for a minute first. I need you to stay here with Caroline. This lady is Trish; she's been taking care of your dad. I bet if you ask, she'll show you all the cool stuff they've been charting about him."

Benjamin looked up at the smiling lady who was waiting to be introduced to him. "I can see Dad's chart?"

"I can even show you a CAT scan and what he looks like inside his head," Trish offered.

Benjamin looked back at Luke. "Okay, for a minute." He reached for Caroline's hand.

Luke followed Trish's directions to Mark's ICU room. He'd been getting hourly updates; he knew what to expect, but it didn't make it any easier as he pushed aside the curtain and saw his cousin. Mark was awake, if fading in and out. He lifted his hand and came as close to a smile as he could, given the pain he was in from the surgery. "You found Benjamin."

Luke rested his hand over his cousin's. "Alive and well; he'll be in to see you momentarily. It's nice to have you awake."

"Sharon —"

Luke shook his head. "No news."

"The five million ransom was due at midnight. The old church outside Benton."

Luke understood the fear in his cousin's voice. "The nurse passed the message on just as soon as you whispered the words in recovery. They'll call again."

Mark looked toward the door then back to Luke. "I can't lose her. I've got to know. What are the odds?"

Not good, but Luke refused to think about it. "They'll call. And I'll do whatever it takes to bring Sharon back safe."

"I know you will." Mark grimaced as he tried to shift his shoulder. "How's Caroline doing?"

"She's a strong lady."

"A good one. You two should have been a number a long time ago." Mark sighed and closed his eyes. "It was a guy on the phone."

"Anyone's voice you recognize?"

Mark shook his head. "I remember the house with the skylight problem, saying good-bye to Al. Picking up the phone to answer the call . . ." Mark's voice drifted off and he forced himself to rally. "That's it until I woke up here. The phone call is part of some foggy nightmare. You've got power of attorney on file. Use it — the business, the house, the land, whatever you need to do when the time comes. I can build the business again; I can't rebuild my family."

"Any names bothering you I should be looking at?" Luke asked.

"No, sorry. You'll have to assume just about anyone is a suspect." Mark's strength was fading. "Send Benjamin in, let me see my son. Then take him away somewhere safe."

"I'm going to keep him very safe. You've got my word on that." Luke stepped to the door and signaled to Caroline and Benjamin to come in.

Mark held out his hand without IVs. "Come here, buddy. Give me a hug."

Benjamin buried his head against his dad's shoulder. "I didn't keep Mom safe."

"Hey, you did great. You were able to tell us what happened. I'm proud of you." He gently tugged his son's shirt collar. "You got yourself a nice shiner."

"I ran into a tree," Benjamin said. "You really crashed the car underwater?"

"Became a scuba diver for a while and had to break the window to get out."

"Wow."

Mark pulled him close and kissed him. "You did good, son."

Luke rested his hand on the boy's shoulder, knowing Mark was at his limit for energy. "I'll bring you back over tomorrow," Luke promised. "Come on, we'd better go take Caroline over to the house now, because she's about asleep on her feet."

Caroline, leaning against the wall, opened her eyes and couldn't stop a yawn as she smiled. "I am pretty tired."

Benjamin walked over to her and wrapped his arms around her waist. "Maybe I could fix you something to eat this time?"

"You can put in a pizza for me."

"I'll have a list of names for you tomorrow," Mark said softly to Luke. "Anyone I can think of who might have motive to do this."

"Tell Trish to call if one more urgent than others comes to mind," Luke said. "I want hourly updates, assuming I'm conscious."

"Not a problem; I'll call every hour." Luke looked at his cousin, an enormous weight of history between them backing his promise. "We will get Sharon back."

"Better believe it." Mark looked toward Caroline. "Take care of her too."

Luke smiled. "I will."

Sharon found the TV worked, but they were blocking any channels that might give her news, might give her a clue of what was happening — it was infuriating to have old movie channels and reruns but no news. She finally settled on the channel showing upcoming programs; at least it gave her the time. Four p.m., and from the show listing, it was still Saturday afternoon. The headache had eased to the point she could turn her head without nausea. She found a coloring book and a blue crayon and used the inside cover as a notepad, trying to think.

- Who grabbed me?
- Is Benjamin safe?
- Where am I?
- Am I really going to be left here alone, or are the men coming back? I need a weapon if they return.
- Can I get out of here? There has to be a door to this room.
- What is in this room I can work with?
- If it is a kidnapping, how does Mark get money on a holiday weekend?

She eased herself from the narrow short bed, knowing a weapon was her first order of business. She had to be ready to stop them.

A weapon, but also an impenetrable defense. I've got the bathroom I can hide in. If I can block the door and their ability to get to me . . . they can't shoot me if they can't see me.

Sharon started in the corner of the room. Food, books, movies, supplies — she ignored those, looking instead at how the shelves had been built. One of those two-by-fours would make a great bat. She'd love to give one of those guys the headache she had.

She pounded on the walls, but the dull thuds told her the soundproofing around this room was thick. She was stuck inside a framed-in box. Since she had power and TV, there might be a way to get access to the wires into the wall, maybe even tug in the two wires of a phone. She didn't know if she was in a basement or an attic. Sharon systematically began taking apart the room.

SIXTEEN

Caroline was sound asleep in the front seat of the car, Benjamin asleep in the back. Luke shut off the vehicle and rested his head back against the headrest, more than ready to join them. "Caroline, we're at the condominium." She stirred.

Luke walked around the car and opened the back door. He didn't try to wake Benjamin, just picked the boy up. He walked with Caroline over to the elevator.

The officer monitoring the phones met them at the condominium door, and Luke nodded his thanks.

"Where's Benjamin's room?" Luke asked Caroline.

"Back this way," Caroline said, and showed him. Luke laid Benjamin down and she moved to take off his shoes and get the boy settled.

"Go on to bed, Caroline. I'll wake you if

there is any news. Jackie will be here, or one of the officers, to listen for the phones."

"You'll get some sleep too?"

"As soon as I check in with Jackie."

He waited until she closed the bedroom door before he dialed his partner. "We're in Atlanta and settled. Where are we at, Jackie?"

"Not much new to report. No leads on the van, and we're still working on tracing the phone call to Mark's car. Get some sleep, Luke, while you can. We're going to get a call from whoever is holding Sharon."

"I just hope it's soon." Luke looked at his watch. "I'll call in four hours."

Luke hung up the phone and went to find somewhere to collapse.

Caroline stirred, awaking suddenly with the awareness something was wrong. The light from the window reflected city lights; it had to be the middle of the night. The shadows slid off a quiet still figure beside her bed. "Hey, Benjamin." She reached out and took his arm as she pushed herself up on one elbow.

"I miss Mom."

She shoved pillows behind her and helped him climb up on the bed beside her. "I do too. Where's Luke?"

"Asleep on the couch. He snores."

"I imagine I do a bit too." She hugged him and looked over his shoulder at the clock. "Getting hungry? We can go raid the kitchen, maybe call the hospital and ask Trish how your dad is doing."

"Can we fix a pizza? I don't remember dinner."

"Tonight, I think we can do whatever sounds good. See if you can find me my fuzzy slippers to go with these sweats."

Benjamin slid off the bed and opened the closet doors. He brought back her slippers. Caroline tugged on a sweatshirt over her T-shirt. "Lead the way."

Caroline followed Benjamin to the kitchen. She opened the deep freezer. There were several pizza options. "Hamburger? Pepperoni? Or something that looks like your mom's idea of Canadian bacon and pineapple."

"Is there just a cheese one?"

"Somewhere in here." She dug one out. "Set the oven to 400."

She got out the milk and chocolate syrup while Benjamin got plates and glasses for them. She was liberal with the chocolate syrup and then slid the tall glass over to him.

"Thanks." He found a straw and settled on the chair to drink the chocolate milk. "How long before they find Mom?"

"It may be a few days."

"They want Dad to pay money?"

"We don't know yet. But I expect that is what they'll ask for. Your dad was talking with Luke about that earlier at the hospital."

"Dad can have what's in my saving's passbook."

She reached over and ruffled his hair. "I know he'll appreciate that offer. Your dad will be able to put together whatever is needed. Did you set the timer?"

"Twelve minutes."

"Why don't you get out a tray and extra plate so you can take the officer covering the phones a late-night snack."

"Good idea." Benjamin slid from the chair to find a tray.

Caroline got up. It was clear Benjamin would be wide awake for a while. She opened the side cupboard and got out the checkerboard.

"I thought I smelled something really great."

She turned and saw Luke leaning against the kitchen doorpost.

"Pizza," Benjamin told him.

"A man after my own heart." Luke pulled out a chair beside the boy. "Got some more of that chocolate milk?"

"We do," Caroline said, smiling. She got down a glass for him. Luke had slept in his clothes and looked rumpled and tired. He'd slept, but not enough to look rested. They needed a few hours of calm to settle the enormous stress of the last thirty hours.

When the pizza was done, Luke helped Benjamin cut it. The boy took a tray to the officer monitoring the phones. Benjamin came back and tugged his chair up to the table. He blew on his piece of pizza to cool it. "I hope Mom isn't hungry."

Luke reached over and rubbed his back. "You can fix her pizza when she comes home. She'll like it just like we do."

"She'll want the one with pineapple on it."

Luke laughed, the sound a bit rusty. "We'll save it for her then."

Mark fought the tug of the drugs. Someone had done this. Someone had wanted to take Sharon from him and had done it for money.

Sharon had to be okay. He wouldn't be able to look at Benjamin if something happened to his mom because she'd married him. Sharon was out there somewhere. Who wanted money that badly? Who wouldn't care who they hurt?

He worked for many who thought money and profit were everything, that the size of the home they built determined their worth, that the size of the company they ran determined their place in society. Was it someone he knew?

He started to think of names. None seemed likely, but at least they were names. He pushed the button beside his hand and held it down until Trish came hurrying in. "Paper. And a pen. Write down the names I tell you."

She was ready to protest but he looked at her, his hand gripping hers, and she nodded. She tugged over a chair. "Go ahead, Mark."

Luke shared a look with Caroline over Benjamin's head, and she pushed back her chair and reached across the boy to pick up the last piece of pizza crust. "Come on, buddy. It's bedtime again if you can roll that way. You ate like five pieces."

Benjamin pushed back his chair and patted his tummy. "I'm really full. Can we have pancakes for breakfast?"

"To bed, you bottomless pit," Luke replied, laughing as he lifted Benjamin to his feet. "Only good dreams allowed for the rest of the night."

Caroline went with Benjamin to tuck him in with a story.

Luke picked up plates and cleared the table. He bet the boy would fall asleep before Caroline finished a few pages of the book. Mark was blessed to have such a good kid as a son.

Jesus, why haven't we received a ransom request?

Twenty-four hours was a bad sign; by tomorrow there would be real doubt Sharon would be found alive. How was he supposed to carry his family if it came down to telling them that kind of news? Caroline would make it as easy on him as she could, and Mark would take it because he had to, but Benjamin — he'd lost a father to a tragedy and found the ability to open his heart to a second dad and love Mark. But if Benjamin lost his mom . . .

Luke washed out the rag and laid it across the sink. Even if Caroline did everything she could to fill the void, she would still only be the aunt Benjamin loved.

Lord, in twenty-four to forty-eight hours optimistic people will instinctively know it's been too long. The optimism will fade and people will start to grieve. I have to do something to move things along before then. I need some hope; I need the phone to ring. And I'm helpless to make that happen. I need a miracle.

Tomorrow was Sunday: more searching, more waiting, more struggling to keep hope. It would be a rough Sunday.

Caroline came back to the kitchen. Luke turned. He wasn't surprised to see the smile she had kept in place for Benjamin fade. She looked so burned out. "Sit for a while."

She pulled out a chair. "He'll be asleep anytime."

"That's good." Luke poured her a glass of orange juice and set it on the table. "You're coping quite well considering."

She gave him a tired smile as she rested her head in her hands. She hadn't brushed her hair since going to bed earlier, and it tangled around her shoulders. The sweatshirt must be borrowed from Sharon, for the sleeves had to be pushed back lest they slide past her fingers.

"Can we talk?"

He pulled out a chair across from her. "Sure."

"I need some answers."

"I don't know that I have them."

"How are you coping?"

He blinked. "I'm okay, Caroline."

"Mark is hurt. That can't be easy to deal with."

He pushed his hand through his hair. Tonight she wanted candor and emotions from him, and it was the last thing he had to give. Luke picked up his drink. "I feel guilty I got Mark back before your sister."

"Luke, it's okay to be relieved."

"I about lost him once before to a fall at a building site. His life is proving more risky than mine. About the only thing I've done is get shot in the foot."

"Jackie will never be able to apologize her way out of that, will she?"

He smiled. "It's nice to have something to rib her about. And we at least caught the guy we were chasing that night."

She spun the ice around in her glass. "Benjamin came home with only bug bites."

Luke held her gaze, then leaned over and gently squeezed her shoulder. "He was really glad you were there."

She leaned her cheek against his hand for a moment, then sighed. "Sharon isn't going to be so lucky, is she?"

"I don't know, Caroline."

"Thirty hours ago we didn't know what had happened; now we do. That's progress."

"And we'll work every lead we have and find ways to generate more." Luke got up, needing to pace. "They will be in touch, Caroline. They wanted money. No matter what has gone wrong with their plans, none of it changes the fact they still want money."

"You're going to get her back alive, too."

"I'm going to try."

"I hate this tightrope of waiting, with emotions that bounce from despair to hope one minute then back again."

"I know. It's going to get even harder tomorrow." He sighed. "One word of advice? Don't fight the emotions. Work through what you'll do if the worst comes to pass, then let yourself feel hope and work through the steps you'll take if she is found alive. You need this time to prepare for both. Because when we get a break in this case, things will likely move very fast. You won't have much time to adjust."

"How long before we know one way or another?"

He didn't want to answer that but she deserved the truth. "If there's going to be a ransom demand, it will come in the next forty-eight hours. After that — this is just a search."

She blinked, took a deep breath, and

nodded. "Thanks for being honest."

"I wish it were a better answer."

She offered a slight smile. "Hope or despair. For this moment, I'll think positively. We'll get a call. We'll get her back alive. And if we get a miracle, she won't be hurt any more than Benjamin is."

She pushed back her chair and pulled a folded piece of paper from her pocket. "I am glad you're here walking through this with me." She slid the piece of paper toward him. "For you. I like lists. We'll be starting tomorrow at the FBI office here in Atlanta?"

"Yes."

"I'll see you in the morning."

"Good night, Caroline."

He watched her leave before he leaned over and picked up the paper. He opened it.

TEN REASONS I'M GLAD LUKE FALCON IS HERE

1. His voice is calm even when he has bad news to tell me.
2. He keeps going and going even when he's exhausted.
3. He knows how to find me candy bars.
4. He loves Benjamin.

5. Benjamin loves him.
6. He doesn't promise more than he can do.
7. He lets me cry and not say anything.
8. Sharon respects him.
9. Mark trusts him.
10. I love him.

Luke — an easy life is fit for easy tasks; a hard life is fit for hard tasks. God knew I would face tonight and the possible loss of my sister, and He knew I would need someone special alongside me.

God needed a warrior, so He made one. I hate the cases you've worked in the past that give you eyes that see reality and know the good and the bad possibilities, that give you no easy place to hide. You're like a tree beaten up by wind and rain that digs in deeper to survive.

God made a man of perseverance. He's been refining in you a hot fire, to pour into you traits not many would need. God knew every case you'd see, how hard it would be, and yet He set you on this course for a reason. He created a man who can keep going in the face of tremendous discouragement, in the face of emotional people and chaos and only scraps of information to work with.

God made a man I needed. In order to answer my prayer for someone who can help my sister, He started decades ago creating you. If it's possible to find Sharon alive, you'll do it. If not, you'll help me through it. You are as ready for this task as God can make a man.

If a day comes when you have to tell me Sharon is dead, it will be okay to just say it. I already know your heart.

Caroline

Luke wiped away two tears. And then he slipped the note into his shirt pocket next to his heart.

SEVENTEEN

"Was it too simple for you? Snatch the boy, make a ransom call, collect the money? This was to be over in five hours, not turn into a circus." Jason Fromm turned his pen end over end, furious. The bank had long ago closed, the staff dismissed that morning so they could join the search while still on paid time. His generosity meant he had the top floor of the building to himself for the day to pace and stew while he waited for this midnight visitor.

Frank put down the elevator repair toolbox he carried as a prop and shoved the oak door closed, making photos of Jason, standing beside several prominent Atlanta politicians, bounce on the wall. "We did what we could to grab the boy, but there was no way to catch him once he bolted to the woods. We grabbed who we could. Ronald made the ransom demand exactly as you ordered."

"And what we have as a result is a mess." His anger had been building for a day, and it was turning into a decision: Necessity might have forced him to hire Frank Hardin, but it didn't mean he couldn't also fire him — in a very permanent way. Just not here in his office, where the blood would get on his new carpet.

Frank paced over toward the window. "So the price goes up for our troubles. Mark is alive, going to be fine, and now knows just how serious we are. We roll with it and we go on. One Falcon or the other, it's now twenty million."

The mention of money helped. "As his banker, I can only see advancing him ten million."

Frank laughed and tossed over the house keys. "I put her in the room and sealed the door. You can't hear her, but you might want to sleep in a guest room just the same."

Jason ignored the comment. She might be in a safe room in his guest house, but it was purely a business decision. The only way to make sure no one stumbled on his guest was to make sure no one could. The cops would never suspect him as being involved, but if by a strange twist of fate they were able to do so, they could search his house if they would like at his invitation, and they would find nothing. It was the men involved who were the risk, and the vehicles. "Where are the others?"

"Nearby, and sitting tight. They won't reappear until you need them."

"Then I think I'll place a condolence call and wish Mark's family all the best and offer any help I or the bank can provide should the need arise."

"When do we deliver the next ransom demand?"

"When I'm comfortable the relief of seeing it will be such that they are eager to pay. Patience is a virtue when you want a lot of cash. We need another drop point."

"They'll have time to be prepared, they'll be watching the drop this time, so we'll have to be more creative. I've got some ideas in mind."

"Get it set up."

Frank opened the door. "My price goes up for every day this drags on."

"I figured it would. Stay near the phone this weekend."

He burst into his own home, gasping for breath, not used to running. He'd hidden his truck in the old barn, afraid to use it anymore, afraid they had seen it. They took Sharon. They snatched her while he took photos of her and Benjamin; they pushed her into a van and took her away. He'd lost them in traffic, and a frantic day searching had left him dizzy.

He hurried into the darkroom, dumping film into his hand. He had to know if he had the pictures he needed. He had to do it fast, before trouble appeared here. Someone might have seen his truck near Sharon's house. Someone might think he was involved. The thought of it was enough to make frustrated tears wet the corners of his eyes. He wasn't involved — he would never hurt them. But he couldn't risk having the sheriff come and see his office and the photos he had taken over the years.

His hands shook as he poured the chemicals. He watched the strip of negatives develop. Ski cap. Ski cap. Partially off ski cap. There! He rushed the development of the photos and pinned them to the board. Track this man, and he would find Sharon.

Caroline had looked frantic on the morning news, and when he helped recover her sister, the gratitude she would feel . . . All he had ever wanted was about to be dumped into his life with one heroic act. He memorized the photo. Find this man, and he had a place to start his search.

EIGHTEEN

The Atlanta FBI offices were crowded with investigators now working on just one case — finding Sharon. Luke picked up the remote and clicked off the security tape taken from the Benton hospital. He looked over at Benjamin. "You and your mom were grabbed in Benton. In a kidnapping, they won't want to travel very far. They will keep her somewhere locally while they wait for the money to be delivered. I'm betting within a hundred miles of Benton."

"So that means Milo and Sandy Hill." Benjamin carefully turned the pencil on a string along the map to define the hundred-mile circle. "How do you search part of a city? The circle cuts through Atlanta."

"You let the local cops search those areas. They know buildings that are abandoned or rarely visited. They have people on the streets who will give them information for money. If Sharon is in the city, someone will have seen them." Luke put in another tape. One of these tapes had to have a picture of the white van.

"Can we go to Benton and help hand out the flyers?" Benjamin asked.

"After we see your dad, we'll drive to Benton, and we can spend all day tomorrow working at the command center talking to the volunteers and passing out flyers," Luke agreed.

Jackie brought over another box of security tapes. "Can I get you anything, Benjamin?"

"Do you have a highlighter I could use? Something yellow or orange?"

"Ask our secretary to show you the supply cabinet. It's got all kinds of markers you can use."

Benjamin headed out of the room.

"I like him."

Luke glanced at his partner. "So do I. Thanks for bringing in your boys earlier; it helped Benjamin, having some kids to hang out with."

"My pleasure. Where's Caroline?"

The mention of her name was enough to have him relax a bit more. "Hopefully asleep on my office couch. She was up with Benjamin last night." He'd long ago said that there were optimists and realists and then there were men like him who lived to do what had to be done. He's accepted that not many people would ever understand him. That had changed in the last twelve hours. Caroline understood him.

No one had ever gone under his guard like that before. And that note of hers would probably wear out before he was done rereading it. He'd seen a lot of ugliness, carried a great weight, and she looked at that burden he wrestled with and not only said it was okay, but that God had made him special. There still weren't words to convey to her his appreciation for that.

He would find her sister. He'd promised himself that. "Whoever took Sharon knew her schedule well." Luke pushed the fast-forward button through another tape. "How many names are in the index now?"

"Twelve hundred. Her patients, office staff, and those on the hospital floor she most often works — Sharon interacts with a lot of people. Add Mark's clients, the firm vendors, construction contractors, his friends from years in Atlanta — there is nothing simple about this search."

"How many on the shortlist?"

"Those who knew her routine, knew she

was heading to Atlanta, knew Mark wasn't with her — we've found two hundred names. Of those, profiling to find someone who has motive for a kidnapping, we've got about fifteen names of men who have questionable finances and questionable background checks."

"That's a thin list."

"Too thin," Jackie agreed. "We need someone able to plan this, target Mark and his family, hire muscle, arrange the vehicle, arrange where to hold her — we're not looking for the guy next door who's committing his first crime."

Luke ejected the tape and put in another one. "We need another ransom demand."

"And if they decide the ransom call is too risky to repeat, and decide to cut their losses?" Jackie asked softly.

Luke knew Jackie was trying to prepare him, but he had already begun to grieve that two out of three might be all they saved. "If Sharon's already dead, nothing we try now is going to change that. I'll find the guys behind this." He paused the video. "Another white van. What tape is this?"

Jackie found the case and searched the logbook. "From the U-Store-It warehouse off I-20, between Benton and Milo."

Luke ran back the tape. It was from a security camera trained on a security fence and an entrance gate. It happened to pick up the frontage road and vehicles passing the business location. The road was pretty sparsely traveled, which was why the vehicle had stood out as it passed. He stilled a frame capturing the van. The time stamp said 5:20 p.m. Friday.

"Is that it?" Benjamin rejoined them and leaned over his shoulder to see the screen.

"It might be. Do you recognize anything?"

"It's got two antennas on the front like I saw."

"Get your map, Benjamin, and let's find this business."

The map had a blue dot marking the motel where a white van had been seen Thursday night, a red dot where Sharon had been taken Friday. Benjamin found the spot of this sighting and put down a yellow dot.

"Maybe fifteen miles outside Benton?" Luke asked Jackie. "If this is the same van, it fits the time and distance constraints. This tape puts a white van at 5:20 p.m. leaving Benton and heading away from Atlanta toward Milo. At 6:19, we have Frank in the Toyota at this gas station, on his way into Atlanta. Two guys, already going different directions?"

Jackie drew a line on the map. "The road that van is on — there aren't many turn-offs. Let's see if we can find another security camera that picked up the van between, say 4:30 and 5:45? With the combination of antennas and that distinct hinge on the door panels, we should be able to confirm we're looking at the same van."

Luke handed Benjamin the box of tapes and checked the log sheet. "Find me ones numbered 74 to 78 and 92 to 99," he asked, choosing businesses down the road from the U-Store-It business. This was probably the wrong white van, but it was in the area of interest during the right time window. That made it a possibility to work and eliminate.

Benjamin handed him a tape. "Try this one."

Twenty minutes later, Luke hugged Benjamin and sent him down the FBI office hallway to join Jackie's family. "Go say good-bye to the guys. Ten minutes, and we'll head to the hospital."

"Can I take this map to show Dad?"

"Sure. Ask Jackie to get you a folder for it."

Luke opened the door to his office, tugged at his tie, but didn't turn on the lights. Caroline was still asleep on the couch. His suit jacket was draped over her arms, for this command center was cool. He hated to wake her. By his tally she'd had about eleven hours of sleep since this began.

He sat on the chair by the couch and gently shook her shoulder. "Caroline, it's coming up on five."

She opened her eyes and yawned. She pushed back the jacket and swung her feet to the floor. "We're heading to the hospital?"

"I just talked with Mark. He's awake and sounding pretty strong. I want to give him an update in person." He handed her the hair clip that had fallen to the floor as she swept her long blond hair back out of her face. Her eyes were puffy. Benjamin was taking his emotional equilibrium from Caroline, and the burden was heavy on her. There was so little Luke could do to help her.

"What have I missed?"

"We're working a possible lead on the van."

She rubbed the grit from her eyes with her palms. "I hope Benjamin wasn't too much trouble."

Luke leaned over and put his finger beneath her chin, encouraging her to look at him. "We're fine. You've got your own handprint on your cheek. A nice little balled-up fist was tucked — right there. You're cute when you sleep."

"I'd rather be pretty when I'm awake."

"A comb and clothes you haven't slept in will help that, and I should be able to help with both of those later. You doing okay? No nightmares?"

"I'm not what you would call steady, but I guess you could say I've stopped thinking about what if and am patiently waiting for what is."

"What we know right now is we may have identified the white van on a security tape about 5:20 on its way toward Milo. The search is focusing in there."

Jackie leaned around the doorway. "Luke, Henry James needs you a minute."

Luke got to his feet, hearing the urgency in his partner's voice.

"I'll be with Benjamin," Caroline said. Luke nodded and headed after Jackie.

"Luke, do you know a Taylor Marsh with the state police?" Henry James asked, hanging up the phone and then reaching for the file on Frank Hardin.

Luke headed over to join the agent running the search. "Yes, he's a good man."

"Marsh found a bar owner who had three men drinking beers from Thursday night until closing on Friday morning. They left his place at three a.m. They were driving a white van."

"Where?"

"East of Benton on I-20. It's a popular place for the construction and contractors crowd to hang out; the bar owner didn't think much of it since vans and trucks are more common than cars. But he pointed to Frank Hardin in a photo lineup and said maybe."

"Three men?"

"Mid-thirties for all three, one tall and thin, one heavy set, and the third a talkative guy with calloused hands who was buying all the drinks."

The lead did feel solid. "Does Marsh think this bar owner can give us composites?"

"I've got an artist on the way out there to join him, and Marsh said he's going to hang out to meet the regulars, see who else noticed the threesome. The bar owner didn't remember ever seeing them before, and strangers are not common in his place."

"One or two could still be locals choosing to meet at a bar they rarely drink at. If Frank Hardin was with them . . . tell Marsh I'll be heading to Benton tonight to see him."

"I'll join you," Henry James said. "The van search is beginning to focus in that area too. I think they went to ground somewhere close to where she was snatched."

Luke nodded. "I'm thinking Sharon was tucked somewhere within an hour. The lack of leads, even false ones, says there just isn't much out there that citizens could have seen. That white van wasn't on the road for long after Sharon was snatched." Luke looked at his watch. "Give us an hour and a half at the hospital, and then we'll head to Benton. Ask Marsh to meet us at Mark's house when he's done."

"We'll meet you there."

Sharon could find no way to stretch out on the short bed that didn't cramp her back. Television at two a.m. on Sunday wanted to sell her odd kitchen appliances that they promised would make her life easier. She gave up trying to sleep, piled anything that was soft behind her as a pillow, and unwrapped another Pop-Tart.

She left the TV on. It was lame, but at least it was a voice talking.

Under her cave of sheets created to block any security cameras, this was the oddest night she had spent in years. Later this morning she would start breaking into a wall in the bathroom. She had found a few items that would survive as hammers and chisels, and she would go after the place with a vengeance where the pipes entered the walls.

Benjamin, Mark . . . she couldn't imagine how they were surviving this. Caroline would be frantic. Had Benjamin gotten to a neighbor and started the search? Had Caroline been the first to realize there was trouble? Had Mark come to the house then realized something was wrong? Had he gotten a call?

Jesus, please give them enough peace to take this hour by hour. Give them each other for support.

She kicked at the opposite wall and added to the dent appearing. Enough hours in here and that weak spot she'd found between studs was going to crack and cave in under the beating. A good two-by-four slamming into the paneling might be enough to pop the nails in the wall out. All she had to do was find the weak spots in how someone had constructed this room. She was going to get herself out of here, somehow.

NINETEEN

The nurse moving around Mark's bed to give him medications paused to smile at Benjamin and then picked up the chart to note the doses. She looked at her patient. "If you keep improving like this, you'll be moving out of ICU in a day."

"I sincerely hope so," Mark said, as he continued to hold his son's hand. "What's the verdict, Benjamin?"

The boy looked up from the equipment and IV drip he was studying. "It has another five minutes to drip."

"That sounds about right," the nurse said. "Good job on the math."

"It's even numbers; it's easy. Do you take out the needle when this is done?"

"No, I just shut it off. Your dad gets more medication later tonight."

Benjamin looked at his dad. "Does it hurt when it goes into your arm like that?"

"A little."

Mark raised the bed into a more upright position, wincing at the movement. Benjamin saw it. "You can have my pillow." He picked it up from the chair.

"Thanks, buddy. Slide it behind me." Mark leaned forward so Benjamin could do so. "There's perfect." Mark adjusted the IV line. "Slide your chair over this way and show me this book Jackie gave you."

"It's from the FBI training academy. It's even got her notes in it."

"I hope it's not scary."

"It's all about identifying bugs. I think I saw a couple of these when I was hiding in the woods."

Luke watched Mark with his son and thought the two of them would survive this, if only because they had each other. He caught Caroline's attention and gestured to the hall. She stepped out of the room with him. "Benjamin should be okay for an hour. You mentioned you wanted to see the list of friends who called in this afternoon? I can get you the list and a phone if you'd like to return a few of them."

"Please." She leaned back into the room to get Mark's attention. "I'll be down the hall returning calls if you need me."

"Thanks."

Luke tugged out his notepad as they walked down the hall, looking for the number of the coordinator.

Caroline covered a yawn. "Calling to say thank you seems so inadequate for the hours they've spent getting out flyers, talking with people, and searching remote buildings and woods."

"They know it could have just as easily been their family. It helps them to be able to do something tangible to help."

His pager went off.

Luke looked down and saw Jackie's urgent code. A crowded hospital hallway was not the place to take this. He saw an empty hospital room and stepped into it, punching in Jackie's number. "I'm here and I've got Caroline with me."

He looked over at Caroline. "We'll meet you there." He closed the phone.

"They found her?" Caroline whispered.

He curled a hand around her shoulder, and since that wasn't going to come close to handling the emotions he felt, let his other hand touch her face. "No. A package was delivered here at the hospital for Mark. Caroline — it's got a photo taped on the back of Sharon."

The package had been moved to a private office in the administrator's wing. Luke shifted his hand on Caroline's back, feeling her tension in how still she stood.

"Preserve the tape; there may be prints."

"I've got it."

"There's a wire."

"It's mine. I don't want that flap to curl back."

The two crime scene technicians were talking around each other even as they cut into the package. It was a generic post office priority box, the label printed, the box stamped, but no cancellation marks indicating it had been actually sent through the mail.

"Patient services has a post office drop off site for letters and packages on the first floor," Jackie said. "They also accept incoming mail for patients and make sure it's delivered to the correct room or forwarded on to their homes if they've just been released. A volunteer working the Sunday afternoon shift found the package still in one of the delivery bins and thought it had been an oversight from Saturday and not delivered since Mark was on his way to ICU. It could have been left anytime after noon yesterday. Security tapes are being checked to see if one covers the area, but employee areas aren't well covered."

"I'm ready to turn it over."

"Hold on, okay. Slowly."

The technician turned the box over and the picture was visible. Sharon was arriving at work, locking her car. It looked like a morning shot.

"It's a photo from early last week," Caroline said immediately, stepping toward the desk. Luke tightened his hand on her shoulder to stop her. "Sharon had her hair styled with bangs last Monday, didn't like it, and on Thursday changed back to a straight part."

"That helps," Luke reassured her.

"The box is heavy; there's more than a piece of paper inside." The technician looked at Luke. "Want to do the honors?"

Luke thought about what might slide out of that package and shook his head. The technician carefully tipped the box. Photos slipped out across the desk, most of them eight-by-tens — Sharon putting groceries in her car, Sharon walking into the hospital, Sharon getting her mail from the roadside mailbox — followed by a folded bulky manila envelope.

"Oh, my."

Luke squeezed Caroline's shoulder and then moved forward. He pulled on latex gloves and picked up the first print. This was someone who had been watching Sharon and Benjamin for quite a while. Luke slid each photo into a plastic sleeve to protect any prints and handed each one to Jackie to show Caroline. "I remember that blouse from Tuesday, that necklace from Thursday morning," Caroline said, her voice shaky. Luke counted thirty-eight photos in the stack.

A single folded sheet of paper lay at the bottom of the stack of photos. Luke opened it holding the corners and laid it flat. He used the tip of his pen to turn the page so Caroline could read it.

TEN MILLION.

They had doubled the ransom amount.

"Mark doesn't have that kind of money," Caroline said, distressed.

"No. But he can get it," Luke reassured her. They'd get the cash together; he was confident of that.

"Where's the drop site and when?" Jackie asked.

The technician finished carefully cutting open the manila envelope. Two phones were wrapped inside.

"It looks like they'll be calling to tell us." Luke opened the phones and found them both the same model with built-in radio handset capability as well as phone. Security in duplication; these guys were thinking ahead. And if they chose to use the radio rather than cell phone capability, tracking them would be that much more complex.

"Ahh, here we go." A three-by-five card was shoved in the side pocket of the phone case. It was covered in small type, and from the look of the letters, an old-fashioned typewriter. Luke slid it into a plastic sleeve.

Nonsequential bills, black leather gym bag, Luke Falcon driving, I-20 exit 157, Burger King, 11 a.m. Tuesday, we'll call.

"They asked for you by name, Luke."

He looked at Caroline's worried face and leaned over to kiss her cheek. "It's what I expected and hoped for. If something goes wrong, I've got a personal motive to see that this ransom gets delivered and they know it. That will make it easier to work out any problems that might arise." He looked through the photos Jackie had spread out. "There's nothing here to prove they have her, that she's still alive and fine."

"The fact they were watching her before

the kidnapping is enough for me to know these are the guys who took her," Jackie offered. "Let's hope they'll be willing to give us proof she's alive before we give over the cash." Jackie read the details again. "They aren't giving us much time to get together the money. And it's a very interesting starting point."

"Frank's sense of humor?" Luke asked darkly. The exit was the same as the gas station just miles from the motel where Karen had been killed. Jackie looked up at him sharply, and Luke shook his head. It was his personal nightmare; the possibility the two cases were linked.

Luke squeezed Caroline's shoulder. "This is the best news we could get short of having Sharon home. Forty-eight hours and hopefully it will be a family reunion."

She leaned her head against his shoulder. "I do love the sound of that."

"Let's hope Mark's banker is in a good mood. We've got some cash to arrange."

Caroline held out her hand to Benjamin. "Let's go down to the hospital cafeteria to get a grape drink while Luke and Mark talk." The boy slid off the chair where he was keeping his dad company.

Luke stepped aside and waited until he

was sure the two of them were down the hall before turning his attention to his cousin.

He handed over one of the photos and the ransom note. "I'll be going to Benton tonight to meet with the sheriff, Taylor Marsh from the state police, and Henry James, the FBI special agent running this case. We're convinced they went to ground somewhere near where Sharon was snatched."

"The money?"

"I spoke with the Benton Bank president as well as your financial advisor. Between what we can collateralize with property, commit from the trusts, and borrow against the partnership, I'll have it in time."

"I wish I could deliver the ransom rather than ask this of you."

Luke smiled. "I'm relieved you're laid up so you can't try. We pretty much decided this question when I pinned on the badge and you went and got yourself married. I get the risks and the fun; you get the wedding ring and the garbage to take out." Luke held Mark's sober gaze until his cousin nodded. Despite Luke's humor, they both knew the risks that were coming.

"I'd tell you not to trade your life for

hers, but it wouldn't be what I wanted if it came down to that choice," Mark whispered. "And it wouldn't be what you would do. Be careful, Luke. I want you both back here."

"They want money, and they want to stay free to enjoy it. This is going to work out," Luke reassured him. "They'll let her go. They have no hope of enjoying the money if anything happens to her, and they know that."

"Tell the doctors to let me out of here tomorrow, no matter what these machines say. I want to be there when Sharon is found; I want to be with her, not stuck here in a hospital."

Luke hesitated. "If the doctors confirm the bleeding has stopped, I'll arrange to have you moved to the house in Benton. But that comes with around-the-clock medical help coming along."

"I'll be good to travel by Monday evening. Sharon's head nurse Amy? Call her. I like her, and Benjamin likes her. Sharon will need familiar faces around when she gets home."

"I'll call her." Luke hesitated. "Caroline wants to ride with Jackie on Tuesday when the ransom is delivered. She wants to be there when we find Sharon."

"Caroline is stronger than she looks. Let her ride along. Sharon needs to be able to see family immediately. Benjamin can stay with me at the house; I think I can keep him distracted for a couple hours while we wait."

"Anything I can do for you before I head out?"

"I'm good." Mark squeezed Luke's hand. "Thank you."

"We'll get her back. That's a promise."

TWENTY

Caroline had moved a planter of daisies inside last night. Luke stepped back from Caroline's patio door, grateful to see the small sign that she had busied herself rather than spend time thinking and brooding about what was to come in the next forty-eight hours.

"Would you like more coffee?" Caroline asked.

"I'm fine." He moved over to the table to pick up the newspaper.

"Benjamin is going to run the hot water empty showering."

Luke glanced up to the sound of the water running and smiled. "I'd say let him."

"I'm making myself poached eggs."

"I'll join you for three."

"And pancakes?"

"As many as you stack," Luke confirmed.

228

Luke watched her fixing them breakfast. It was as normal a morning as they could have, and the peacefulness of it so striking given what would come later today. He was glad Benjamin had wanted to spend the night over here. The task force was busy around Sharon and Mark's dining room, working out the logistics to get the ransom money together. He needed this excuse to walk away for a few minutes, this break and return to normalcy for a short time.

Caroline paused beside him and set down a large glass of orange juice. "Turn to the comic page, would you?"

He obliged.

Her hand resting on his shoulder, she leaned over to read her favorite ones. He loved the simple joy of having her close. "Do you always start reading the paper with the comics?" he asked, amused.

"I prefer the good news first." She squeezed his shoulder before stepping back. "What kind of jelly would you prefer on your toast?"

"Strawberry."

"I'm sorry for what I said at the clinic Friday night."

He looked over, caught by surprise that she would bring up the subject.

"We're okay."

"I was cruel, Luke. I try never to be cruel."

"Friday night you were past the limit of what you could absorb. You liked me well enough to blow up toward me rather than a stranger. I took that as a compliment."

"Unfortunately you were there."

"I'd like to always be there."

It was too far, the simple words, but he watched her absorb them and not look away. When this was done they were going to pick up a relationship so far different than it had been before this weekend began. They had been dating for a year, feeling out who the other was. This weekend they had gone past those layers. Luke liked what he saw in Caroline when she was under the most pressure he could have ever envisioned.

"I promised Benjamin he could help distribute flyers this morning," he told Caroline, moving them back to safe ground. "Then I need to be back when the ransom money is ready to be picked up this afternoon."

She turned back to the eggs. "I thought I'd work at Mark and Sharon's for a bit, get it ready for Mark to come tonight, and straighten up for Sharon."

Benjamin came sliding down the hall.

"Aunt Carol, I'm hungry. Do you have any Pop-Tarts?"

She laughed and pointed to a chair. "Sit, my man, let me see if I can fill you up."

"When are we going to hand out flyers?"

"Just as soon as you eat," Luke said. "You're going to need your energy."

After the mall, Luke took Benjamin to the largest grocery store in town.

"Ma'am, have you seen my mom?" Benjamin held out one of the flyers. "She's pretty, she's missing, and I'm trying to find her."

The lady stopped loading groceries into her car trunk to stop and take the flyer, study it, and then study Benjamin. "I'm sorry, I haven't. You're the Benton boy whose mom was taken?"

"Yes, ma'am."

"I'll take your flyer and show my friends. Maybe one of them has seen her."

"Thank you." Benjamin walked toward the next car where the lady was just getting out and gathering together her coupon box. He presented his flyer again and repeated the question.

Luke, following the boy on the opposite side of the row of cars and asking the same questions, could tell Benjamin would keep going without a break until he literally dropped. They'd been giving out the flyers for coming up on four hours, and the boy was digging deep to find the energy to continue. Luke had never been so proud of a boy as he was of Benjamin.

Luke tucked his last two flyers under the windshield wipers and crossed between cars to join Benjamin. "I'm out of flyers. How 'bout you?"

"Ten more."

"Split me half?"

Luke spotted a postal uniform, the lady loading cases of soda in the trunk of her car. He knew a strong prospect when he saw one. By the time he finished the conversation with her, she'd offered to give flyers out to other route drivers.

Benjamin came to join him. "Can we go get more flyers? No one has seen anything useful yet."

Luke knelt and offered one of the orange sticks he had picked up at Caroline's that morning. "I think we should head to the Benton command center and look at more security videotapes. Then we need to pick up the ransom money and work on the maps for the money drop tomorrow. I'll need really good street maps for not only Benton, but Sandy Hill, Milo, and the north side of Atlanta."

Benjamin took the orange stick.

Luke tipped up the boy's chin. His lower lip wasn't quivering, but it was coming close and his eyes were wet. "You are finding your mom, Ben. Every person you talk to who doesn't know something means the odds are better that the next person you talk to will. This is what it means to search."

"She's out there somewhere, and she needs me. I need her."

Luke wrapped his arms around Benjamin and picked him up. "I know, buddy. I know."

Frank Hardin carried clothes out of the master closet and took them into the guest bedroom to hang. Jason had too many suits. Frank would lay them across the bed to save time, but Jason would growl about the creases. Frank shoved back the last obstructions: the built-in shoe shelf that actually moved aside and the tie rack. He finally reached the first of two doors going into the safe room. The panel swung open into the closet without a sound. He pulled out the soundproofing pieces, wishing he had a longsleeve shirt on as the particles coming off the foam would leave him itching. He reached the inside door. "You got the spotlight ready?"

Ronald clicked it on to show the batteries were good. "Yep."

"Then put on the ski mask, kill the lights in this room, and I'll open this door. Remember to shine that in her face, not mine."

The inner door jammed when Frank tried to open it. He shoved again and felt the door meet resistance. He turned and hit the door with his shoulder and body weight to force it open but barely got it to move.

"What's wrong?"

"She's jammed it from the other side." Frank finally stepped back. "Did you already strip that security camera wire?"

"No. I just disconnected it."

"Get it back on and find out what she did."

Ronald walked over to the television set in the master bedroom, searched through wires lying disconnected behind the satellite dish receiver, and changed plug-ins. He turned on the television and punched a button on the box. The screen filled with a faded yellow. Ronald started checking the wiring.

Frank cursed. "It's not the camera. She's

got something in front of it. That's fabric."

Ronald stepped back and scowled. "Why don't we just leave her in there? We can walk out of this house tonight, check into a hotel, pick up the money Tuesday morning, and just keep going. Let them try and find us, find her."

"I'm tempted." Frank kicked the door. "Can't anything be simple about this?"

Ronald undid the security camera feed. "I can force my way into the room; it's just going to be messy and noisy. The outer door is still in good shape. When the shelf is moved back, no one will ever know the room is there."

"Do it. Tomorrow and ten million are not going to get here soon enough."

Luke watched Caroline move between rooms in Mark's home, carrying fresh flowers. She wanted the home to be welcoming for her sister's return. He watched and then turned away. Her nerves had to be raw; his were, and he at least had a leading part to play in this final act to focus on. Caroline could only ride along with Jackie tomorrow and listen in. He stepped into the study.

"She's a nice lady."

Luke glanced at Taylor Marsh, working

on the transmitters for the gym bag. Luke picked up the transmitter being threaded into the gym bag handle and checked the transmission strength. "Yes, she is."

He unbuttoned his shirt.

Benjamin came rushing down the hall and slid on his sock feet into the room. "Luke, what about this one?" He held up a gray shirt of his dad's.

Luke took it. The shirt had a good collar to clip a microphone to, good cuffs for anything he might need to quickly conceal, and a good shirt pocket that would hold a second phone. "That's perfect."

"I hope it fits."

Luke changed shirts. "Perfect." He started threading the transmitter and microphone he would be wearing so he could talk with Jackie without special effort.

"Benjamin, find us a pad of paper, and we'll start recording the money packet numbers," Marsh asked.

Benjamin found one. He leaned against the desk to look at the money stacked in the black gym bag. "Do you think this is enough money for them to give Mom back?"

"Do you know what a lot is?" Luke asked.

Benjamin nodded.

"Double it, and that's about how much money is in the bag. It will be enough to get your mom back," Luke promised.

"I haven't seen dollars like this before."

"They're big denominations."

Caroline came in with a vase of flowers for the desk. "Could you give me a hand?" Luke asked.

"Sure."

She came over to fasten the cuffs for him. The odds of something going terribly wrong so that he didn't come back were slim, but he wasn't going to miss every moment he could get with Caroline when the opportunity presented itself. "Thanks."

"You're welcome. When did you say Mark is arriving?"

"You've got another forty minutes."

"I wish I could have ridden in the ambulance with him," Benjamin said.

"Someday when you get older, you can be a paramedic and drive one," Caroline offered.

"Do you think they'll use the sirens when they bring him home?"

"Maybe up the driveway, just for you."

"That would be neat."

Caroline looked at Luke. "I need to go home for a couple minutes and pack a bag for tonight."

"Want me to come with you?"

"Benjamin will walk me over."

"Take an officer with you."

Caroline nodded. Luke smiled as he watched them leave.

"Like I said, nice lady."

Luke glanced at Marsh. "Very nice." He rubbed his chin. He'd have to bug Mark tonight for a razor he could borrow. He needed a shave. "You really want one of these bugs in my shoe?"

"I don't plan to follow you at more than a comfortable jog."

Luke took off his shoe. "Are we ready, Marsh?"

"We'll be wishing Sharon a welcome home by tomorrow afternoon."

Her jaw hurt. Sharon felt it and decided the knot under the swelling would take several days to go down. Trying to tackle a guy twice her size in a space a mouse would find cramped had not been a good move. She struggled to shift the blanket over her head farther away so she could breathe easier.

Her new accommodation was not so nice. The car trunk wasn't nearly enough room for a person. Why had they needed to move her? Why put her in a car, drive her, then leave her? Had the ransom been paid? Was this already over?

Her bound hands had begun to bleed. She rested them against the blanket, unable to see how deep the wounds were but afraid her wrists would become infected. She picked up one of the plastic bottles that had been rolling into her throughout the trip. She gingerly opened the top, sniffed suspiciously, and found no scent. She touched it and tentatively tasted her finger. Water. She hesitantly took a sip from the bottle. Tepid water at that.

She awkwardly tipped the bottle to pour part of it across her wrists, accepting she was drenching where she would be lying in order to get some relief. She recapped the bottle. She felt around and found a few other plastic bottles still on their eight-ring plastic holder. She had enough water for two, maybe three days. At least the car had stopped moving.

Her hands closed around a short jack iron she had pinned down with her knee. Whoever opened that trunk was going to have an equally aching jaw. What day was this? Sunday? Monday? Tuesday? It had been going on too long. It was cold now, and she could faintly hear the sounds of the night. When the sun came up . . . this would be a metal box oven. She would bake in hundred-degree heat. There had to be a way out of the trunk, but she couldn't find it.

Jesus, I want so badly to hope. Either I'm going to be free and see my family soon, or something has gone wrong and I'll soon be dead. Get me out of this alive.

TWENTY-ONE

Luke put the gym bag of cash on the passenger side floorboard and then started his car, letting it idle with the air-conditioning on. He would need as cool a car as he could get to handle the tense sweating hour coming up. The bulletproof vest was already hot and annoying. The thing inevitably gave him a rash and left a patch of raw skin on his side.

The chase van with the tracking gear was idling in the drive, the side door open, Jackie and Caroline sitting on the riding board watching the cops sorting out the route they would follow.

Luke figured he'd head that way to say good-bye before long, but hopefully when he could manage at least a bit of privacy. He walked to the porch instead to have a final word with Mark. His cousin shifted the crutches he was using to stay upright.

Luke met Mark's gaze. "I'm ready."

Mark held out his hand. "Godspeed."

Luke held it a long time. "If something happens . . ."

Mark nodded. "I'll take care of them, buddy."

Luke knelt to be at Benjamin's eye level. "I'm going to go get your mom."

"Are you wearing your gun?"

Luke moved back his jacket to show Benjamin his sidearm. "I don't think I'll need to use it today."

"The vest looks hot."

Luke laughed. "It is. Be brave today, Benjamin. I'll be back as soon as I can. Just be prepared that it might take a while after I drop off the money before we know anything about your mom. Sometimes they tell us where to go get her, and sometimes they decide just to let her out on a road and give her quarters to call home."

"I'll try to be patient."

Luke straightened Benjamin's tie. He had insisted on dressing up for his mom coming home. "I think you look extra sharp. Is your aunt watching me?"

"Pretending not to, but she's watching you."

"Good. I think I'll go say good-bye to her now."

"Are you going to get mushy again?"

Luke quirked an eyebrow at him. "Again?"

"You were leaning against the kitchen counter last night twirling that flower while she did dishes just so you could give it to her when she got done."

"True, but she's wearing it this morning isn't she?"

Benjamin looked. "Yes."

"Now I get to go mention how she looks like a pretty flower and kind of ease into saying good-bye that way." Luke nudged the junior agent badge on Benjamin's pocket straight. "If anything happens today that's kind of bad, if I get hurt, you'll give Caroline one of your super hugs for me?"

Benjamin held his gaze and nodded.

"Good man." Luke held out his hand. "You did an awesome job running when your mom said run. Do an awesome job now taking care of your dad for me."

Benjamin's hand disappeared into his. "I will."

Luke stood, and after a final nod to his cousin, he walked down to the van to say good-bye to Caroline. The odds that something bad would happen — trouble happened. And a smart man didn't leave things unsaid.

"How are we doing, Jackie?"

"I've got everyone dialed in. We'll plan

to stay about two miles back most of the time with others paralleling you."

"Sounds fine." He knew Jackie; there was no way she would lose him. Luke looked at Caroline. "Think you'll be comfortable with Jackie?"

"As long as I don't accidentally touch anything."

"It does get to be like a can of sardines in there." He offered his hands and took both of hers, tugging her a few steps away from the others. "Come to dinner with me when this is over."

She blinked at him, and then a small smile appeared as she relaxed. "I could work on a list of ten reasons I should say yes to dinner while I watch you run around with this bag of cash."

He grinned. Get her comfortable enough and her sense of humor started to peek out. "I'm thinking I would love to get another one of your lists." He wanted to kiss her but now wasn't the time to cross that line. If he were blessed to come back, fine, he had plenty of time, but if this day went bad, he would rather leave this parting on a light note. "I've gotta go."

"Be careful."

Luke nodded. "And I'm bringing Sharon home."

TWENTY-TWO

Luke slipped on his sunglasses, picked up the gym bag, and got out of the car. He walked across the parking lot and into the state visitor's center to the display of maps, the cellular phone in his hand pressed tight to his ear to hear the distorted words directing him. "I'm here."

"Pick up the next to last trifold for the Savannah Home festival."

Luke retrieved it and opened it. A small white piece of paper with four numbers on it slid out. "Go to locker seventeen at the bus station. Tell me when you're there."

Luke tightened his jaw to eat the words he wanted to say. This idiot had been taking him in circles for almost an hour. This was getting very old. He walked back outside to his car and put the cash on the passenger side floorboard, the sunglasses on the dashboard, and the car in gear. The bus station. Where was that?

He picked up the map and drove to the bus station. Only four cars were in the lot. Luke parked by the front door, walked inside, and saw a wall of lockers. Number seventeen was near the floor by the exit. He knelt and wrestled with the rusted lock. The door opened and he pulled out a copy of today's newspaper. "I'm here," he told the guy on the phone. He hadn't placed an age to the voice yet, but it wasn't particularly old or young.

"Page six, the circled ad. Go to the new Sandy Hill mall, the food court. Buy two; I'm hungry. Let me know when you're there."

Luke yanked open the paper to page six and saw an ad for steak sandwiches circled. Luke stood, kicked the locker, and headed back to his car. This guy was going to make him buy him lunch out of his own pocket before he'd say where to put the ten million. Luke understood driving odd places in order to figure out how many chase vehicles were around, but this was childish. And he was getting mad.

The new mall was miles in the other direction. Luke put the bag of money back in the car again and headed to the interstate. He pushed his speed to the edge of what traffic was flowing. *Hold on, Sharon. I will deliver this and get you back, even if I have to strangle this twit through the phone.*

Labor Day shopping traffic was heavy around the mall. Luke finally found a parking place four rows down from the department store. He checked the bag to make sure it was fully closed; the last thing he needed was some curious shopper realizing he was carrying a bag of money. He slid on his sunglasses and headed into the mall. He stopped at the mall map to check directions to the food court.

"Go right and up to the second floor. The food court is by Nordstroms," Jackie commented in his earpiece. "They have a wonderful shoe sale going on."

Luke headed to the escalators. Jackie was riding in an air-conditioned van drinking a cold soda and listening in while he baked in this vest. He reached the food court, found the Steak and Co. counter, and pulled out his wallet to buy two steak sandwiches.

He stepped away from the crowded counter. "I'm at the food court and I have your sandwiches. Where now?"

"The Employee Only door between Steak and Co. and Taco Bell — walk through it, turn right. Open the third door on the left marked Utilities and step inside."

Luke's adrenaline spiked. The trade was going down here. He shifted the phone, took a grip on the gym bag, and tried to move the sack with the sandwiches to the same hand in order to keep his gun hand free — only he couldn't juggle the three items. No wonder he'd been told to buy the sandwiches.

He walked through the employee door and found a concrete floor and tile hallway. He turned right, smashed the sandwich sack in his hand with the gym bag and phone, and reached for his gun. Putting his hand on the doorknob for the third door, he turned it, pushed the door open with his foot, and as the door swung open he tracked with his gun.

It was a service utility room. A conveyor belt ran by with blue plastic bins snapped into lock points on the belt, each bin labeled for its destination restaurant. He saw a sixty-pound bag of frozen French fries flow by. The supply lift was bringing goods from the freezers and refrigerators to the various food bar storefronts. The room was empty. "I'm here."

"The bin for Potatoes and Co. Put in the gym bag and close the lid. Don't forget to include the steak sandwiches."

"Where is Sharon?"

"Money first. I open the bin and get the bag, then I tell you where she is."

Luke watched the conveyor belt for the proper bin, put in the bag and the sandwiches, and slammed the lid closed. The bin disappeared along the conveyer belt under felt strips that kept temperatures between rooms steady.

"Nice doing business with you. Open the other phone."

Luke pulled it from his shirt pocket and flipped it open. The phone switched to a radio frequency and automatically connected.

"Thank you, God," Sharon's soft voice echoed clearly on the line. "Who's there? Who am I talking to?"

Luke had to stretch out a hand to brace himself against the wall, feeling like he was having a heart attack. "It's Luke, Sharon. And I am very relieved to hear your voice." He slammed through the hallway. "Where are you?"

"Benton, I think. My own car trunk. Hurry please; it's getting hot. Is Benjamin okay?"

"He's great, Sharon. He's just great. Keep talking." He tore across the food court and took the stairs down two at a time. "How about you, are you doing okay?"

"Just tired."

She sounded pretty weak, and he could hear her crying. Relief tears, those were good.

"They were planning to kidnap my son."

"He ran just like you told him; he did great. Your own car, Sharon? You're sure?"

"It's my own junk — four old tulip bulbs I forgot to plant, Benjamin's baseball glove, the black shoes I meant to give Caroline . . ."

"Is there a safety trunk lock? To keep kids from getting locked inside? Can you spring it yourself?"

"Someone damaged it. I've been trying to pry through the backseat padding."

"Have you been in the trunk all this time? It's Tuesday, about noon."

"A small room first. I couldn't stand up in it, but they had a bed, TV, these bins filled with stuff to keep Benjamin entertained, a tiny bathroom. They moved me several hours ago." She started coughing, the sound painful to hear.

"Easy."

"I've screamed and pounded for attention but no one comes. I heard owls last night, and I think water is nearby, a stream maybe. It got pretty cold. I think I'm outdoors but I can't see sunshine through the cracks around the trunk."

He cleared the doors to the mall and headed toward his car. "It's sunny out right now," Luke confirmed for her. "I'm in Sandy Hill heading toward you. It may be the Benton sheriff who reaches you first."

Jackie's voice came tense over his earpiece. "Luke, she's not in Benton like she thinks; she's well south. Head back on I-20. I'll try to get you the closest exit."

"We're tracing your call right now, Sharon. We'll get a fix on your location."

"The phone batteries are running down."

"We'll just talk as long as the batteries last. We've already started to home in on you."

"I've got notes for Mark and Benjamin and Caroline. I wrote them the first two days and kept them folded in my pocket so I would have them with me."

"I know they will love to read them. Do you have any idea who did this, Sharon?"

"One man drove my car, two men in the van, and I think I heard a different fourth voice when they were arguing as they moved me from the room to the car. They always wore ski masks."

"It's good that they were careful. The ransom exchange is easier."

"How much?"

"Mark thought you were worth more."

"That's sweet. How much?"

"Ten million. If they can run far enough to try to spend it."

Luke signaled for the interstate merge, got into the flow of traffic, and hit the police lights, dropping his foot down on the gas to jump the car through seventy and eighty before finding a cruise speed just under ninety-five. "Sharon?" She'd gotten too quiet.

"He really put that kind of cash together?"

"Trust me, he would have come up with a whole lot more." Luke debated telling her what had happened, but thought on the whole she'd be better with all the truth. "Mark had a car accident Friday, serious enough that they airlifted him to Atlanta. He's already home in Benton waiting for you with Benjamin. We think they called him to say they had you just before the accident happened. His car ended up in a pond."

"It's never been smart to distract him while he's driving."

Luke laughed. "I hear you."

Jackie's voice broke in again on his earpiece. "Exit 161 and head toward the state park. She's somewhere south of Billmar Road and west of Highland." Luke eased off the gas to scan the map. That was still a huge swatch of land, not much of it developed. Cellular and radio towers would be a long distance apart, making her location hard to pinpoint.

"How's Caroline coping?" Sharon asked.

"Like a trooper."

"I'm glad. I have a —" The phone cut out briefly on her words. "Tell . . . I love them."

"I will. If we lose this call, know we're coming." He heard only static. "Sharon? Can you hear me, Sharon?"

The call was gone.

"Jackie?"

"The best we can do is about a two-mile grid," Jackie said, and Luke heard unexpected tears in her voice. "We're about three miles south of you, triangulating the call."

"Two hours, Jackie. Enough men, we can search the grid and find the car within two hours. What happened at the mall?"

"The transmitters showed the bag stopped moving. Guys started to move in, and someone pulled the fire alarm. People in the mall panicked."

"Let me guess, he dumped the bag."

"They found it in the bin you had placed it in. He must have shoved the cash into another bag, then pulled the fire alarm. There may have been a couple people splitting up the money to make it easier to carry out."

"They won't get far, not with the trail they left us with this drive around."

"That last locker was a mistake. The bus station has a permanent guest in a homeless man, and there's a sketch artist already working with him."

"How's Caroline doing?"

"I'm bawling, Luke," she replied, her first words on the line. "I've been passing on Sharon's words to Mark. He's on the other line."

"I figured you might. Let's meet up at —" he found a restaurant near the search area and gave directions — "and you can ride with me. Sharon will be fine, Caroline. We'll find her."

TWENTY-THREE

Luke's car idled at the junction of park roads. Caroline used binoculars to scan the area and the campsites. "There are too many back trails in this state park. She could be anywhere."

"Think it through; it's not as big a search as it appears. The car will be near a camper or a tent. It won't be off on its own where a park ranger would have noticed it as abandoned. But the site will also be somewhere that Sharon calling for help wouldn't have attracted attention in the last day or two. That means it has to be one of the more remote sites. Eliminate clusters of campers; eliminate vehicles out on their own. You're looking for probabilities."

"Let's try the south branch of this road and go into the valley. She couldn't see the sun but she could hear water. That suggests one of these smaller tributaries flowing into the lake."

"Good."

Luke turned that direction.

"I want so badly to be the one to find her."

Luke rubbed her tense arm. "We're close, Caroline. We're close."

"We got it!" Taylor Marsh broke in on the radio. "Two troopers just spotted Sharon's car. It's back on lot MA-8, one of the primitive camper sites that has a concrete pad, picnic table, and water, but no electricity or sewer. The troopers are trolling the shoreline in a fishing boat. They can see the car parked under trees, a mini-motorhome on the campsite. A pickup truck and a gray sedan are also on the lot. There's an empty boat trailer. The site looks deserted. The occupants may be out on the water, but the troopers don't see a boat tied up nearby. It's a high embankment; they can't beach near the site."

Luke picked up the radio. "Tell them not to even try. Tell them to just keep trolling and to set up a ways down the shoreline, so they can tell us if anyone comes near the site from the water. Send two men to walk in silently and get binoculars on the site while we close the roads."

Luke found a place to back up, turned the car around, and drove to the closest crossroad to the campsite. He pulled in behind Marsh. As he parked and reached in the backseat for his vest, more patrol cars rolled in.

"You have to stay here, Caroline. Stay with the deputy."

"I know."

He leaned over and hugged her. "Pray hard."

He got out of the car to talk to Marsh as Henry James and Jackie both arrived.

Marsh set down his radio. "The site appears deserted. No movement in the camper windows, no sign of anyone around the lot there. And that is definitely Sharon's car, down to the hospital decal on the back window. That truck is registered to Ronald Parks."

"Frank Hardin's old pal. Which suggests Frank has indeed been here," Jackie said for them all.

"I hear you." Henry looked at Luke. "How do you want to play it?"

"Send three men to the front and three men to the rear of the camper to stop anyone who might try to exit the vehicle. Jackie and I pop the trunk of the car and

257

get Sharon out of the line of fire, then you take down anyone in the camper. Snipers cover us."

Henry looked at Taylor and got a nod of agreement. "Okay. Let's do it. Marsh, you lead the group to the front; I'll take the rear. Let's get the snipers in place."

TWENTY-FOUR

Midday sun suggested siesta time as they crept through the woods to the campsite. Luke wiped sweat from his forehead and dried his gun hand again on his jeans. Sharon was in sight. Where the foliage lightened he could see the side panel and rear fender of her car. The car had been parked near the woods, making it easier to approach as they didn't have to traverse over several feet of crushed rock.

Henry James moved his FBI group in to cover the back of the camper. Taylor Marsh moved with his officers to the front of the camper.

Henry nodded. Luke and Jackie crept toward Sharon's car. The silence from the trunk both concerned and comforted him, for his biggest fear would be Sharon hearing something and calling out, unintentionally alerting anyone in that camper to their presence.

Luke knelt by the car. "Sharon, it's Luke. Stay real quiet. We're popping the trunk."

He slid the tool into the lock and used his muscle to force the mechanism, his hand stopping upward movement as the trunk popped. "Stay still."

Luke lifted the lid.

He bit back bile. His expression spooked Jackie and she rose to see into the trunk.

It was empty.

The wind blew small pieces of paper around inside, scrawled writing on both sides — the notes Sharon had mentioned. Luke picked them up so the wind couldn't blow them out to the lake. All but one of the water bottles rolling around in the trunk were empty. The phone Sharon must have been using lay on the trunk mat.

Luke lowered the trunk lid. He used the car as cover and moved with Jackie to join Henry. "She's either in the camper, or they've already moved her on the water."

Henry quietly cursed, echoing what Luke was feeling. Taking a deep breath, he leaned around to study the camper door. "Luke, you and I, we open that door nice and quiet and go in with Marsh and his guys covering our back. My guys will force the driver and passenger doors to take the front of the vehicle."

"Let's do it."

Luke took up position behind Henry, and they eased around to the camper door. Henry put his hands on the door and lock, Luke nodded, and Henry forced the lock and opened the door. Luke moved in.

He recoiled at the smell and yet kept moving forward. He'd smelled that odor too many times in his life. Henry James did too, and he tightened his grip on his weapon. Luke took the two steps into the camper in one big step, his weapon sweeping ahead of him.

The first man's body had fallen in the small aisle before the small kitchen sink and counter, a cup of coffee staining the center of the man's shirt, his hand still loosely curled around the cup.

Two more men were dead, one seated on the bench seat of the back table, the other the only one who looked like he'd been able to rise and attempt to react. He'd been killed by two shots, one to the face and one to the back, collapsing him across the first man's boots.

They were dead. Two unknown young men. Ronald Parks. And a gray backpack was sitting open on the table, stuffed with money, splattered with blood, attracting flies.

TWENTY-FIVE

Luke stepped outside the camper, walked halfway to the car where Sharon had been, and lost it. The post he kicked splintered, the picnic table crashed to its side, and the fishing boat trailer rolled back until it hit the railroad tie marking the edge of the campsite.

Marsh wrapped him up from behind before he could hit the grill and break his hand. "Don't, man. It isn't worth it."

"I was just talking to her!" Luke choked on the words.

Marsh leaned on him, using his strength to stop Luke from breaking free. "You can't help her if you lose it. Sharon will need you even more in the next few hours than she did before."

We were so close . . . so close.

Luke felt the explosive emotions coming back under his control, and the fist ready to strike the grill relaxed and dropped to his side. Marsh loosened his grip and Luke took a deep breath. "I'm okay."

Marsh squeezed his shoulder. "We found her once; we'll find her again. Remember that."

Luke walked through the woods back to the road, trying to figure out how to tell Caroline he'd failed. She expected him to walk out with Sharon. Instead . . .

No matter how much she braced for news, there was no way to be prepared for this. How was he going to tell Mark he was bringing back his millions but not his wife? How was he going to tell Benjamin he was coming back without his mom? And Caroline, to know her sister was gone and one real possibility was that she was dumped in the lake — Luke felt sick. *Jesus, is Sharon still alive? Or was I the last one to talk with her?*

He took the final turn in the trail and stepped out onto the road. Caroline stood with the deputy by the cars, rocking a bit on her heels as she watched the woods where they had originally entered, waiting, not yet seeing him. The deputy saw him first and said something. Caroline turned. She knew, just as soon as she saw only him coming back. He watched the realization blanch her face, and then she walked toward him, and by the final steps she was running.

He caught her and wrapped his arms tight, feeling bony elbows bump him and her chin bone collide with his chest. "She wasn't there." He rocked her and said it again, unable to explain this. "She wasn't there, Caroline. We opened the trunk where she had obviously been held and Sharon wasn't there."

"They took her with them?"

He picked her up rather than release her. He nodded to the deputy who opened the door of the squad car for him. Luke set Caroline down on the seat and knelt to lean against the side of the door beside her.

She hurriedly brushed at her tears. "I'm okay," she whispered. "Tell me."

"The trunk was empty. Sharon had been there, but she's been moved. There are three dead men in the camper, shot, apparently taken by surprise. The money I paid is sitting on the camper table."

"Did Sharon shoot them?"

He blinked. The idea had not even crossed his mind. "No. Someone had to force the trunk lock to get her out. We think one of them arrived with the money, they sat down to distribute it, when someone opened the camper door and shot all of them, very fast. Then he went to the car and forced the trunk to get Sharon out."

"Someone rescued her? Or took her?"

"I don't know. I'm sorry, Caroline. If it was a double-cross, they would have taken the money and left Sharon. But they left the money. We don't know where she is; we don't know who took her. And it's going to be a long confusing time sorting this out."

She leaned over and wrapped her arms around him. She didn't say anything for so very long. He reached up and rested his hand on the back of her neck, wishing he could say this was a nightmare that was a dream and not real.

Caroline took a deep breath and let it go, then sat up. "You didn't tell me she was dead. She was alive at noon today, and not badly hurt. You didn't find her, so she's likely still alive. I'll take that. It's enough that I'll still hope for the next hour."

He didn't deserve the quiet comfort she offered. "You're tougher than you look, Caroline. Strong like a willow that bends and doesn't break."

"I'm learning from you. You'll cope with this. I know you."

He dreaded what he now had to do. "I need to call Mark."

"I'll do it for you."

He shook his head, knowing this news had best come firsthand. "I need to be the one to tell him."

"How can I help without being in your way?"

"We're shutting down the park and throwing up roadblocks all around the area. This happened recently; Sharon can't be far. You can stay with Jackie if you like."

"Please."

He leaned against her a moment to find some strength, then picked up his phone and walked away to call Mark.

TWENTY-SIX

Luke could feel the sun burning down the back of his neck. Sharon must have baked inside that car trunk. He walked across the campsite and down the road to the command post they had set up. Jackie leaned out of the communication van to hold out a fax.

"The third guy is also from Atlanta — Billy Klein," Jackie confirmed. "A distant cousin of Ronald Parks. Maybe he was the one who set up the campsite? We know three people grabbed Sharon. Is another guy involved who just shot all his accomplices?"

"The money was left behind. Whoever shot these men and took Sharon — I don't think he was ever part of the kidnapping ring. It doesn't make any sense to me — gun down three people and leave the money?" Luke asked.

"Marsh said some of the cash was missing."

Luke ran a hand through his hair. "Four packets, four hundred thousand, and that may just have been sloppy handling on the part of the guys who brought the ransom here. Or one of the couriers pocketing a little extra for himself."

"If Ronald was involved, I think we have to conclude Frank Hardin was also part of this kidnapping," Jackie said. "We know he's connected to a white van. Was this shooting his handiwork?"

"The one thing we know about Frank is he loves money. He wouldn't leave that kind of money behind." Luke thought about it, and the only thing that made sense made this unrelated to the kidnapping. "Tying up the details of the kidnapping isn't going to help us Jackie; it's looking back in time. We need to be looking forward to who would kill these people and also leave the money behind." He could feel that precious time slipping by.

"Forensics will give us a lot. The murder weapon used may already be in the system, and there are likely going to be prints."

"I know, it's the time involved to develop those facts that is against us." Luke looked across the campsite to the picnic table where Caroline sat, nearly motionless as she watched officers move around the crime scene. They would be moving the bodies soon, and Luke didn't want her to see the body bags coming out of that camper. He motioned for Jackie to join him, and he walked over to Caroline.

The hillsides and lake echoed with the sound of an approaching police helicopter, and conversations stopped as it came in to land at the open field north of the campsite. As rotors spun down, four officers ran to meet the helicopter, loading the evidence bins. Two officers climbed aboard. It was on the ground for only a minute before rotors began to turn again, and it lifted off.

"If Sharon wasn't taken out of here over water, is she still somewhere in this state park, or was she driven out?" Jackie asked, going back to the question they were all trying to solve.

"When did her phone go dead?" Luke asked.

"12:32."

"And the campsite was spotted when?"

"3:10."

"The shots had to echo on the water, through nearby campsites. Someone we interview should be able to give us that time. We need to know how much of a lead he has."

"Do we have a vigilante in our own group?" Taylor Marsh asked, joining them. "Someone who knew we were searching this state park for her car and decided to take matters into his own hands? A rogue cop who could take these guys by surprise?"

"If someone wanted to be a hero, Sharon would still be here," Jackie pointed out.

Luke shook his head. "I think we're incidental to this. I think this guy was already watching them, and already following them. They were so busy absorbing their newfound wealth, they didn't realize they brought trouble back with them."

Luke got up from the table and looked over at Caroline, distressed by the conclusion he had reached. "I think your stalker just killed three men in order to take Sharon. And I don't think he's going to be interested in giving her back."

TWENTY-SEVEN

Luke walked down to the lake to watch the water. Six hours since he last spoke with Sharon, roughly four since someone had taken her out of the car trunk and disappeared with her. The sense of sickness inside him grew stronger with each hour. So close. And now they couldn't find even a thread of a lead to work.

"You really think this is the work of my stalker?"

He turned his head, watching Caroline walk toward him with her hands in her pockets and a jacket borrowed from Jackie draped across her shoulders to protect against the wind. Luke met her gaze, then looked back to the water. He'd lost her sister. He didn't deserve the sympathy he saw in her eyes.

She stopped beside him and after a moment reached over to touch his hand. "You need a strip of tape on that."

He looked at his knuckles and the still-bleeding scrape. "It will heal. Don't be kind, Caroline. Right now it's like salt in a wound."

She leaned her head against his shoulder. "You couldn't win today. No matter how determined you were in what you set out to do this morning, the fix was already in. She was alive, as of six hours ago. Hold on to that hope. I know you'll find her again."

"Had I resolved this last fall, it wouldn't be coming back."

"You didn't miss anything last fall. Whoever this is, he never came far enough out of the shadows last year to catch. He hasn't bothered us in months. This weekend was the work of a bunch of guys who wanted to get rich at our family's expense. And if you got mad and reacted as the law allowed, he got mad too; he just reacted outside the law. You told me that a stalking is not an impersonal action. I think this guy cares about Sharon because he knows she matters a great deal to me."

"First disturbed, now a murderer. He won't be calling to ask for a ransom. He's not going to be coming forward to give her back."

"But the odds that he would hurt her?" Caroline shook her head. "I'll take those odds. You can find this man."

This was going to go on for days, weeks, and he had to find the energy to face it. He was so tired. "It's going to be slow work. And that assumes my leap to say this is your stalker is even in the ballpark of being true."

"Let the evidence confirm that answer; it will, one piece of news at a time." Caroline tucked her hand under his arm. "Come on, let's go home."

"I don't deserve you, Caroline."

"On the contrary, I think I got the better deal. You'll just have to trust me on that."

Luke knew what it was to receive grace. It was to sit on the back porch with a little boy who was still missing his mom and not find himself blamed. Benjamin pushed the heel of his tennis shoe at the lower step.

"You weren't able to find her?"

"No. But I talked to her. I tried to get to her, but something happened and someone took her away before we could reach her."

"And bad men are dead?"

"Some are."

"I wish I could have gone to see where she was last at."

Luke brushed back the boy's hair. "She was thinking about you and your dad. She really misses you too."

"I read the note she wrote to me." Benjamin leaned over and wrapped his arms around Luke's neck. "Take me to see my future tree house. Please."

Luke reached for the boy's hand.

"I don't like to cry around my dad. He's sad enough."

Luke blinked away a couple tears of his own. "I know. But it's okay to be sad, Benjamin."

"I miss Mom. She always tickles my toes to wake me up."

Luke walked with Ben down the path to the woods and the tree where the tree house would be built.

"I was thinking that maybe when Mom came home, she might like me to have done something with my time rather than just be sad. I thought I might start on my tree house."

"She might like to hear that you were sad and that you worked on your tree house. You can do both."

"Would you help me?"

"I'll be glad to try. We can move brush and stuff until your dad can walk down here and help us read the blueprint so we can build the flooring."

"It's a good place. A nice sturdy tree."

"Dad says it'll last a long time." Benjamin walked around the tree trunk, looking at his tree. "Do you still like my aunt?"

"A lot."

"She's going to miss Mom so much."

"I know."

Benjamin sat to rest against his tree. "Mom was going to make me the ladder for my tree house."

Luke sat beside the boy. "I hope she's back soon to do so."

"What does he want? More money?"

"I don't know what this man wants. I think he likes your mom and was risking his own life to help her when he rescued her."

"Then why doesn't he bring her home?"

"Maybe he will, or we'll find him. I do know your mom is a brave and smart lady, and she will do everything she can to come home soon. She loves you so much."

Benjamin leaned over, and Luke felt the boy's shoulders begin to shake. "Can I give out more flyers?"

Luke lifted the boy on his lap and let him cry. "I'll give them out with you." He had nothing left inside after this day, or he would cry along with Benjamin. Luke knew what it felt like to be a failure.

TWENTY-EIGHT

Luke took a legal-size notepad with him to the kitchen table and set it down. He poured himself a cup of coffee. The house was finally quiet, Mark and Benjamin in bed, and Caroline napping on the couch not wanting to turn in. There was work to do now, the kind of thinking best done when it was quiet.

Luke drank his coffee, picked up the pen, and started to write.

STALKER PROFILE:
1. This guy is older. He's probably known Caroline and Sharon for several years. Lives in the area. Comfortable with Caroline's routine. Able to blend into her life last fall to leave small gifts, to call when she was just getting home, to know her favorite flowers.
2. Caroline likely knows him without realizing it. She probably smiles when

she sees him, stops to casually pass a few minutes in conversation. Those events fed his broader delusion of them being together. He focused on Caroline last fall. RESULT? He spooked her and backed off.

3. Roses sent to Sharon's office Friday suggest his attention had recently turned to Sharon. Perceived as a way to expand his connection to Caroline by getting to know her sister?

LINK TO KIDNAPPING:

1. Was he watching Sharon on Friday and saw the snatch? BIG IF. It would explain aggression at the campground. He saw who made the snatch, didn't know where they had taken her, where the white van went, but knew who to tail. Stayed with them until they led him to Sharon.

2. Guys milling around campsite enter the camper when the money arrives. Stalker moves in. Fearing for Sharon now that ransom has been delivered, he moves in to protect and take her. Events of this weekend must have seemed like fate — a way to heroically prove his commitment to Caroline by saving her sister. He's a troubled man

driven by intense emotion. Escalates to killer. He won't be afraid to act now, to make what he wants happen. Long ago he made his interest in Caroline clear. Sharon isn't a substitute, but a new dynamic in a bigger plan?

IMMEDIATE GOALS:

1. Forty-eight hours of adrenaline-induced flight driving him — he wants to get away from campground while trying to keep on top of news developments. He'll get to a safe place and take steps to make sure Sharon won't be taken away from him. Maybe head to same place he's envisioned taking Caroline? Remote and a place he's very comfortable with?

DELUSION VERSUS REALITY:

1. He has always been the one entering their world. Now he will bring Sharon into his. He will want to please her, make her comfortable, happy. If Sharon is smart, she'll walk that fine line and sincerely appreciate his efforts while waiting for the moment to get word out as to where she is.

2. In a few days the reality of shooting people will hit him, the doubts: Does he

have enough cash? Food and clothes? Delusion and reality are rubbing against each other. Stress will build. What he once thought he loved he may now hate. Will he snap and lash out at Sharon in violence? Or snap and just abandon her?

3. How long that destructive spiral lasts has variables — how well Sharon understands what's happening . . . how many steps he takes to match his dream with reality . . . stalker's tolerance for setbacks. Time measured in weeks and months, not days.

4. Of course all this assumes he's not crazy. If he is crazy, he may simply kill Sharon, his Caroline substitute, and himself so they might be together for-ever.

Luke set down his pen. He knew what was coming. How did he get ahead of it, where did he step into its path to stop it? They wanted Sharon back. This guy wanted to keep her. Where they collided and how determined how many people might get hurt.

Caroline, will you understand the risk that will have to be taken? When it came down to it, Luke was confident Sharon would at least walk away. He would give his life for Sharon's if necessary, to return her to her family. He looked at his summary of the man he thought had her. *I know you. Now I need to know your name.*

There had to be a way to put together what had happened last fall and what had happened recently to identify who this man was.

Luke saw car lights coming up the driveway. He closed the pad of paper and went to meet the sheriff.

Luke looked through the original stalking report from last fall, searching for the one detail that would give him a place to work. The sheriff, sitting on a chair across from him, turned the last page in Luke's handwritten assessment. "It's a big jump to go from working a kidnapping to now working a stalking. I understand the FBI task force doesn't see it your way."

Luke kept reading. "They think there was a falling out among kidnappers, and we are going to get another ransom demand for even more money."

"But you think we've got a stalker who took Sharon."

"Yep." Luke closed the folder. "And since it keeps me out of their way as they work the kidnapping angles, I've got their full blessing for Jackie and me to chase this idea."

The sheriff tapped the document Luke had written. "I've never met a kidnapper who would leave a ransom behind. If you're not 100 percent accurate in your guess, you're probably 80 percent. I wish I did have a name for you. Whoever we're dealing with, it's not going to end well."

Luke set aside the file. "I'm afraid one of the officers searching for Sharon and manning one of those roadblocks will encounter them. This guy is over the edge. We can't afford an unplanned encounter with him, not while Sharon is with him."

"He may not have tried to go far. I agree with the assessment that he's from this area," the sheriff replied.

"This snatch began Friday after four p.m. If he's been watching the kidnappers, it's very likely he had stepped out of his normal routine and essentially disappeared. We need names to eliminate until we find the right guy, and we don't have a lot of time." Luke knew what he was asking of the man, to name men he knew as suspects, who might have killed three people today.

The sheriff got up and walked over to

the window. "Maybe he hasn't disappeared, but he hasn't been seen around over the holidays, and I'm a bit surprised at that — Mark Medton. He's older, an iron worker from before the mill closed."

The sheriff walked back to the files he had brought and searched for a photograph.

"Any registered guns?" Luke asked.

"He's an avid hunter and camper. He would know that campground well."

"Let's check him out in the morning. Who else?"

"Gary Gibson hasn't been around. I wouldn't place him as your shooter though; I doubt he's ever owned a gun. He's a bit of a recluse after being badly burned in an industrial fire. He's had more surgeries in three years than most men could ever survive. I know he's a pretty good photographer, has his own darkroom, and the like. He's not a violent man and he's friendly enough, just not very social." The sheriff passed over another photo.

Luke studied the photo of a man scarred by fire. Someone who had lived through that kind of pain . . . He understood the eyes. Gary had emerged a survivor. Whatever had to be done could be endured because it was necessary, even crossing the line of morality to kill a man. "You don't need to be an excellent shot to kill a man if you pull the trigger at close range before he starts to react to the threat. Three deaths were fast. The two at the table couldn't have gotten away even if they wanted to, and the last man was hit twice and somewhat wildly with about four shots fired in his direction. Gary lives around here?"

"He now owns his parents' property east of town. And I heard the settlement for his accident was six figures; he could have bought something else recently."

"It can't be Gary."

Luke turned to see Caroline in the doorway. "I thought you had turned in for the night."

"I couldn't sleep. Gary's a nice guy; Benjamin likes him. He wouldn't do this."

Luke got up. "If we are to find him, we have to consider even names of those you think of as friends. For Sharon's sake we have to."

"I know that. But it doesn't do to waste time."

"It's still worth a visit to see him," the sheriff said, looking at Luke. "If he has an alibi for the afternoon, his name comes easily off the list."

"We'll check him out," Luke agreed, looking at Caroline and knowing how like a knife this must feel to her as he investigated those she knew. "Who else should we be talking with?"

"Adam Reece."

Luke added him to the list. It would be a long list before they ended work tonight. Beginning tomorrow, he planned to check out every name in great detail.

Caroline settled in the guest bedroom to get a few hours of sleep, the door cracked so she could hear Luke and the sheriff's conversation. She didn't want to think about last year and what it had been like when the stalker appeared in her life. But the memories of last fall were already returning of their own accord, a mix of emotions as she thought about the night that had become the turning point in her relationship with Luke. The night had begun with so much promise . . .

Was she dating Luke or not?

There were days Caroline didn't know how to answer that question. She slowed her car and pulled into her driveway, tugging out a soft pretzel stick from the deli sack rather than wait until she was inside.

He'd cancelled a date again, for dinner and a night at the theater. Her replacement plans for the evening had turned out to be two hours with Sharon, helping move bookcases around Benjamin's room, followed by a stop at the grocery store. It wasn't the same.

A car was parked off to the side of her driveway. Caroline tensed until she saw the license plates. Luke. She searched the shadows and saw him, sitting on her front porch steps.

She parked beside his car, considered the groceries in the trunk, and decided nothing needed to be carried in immediately. She pocketed her keys, left her purse on the front seat, and picked up the pretzel sack.

He didn't say anything as she approached. She considered inviting him inside, but there was something nice about the silence outdoors. This day hadn't gone particularly well since the moment she got up.

She sat on the porch beside him. Luke offered the sack he held and she tugged out a pot-sticker. "Tell me again why you love carry-out Chinese food so much," Luke said.

"It stays hot better than most take-out

options. Hamburgers and fries, they tend to go cold first; pizza's not far behind. And those taco things, it's not even worth mentioning what cold refried beans taste like."

Caroline offered her deli sack.

"Pretzels? It's been a while since I had one of these."

"They aren't bad."

"I'm sorry about canceling our plans."

"I bought a new dress."

"Now I'm really sorry."

"Was it work?"

"It always is." Luke pulled out another pretzel stick. "You're right; they are good."

Caroline traded him sacks. "I'll take the last of the pot-stickers."

"I bought a double batch for you."

She ate them slowly, pausing when she finished one to stand the sticks upright in a neat little line, the tips wedged into a crack between boards of the porch.

Luke leaned back against his hands and stretched out his legs. "They say it will be a full moon tonight."

"It's cloudy enough I doubt we get to enjoy it. Why the late-night stop, Luke? Not that I mind. It's nice to see you."

"It was a kid tonight. One of those tragedies that is never supposed to happen in life."

He never talked about work in detail. It was about as clear an unwritten rule as she had been able to figure out about him. He would talk dispassionately about his job in general, but never about the specifics of his day or the case he was working on.

The cases themselves — she'd long ago reasoned they broke his heart. He was too often lost in thought and almost brooding for her not to know he was absorbing an enormous load that weighed on him long after he went off duty. She didn't like being shut out, but she did appreciate the fact that his job was more than just a job for him.

"What happened?" she asked quietly.

"Someone pushed an agent's kid under a train."

"Luke . . ." The shock of his words cracked her heart.

"It happened up in New York, but the agent's family was from here. They asked us to stay around and help locate the relatives tonight before the national news carried the name."

He glanced at her and then away. "So I stayed and dialed numbers, and when we finally located the grandmother, Jackie went over to break the news and take her to the airport."

"I'm sorry."

"The girl was twelve. According to several of the eyewitnesses, she was on her way with her older cousins to an orchestral recital. They got to the subway station, and someone hollered, 'Are you Kaci Lewis?' When she swung around in surprise to say yes, they shoved her onto the tracks. All because she was Jack Lewis's kid."

"Who did it?"

"It looks gang related, likely tied to a case he testified at last month."

She didn't know what to say. What was there to say? She leaned her head against his shoulder.

After a moment, Luke settled his arm around her waist. "I didn't feel like going home."

"I'm glad you came here."

He split the last pretzel and handed her half.

"What happened in your day?"

Caroline sighed. "Nothing as profound, I'm afraid. I found Kelly crying in the bathroom during third period, because someone teased her in a particularly cruel way about her new haircut. Then Rick and Tom, best friends since kindergarten, decided to hate each other today and got into a fistfight over a baseball dispute and got themselves suspended. My geography lesson plan turned out to be a washout; it's never good when you lose control of the class ten minutes into a lesson. For a fifth grade teacher, it was a pretty bad day."

"You don't need to qualify it. It was a bad day. And a cancelled dinner didn't help it end any easier."

"The dinner part just got salvaged." Caroline smiled. "Would you like to go for a walk or something?"

"Or something. But I'll settle for a good-night kiss and a peppermint candy stick from your jar."

She angled her head just a bit to see him, and confirmed the smile she heard. "I'm out of peppermint."

"That's a shame. I'll have to settle for a good-night kiss then."

He lowered his head, and after a moment's time to let her draw back, closed the last inches to softly kiss her.

She couldn't wait to kiss him again, but it didn't make sense to ruin the moment of a first kiss with thoughts of the second. She leaned back when he did and smiled at him. "I might have a toffee stick."

"Not a bad second choice." He got to his feet and offered his hand to help her up.

She scooped up the pot-sticker sticks first.

"Why do you keep mementos like that?"

"Because I want to."

He laughed. "That's simple enough logic. Give me your car keys, and I'll carry the groceries in while you unload them."

She dug the keys out of her pocket. "Deal."

He walked back to her car and she went to the back door, pushing aside the small box she saw sitting beside the step. Another unannounced gift; they were getting to be a regular occurrence. If she took it inside now, Luke would just comment on it. She'd get it later, along with her mail.

She turned on lights in her kitchen, glad she had taken the time to set out another four of the tall glass canisters of candy sticks that Benjamin and, surprisingly, Luke enjoyed. "Toffee or almond?"

She offered the options as Luke carried in the first load of groceries. "Toffee." He piled the sacks on the counter. "Another white box, Caroline? Not mentioning it doesn't change the fact it came. How many does that make?"

She thought about lying, but it was a stupid way to avoid the matter. "Five."

"I'm installing that security system this weekend."

"I'll just set it off and have the sheriff

291

running out here to answer false alarms."

"Better that than you continuing to ignore the problem." He pulled eggs out of the sack, and she wondered how many cracked under his grip. "Don't argue the point; it's going in."

"Okay."

He looked at her and frowned. "You'll use it? No saying you forgot or ignoring it's there?"

"Put it in and I'll use it." She wasn't going to fight with a guy whose job had him calling family members of agents to say a child was dead because of what his dad did for a living.

"Thank you."

She stopped behind him to hug him, then reached around him for the ice cream to put in the freezer. "I'm not entirely dense. If it will make you feel better, I'll use the security system."

"I want you to get a car phone too."

"Luke, there are limits. I don't need a car phone."

"When you're stranded on the side of the road, you'll need a car phone."

"If I get stranded on the road, I'm either close enough to town or to my home that I can easily walk the rest of the way. It's not like I spend my weekends visiting antique shops across the county."

"It would make it easier for me to get in touch with you."

"The answering machine, which you talked me into just two weeks ago, does a perfectly good job of recording the message that our plans for the evening have changed."

"Caroline —"

She smiled at him but firmly shook her head. "Let it go, Luke. I don't need or want a car phone or a cellular phone or for that matter a pager. I like not being in touch for ten minutes of my day while I drive to and from work; it's my time."

"Then make it temporary. What's it going to hurt to have one for a few months?"

She put down the sack she was folding. "Why are we fighting about this?"

"Because you need to say yes."

"You need to take a no as no."

Luke leaned back against the counter and folded his arms.

Caroline frowned. "Do you know how annoying that is? Lean back, fold your arms, wait for the obstacle to pass — not every subject in the world has to be resolved with your point of view prevailing."

"There's no logic in your refusal."

"And there's logic in your request?"

"Someone is leaving those 'gifts,' and I use that term loosely. One day he's going to approach you and say, 'Hi Caroline. Did you like what I sent you?' And you're either going to be looking in the face of a creep or a very dangerous creep. Get it through your head that this is not something to ignore and deal with it."

"I am dealing with it. I'm careful. I watch where I am and where I go. But I'm not changing from being who I am just because someone else needs some help."

Luke dropped his hands. "I'll be by early to install the security system. It would help if you called the monitoring company before then to give them your contact numbers. This is their number."

"I'll do that."

"I'll get the last of the groceries and let you get some sleep tonight."

Ten minutes later, she stood at the back door and watched as he pulled out of the driveway and turned onto the road. It had been stupid to fight about something as basic as her safety, and to do it tonight of all nights. She shut off the outside lights and closed the door, turning the perfectly good dead bolt.

He thought she couldn't take care of

herself, couldn't handle the details of the cases he worked, couldn't handle being more than just the lady he occasionally dated. He'd smother her if she let him; smother her in the concern built up and reflected from all the stresses of his job. She wasn't fragile, threatened, or avoiding reality. She just saw it differently than he did. And she didn't know how to convince him that when she needed to be strong, she could be as strong as he needed her to be.

I always said I wanted a complex man in my life, with layers and depth. Luke is all that and more.

She picked up a candy stick for herself and undid the ribbon and plastic wrapper. It had been a nice kiss. They hadn't bumped noses or any of the other awkward figuring-each-other-out movements she had expected that would mar a very sweet memory. She smiled. Six months. He'd taken his time with that first kiss. If it was another six months to the next one, she was going to kiss him instead of waiting.

She tied the short piece of ribbon off her candy stick around the pot-stickers and took them upstairs to add to her memory box.

★ ★ ★

Caroline woke up when she heard the sheriff move into the hallway, preparing to leave. She listened to Luke, hearing the tension and fatigue in his voice as he made final plans to meet up for the search tomorrow. The door shut, and minutes later Luke came upstairs and walked down the hall to check on Benjamin.

It's going to be okay, Luke. We'll survive this. If finding her stalker was the next step they had to take, they would take it together.

TWENTY-NINE

Luke pulled into the driveway of his home in Sandy Hill very early Wednesday morning. He needed to pick up a change of clothes and search out the document copies from his safe, as Mark was in no shape to visit the bank deposit box to retrieve the originals.

Neither one of them wanted to risk the paperwork not being in order should a question arise regarding Benjamin's legal guardianship while Sharon was missing. Reporters were digging into anything that could be behind the snatch, and the task force had already had to dodge questions about Mark's partners and his recent marriage. Before he unlocked the front door, Luke picked up the newspaper from the stoop and lifted the lid on the mailbox to confirm his neighbor was picking up his mail.

The Friday paper still sat open on his

kitchen table, a pair of scissors marking the comic page. Dry cleaning hung on the coat rack ready to go out the door with him, and the smell of lemon oil hung faintly in the air. Helpless bachelor didn't fit his lifestyle. Luke set down the current day's newspaper and glanced at the pile of mail on the counter. It would wait for another day.

He moved through the house turning on lights and took the stairs two at a time going upstairs. There was no reason to have a place with four bedrooms and two baths except for the fact he liked having the space. His one concession to the job, the travel, was the fact he had bought a house in a co-op community so he didn't have to keep up a yard.

He took a fast shower, washing away the grime, and returned to the master bedroom. It would be a day spent with the sheriff interviewing people. Luke pulled out a blazer to go with the dark slacks and white shirt. Out of habit, he reached for a tie.

He listened to the weather report as he stopped at his chest of drawers, picked up his wallet, and slid it into his inside coat pocket. The handgun in its holster was clipped to his belt, with two additional clips beside it. He picked up his badge and polished it, then slipped it onto his belt beside the gun. The Bureau should pay him more, but otherwise he had few complaints. For all the problems a bureaucracy as large as the FBI created, it still had room to let him be a lawman first and foremost.

He met his eyes in the mirror as he combed his hair, accepting the shadows he saw and their cause without dwelling on the emotions. Luke set down the comb and nudged Mark and Sharon's wedding photo from last year back into alignment with the one of his parents. They looked so happy in that photo.

He clipped a small flag to his lapel, a gift from Benjamin, and then slid a handkerchief into his pocket, figuring if he didn't need it before the day was over, Caroline might. *God, what do You think? A quiet day with a successful outcome? You know what's coming.* Luke looked at the wedding photo again as he slipped on his watch then stepped away from the dresser. He efficiently packed a bag to keep him going for a week.

Luke headed to his private office. Case notes were stacked beside his laptop. He often worked here for a brief time before heading to the office in Sandy Hill. Jackie was one of the few agents he'd met who routinely kept the same early hours as he did. They'd chosen each other as partners out of a desire for sanity; they both preferred to do a day's work before lunch. He punched in her number on his phone as he knelt to open the safe.

"Jackie, what are the headlines?"

"We got a couple more possible sightings of Frank Hardin overnight. I'm running them down."

"Where?"

"Milo, which makes them interesting."

"Putting him back in the area. Anything I can help with?"

"I've got it covered."

"The sheriff and I are going to work names off that stalking list this morning unless something more urgent comes in."

"Henry James is focused on the roadblocks and media right now. It's going to be midday before a lot of the forensic data will be available from the campsite."

"I'll plan to be by this afternoon to update on whatever the sheriff and I find."

"I'll stay in touch, Luke. I've got a call coming in, gotta go."

He hung up the phone, satisfied his

partner was plugged into the latest news at the task force.

Luke sorted papers and found the document copies he sought. Mark's adoption of Benjamin had just recently been approved by the courts. Luke knew he was listed in Mark's will, and Caroline was listed in Sharon's, setting up dual guardianship and administration of a trust in Benjamin's name should anything happen to Mark and Sharon. It would help to have a dual power of attorney designation added specifically referencing Benjamin and any medical care he might need.

He slid the papers into his briefcase and closed the safe. He spun the dial.

He glanced at his watch. Caroline should just be getting ready to take Benjamin out to distribute flyers. He tried her cellular phone. "It's Luke. How was breakfast?"

"I'm a fan of donuts which I think you knew. Thanks for buying the chocolate-filled kind."

"They're another thing we have in common. I'll stop by and pick you and Benjamin up at the community center around noon. I've got Mark's prescriptions. Anything else you need me to bring?"

"That will do."

"I think your phone battery is going dead."

"I'm going to see about getting a new one today; this battery won't hold a charge anymore. Noon at the community center; Benjamin and I will be ready."

"See you then," Luke replied, letting her go. He turned off lights and locked up his home again. It was odd to realize Caroline had never been here. He'd have to fix that one day soon. It was a nice place to entertain, and he'd enjoy having her at his side hosting an evening for their friends. One day . . . This storm was going to end, and life would return to normal. He had to hold on to that hope.

Luke held the squad car's rear door open for Caroline. "I wish you had stayed with Mark and Benjamin." The list of names in his pocket the sheriff had helped him put together was slowly being crossed off as they gathered enough information to either clear a person or move the name to a list to investigate further. He hadn't vetoed Caroline's request to ride along with them, knowing it was easier on him to have her around as this day unfolded. But now he was regretting that decision. As the list dwindled, Caroline grew more and more tense.

"I need to do this. I'm okay, Luke, just tired."

He let his hand rest reassuringly on her shoulder for a moment, then he closed the door. In some ways it felt their roles had reversed overnight. He had something to work, and in the activity there was some relief, while Caroline was now the one able to only watch events and feel the weight of what they might discover today. Luke feared word would come about Sharon today and be the worst kind of bad news.

Luke picked up the stack of folders. "Who's next on the list?" he asked the sheriff.

"Gary Gibson. We'll try the farmhouse first."

The drive took only five minutes, and during the short ride, they passed two volunteer groups who were walking the roadsides, looking for anything out of the ordinary. If only they had something to go on to give those volunteer groups a chance of turning up good news.

"I'd like to stop by the volunteer center later today," Caroline said.

"We'll go in tonight and help serve dinner for the volunteers," Luke offered.

The sheriff turned off the main road onto a graveled winding road. Luke felt uneasy and couldn't put his finger on why. "It's a large place." Cattle grazed in the expansive pasture coming down to the edge of the road, and it looked like acres were planted with corn and beans.

"Most of the land is rented out to be farmed."

The road turned to the right and the farmhouse came into view. The two-story home looked to be built in roughly the same era as Caroline's home, but it did not appear well maintained. The roof looked reasonably new and a breezeway off the side of the house looked like a recent addition.

Luke checked the file. "Gary has only one vehicle, a gray pickup truck with blue trim?"

"Yes."

Caroline turned to look back toward the barns. "I don't see it."

"Neither do I."

The sheriff parked in front of the farmhouse. "Gary isn't one to be out in the fields or checking on the cattle. If he's around, he'll probably be near the house."

Luke got out of the car. "Why don't you stay put, Caroline? This may be a short stop." She nodded and Luke closed his door. He walked with the sheriff up the walk on to the porch. Chimes mounted on the top of the well moved in the breeze.

The sheriff knocked. "Gary, you home? It's Rob. I need to talk with you."

No answer. Luke walked down the porch and around the house to look in the windows. The living room looked deserted. He saw no sign of a light on inside. "You said he had a darkroom?"

"I believe so."

"He probably built it in an interior room of the house that already had no windows. Why don't you check the barn for his truck. I'll walk around and try the back door. I'd hate to leave only to find out later he was here and working."

The sheriff nodded.

Luke walked through the tall grass around the house. Why did the man keep flower beds if he never weeded them? The two concrete steps to the back door had begun to chip. Luke knocked on the back door, then opened the screen and knocked again. "Gary, are you home?" He listened but heard no sound of movement. Not entirely surprised, Luke stepped back to the yard.

A kitten appeared briefly from under the stoop and disappeared again. Luke knelt to

305

coax the kitten into coming back out. The guy liked cats; Luke supposed that was to his credit. This one looked to be about three months old. Luke picked the kitten up and carried it as he walked the west side of the house, checking windows. He stepped around a rosebush to see in the window of what he guessed would be one of the back bedrooms.

"There's still no sign of his truck," the sheriff said, walking over.

Luke slowly lowered the kitten to the ground, then stepped closer to the window, raising his hand to stop the sun's glare on the glass. "Get us a warrant. We've got probable cause."

Feeling a bit sick, Luke stepped back so the sheriff could see.

Luke walked the hallway of Gary's home, studying the photographs lining the walls. Gary had spent a lot of time documenting a house fire. A few photos showed firefighters at the scene as the fire burned and part of the roof collapsed. The rest of the photos were taken in the weeks and months afterward, as the remains of the home weathered with time.

Gary had used the burned-down house as a photo study, projecting his own moods onto the burned-out wood. Twisted beams still reached into the sky set against the blue of a noonday sky. Ash drifting away in a breeze. A slim blade of grass poking up through the rubble. A flower in bloom projecting up through a broken picture frame. "This guy has talent."

"Photography is probably the only safe outlet he has for his emotions since the accident," Caroline said. "He'd occasionally show me the photos he was having framed."

"I don't think you should come any farther."

Her hand in his tightened. "I'll cope with it. It's not going to be worse than I have imagined."

Luke stepped into the office he had seen through the window. The room had tall ceilings and narrow windows, the lighting good and the furniture sparse. Only a couple dozen framed photos hung on the walls, but they were enough to get them a warrant.

Luke stayed by Caroline as she paused in the doorway and took everything in. They were clearly photos taken without Caroline or Sharon's knowledge.

There were photos of Benjamin going back to when he and Sharon had lived at Caroline's home. "You can tell when he found the zoom lens and mastered it. He's

307

putting himself in your lives." Luke stopped at one of the photos. "This one looks recent."

"That sweatshirt — it's from last fall. And from the lighting, he had to be watching me sometime around dawn. Do you think he was making those phone calls?"

"Probably."

Caroline stopped by one of Sharon putting groceries in her car. "We never saw him."

Luke rested his hand on her back. "You didn't see him because he didn't want either of you to notice him." There were empty places on the wall. Luke stopped and touched one of them, seeing the different amount of fading on the paint from the sunlight. "This one was removed recently. He must have taken his favorite photos with him."

"Can we find his darkroom? See if there are negatives still here?" Caroline asked.

"It's set up back in the second bathroom," the sheriff said, rejoining them. "Based on the trash creating a stench in the kitchen, Gary left fast and he hasn't been back here in a few days."

"With those kinds of burn scars, he's not going to be exactly inconspicuous as he travels. So where would he be heading?"

"I don't know if he owns property beyond this farm."

"What about the insurance settlement after the accident? Didn't he receive that recently? Has he spent any of it in the last months?" Caroline asked.

"I'll start making calls to find out."

Luke led the way to the darkroom to see what they had to work with. Several strips of negatives hung from the shower curtain rod. A small counter had been built out from the wall, extending over the bathtub to form a stand for the photo wash trays. Spiral-bound books of negatives sat stacked beside the stool next to glass jars of developing solutions. "This place is a fire hazard."

He picked up one of the spiral-bound books and started turning pages of the negatives. Caroline stood at the doorway and watched for a minute, then she disappeared into the adjoining bedroom. "Luke, look at this."

He stepped to the doorway. Caroline had opened the bedroom closet doors. There were four file cabinets inside. Caroline opened one of the drawers and pulled out a folder. "The folders are dated by date and locations. He's been taking photos for years. Do you want to take these photos with us?"

"Stay focused on things related to where he's traveled in the past and where he might go again. Or if we are lucky, any photos he has taken since Friday. Maybe he was back long enough to use his dark-room one last time."

Caroline opened file drawers. "The most recent file I see is from last month."

"The recent stuff is probably in here or possibly in his office."

"I'll search his desk."

Luke picked up the binders of negatives still in the darkroom. "Caroline, find a box or sack and gather up whatever papers or receipts you can find when you look through his desk. See if he has a rolodex or a calendar book. We'll take them with us to review. He's going to be heading to some-where familiar."

She nodded, clearly relieved to have something concrete to do. "I'll bring you something to carry those in too."

"Thanks."

"Luke, what about the kitten? If Gary has fled . . ."

It took him a moment to catch up with what she was asking. He smiled. "Find as many of the kittens as you can, and hope-fully their mother. We'll take them with us."

THIRTY

Caroline ate a few fries because they were left from dinner but put the last two hamburgers in the refrigerator. She found paper towels and the cleaning spray and set about wiping down the kitchen table.

"Benjamin has the momma cat and her kittens safely tucked away for the night in the laundry room."

She turned to smile at Mark. "That's good."

"I can see I'll be buying both a cat and a dog when this is over."

She offered him the pills Amy had set out for him after dinner, and he swallowed them dry. "Benjamin should be asleep soon; he was fighting to keep his eyes open even as I read his bedtime story. I think I'd better turn in too. Is there anything I can do for you before I go up?"

"I'm fine, Mark. I hope you're able to sleep well."

"I'm the lucky one I think; those pills knock a person out."

She knew he was in pain and running a slight fever again, that every breath had to feel like it was on fire. But she understood why he never said anything in complaint. "I refilled the ice bucket upstairs and left you a bottle of ginger ale. Sharon had the hot pad stored in the guest bathroom; I set it on the nightstand for you. It might help that shoulder some tonight."

"Thanks. Amy's back at first light with the doctor, so I'd best be on the road to recovery by then. The last thing I need is to be prescribed more pills. If Benjamin cries at all and I don't hear him, please, wake me."

"I'll do that. Good night, Mark."

She watched him leave, using a cane and leaning a hand against the chair then the wall to keep his balance as he walked. He'd pushed himself coming out of the hospital earlier than was wise and dealt with the fact his wife didn't come home.

In his place, she would have cracked under the pressure a long time ago. She turned her attention back to the kitchen, keeping busy to help pass the long evening.

"Is there enough in Gary's files to help us find him?" Caroline asked.

Luke looked up from the papers he was sorting through. She looked ill from the lack of sleep. He'd hoped that she would lie down for an hour after dinner. He tugged out a chair at Mark's dining room table for her. "We've got credit card receipts, cancelled checks —" he held up the receipts he had taken from Gary's files — "tracing where he's been in the last year won't be so hard. We'll figure out where he might go again."

"He had to have taken her somewhere within driving distance. He's not going to fly her somewhere. How far does he run?"

"I don't think he will try to go more than a day or two before he hunkers down. He'll need access to more cash, and that will help us spot him. Or the flyers will pay off and someone will report seeing them. How's the distribution coming?"

"Jackie has the new flyer out with the media, and the volunteers are starting to distribute it now." Caroline's voice broke and she wiped at the tears. "Sorry."

He nudged his sandwich her direction, silently encouraging her to try to eat some more. She was holding it together, but her emotions were fraying as the stress never abated. "You need to get some sleep."

"I tried. It doesn't come."

She picked up the sandwich to nibble at a bite. "Mark doesn't look so good. You need to speak with him, Luke. He's been going through the negatives we brought over, seeing how many locations he can identify where Gary was watching Sharon or me. He can't do that kind of thing to himself, not when he needs to be recovering. He went up to bed, but I'm afraid he'll just get back up again soon and go back to it."

Luke set down the papers he held. "I've tried, Caroline. He needs to do something, and to be out searching the roads is beyond his strength right now. I had a hard time convincing him not to pick up his car keys and drive through the night."

He leaned over and rubbed her hand. "Right now we make progress by generating and dispersing information, increasing media coverage, and following up on leads."

"It's so hard, this part of your job. Sharon's out there somewhere, and we're helpless to end this without a break coming our way."

"We'll get that break through a lot of

hard work. How's Benjamin holding up?"

"He's frightened, scared, trying hard not to cry in front of his dad. I'll take him out tomorrow to pass out more flyers. That seemed to help him, having something tangible to do."

"Keep up your courage, Caroline. Sharon is out there, and we *will* find her."

She offered a smile that faded and set aside the sandwich. "I thought I might go back to my place for a couple hours and see if I can sleep there. Benjamin finally nodded off and Mark's resting."

Luke pulled out his car keys for her. "Call me when you get there, okay?"

She leaned over and kissed his cheek. "Thanks, Luke."

She headed toward the door.

He watched her go. He'd been afraid she wouldn't have the strength to make that decision to step back for a couple hours, the wisdom to make it. He should have known she'd do the smart thing.

Luke sighed, wishing he could give Caroline something, anything that would be positive news. He looked at the spread-out papers. If Gary had a place he was heading to in mind, he either owned it, had stayed there before, or could easily access it on short notice. It wasn't obvious in the first look at his accounts where that place might be.

Gary obviously bought a lot of film and development supplies. But the cash trail for those hadn't been discovered yet either, which suggested there was another bank, another account somewhere. But where? Luke returned to the search.

It felt odd being home. Caroline took a mug of hot chocolate out to the back deck and sat down to watch the night sky. The forecast spoke of rain in the next few days, but tonight the sky was clear and the stars bright. The sleep she desperately needed was so far away.

Where was Sharon? Caroline had sat out here with her sister so many nights, talking about life and laughing together.

Jesus, I've survived the first punch of this storm, but it is not letting up and it's like being in a hurricane. I don't know how to cope anymore. I'm losing hope that this will ever end.

Luke kept moving through this, one step at a time, his emotions held just below the surface. She, on the other hand, just felt overwhelmed. She couldn't match Luke's control, but she had to find a way to do so. *How long, Lord? Will we find Sharon tomorrow? In a few days? Does this go on for weeks?* She didn't know what to prepare for.

Luke will do anything he has to in order to save my sister. For that matter, so would I. And I'm scared for him, for what this might require before it's over.

The awareness sat just below her conscious thoughts through the days, as she watched Luke, as she saw him focused on finding Sharon. Caroline knew with each unexpected turn in this case, the odds increased that Luke might be hurt before this was over. *We need this to end, Lord. We need Sharon home.*

What happened if Sharon didn't come home? Caroline thought about Benjamin, about what it would be like having to step into Sharon's shoes for a while — to help Mark with the day-to-day routine, to watch Benjamin after school. What did she know about being a mom?

She could be an aunt, keep an eye on Benjamin, help him with schoolwork, listen to his day and help take him to events. But when it came down to the important things — it would never work. Benjamin had to have his mom come home. He'd already lost his dad to an accident and was having to adapt to a new dad. If Sharon didn't come home, Caroline feared

Benjamin would withdraw into his shell and not let himself love anyone for fear he'd lose that person.

Could Mark even go on with his life if Sharon was never found? How long did they search before making the painful decision to stop? How long would it be for the courts to consider Sharon dead, making Mark a widower by decree? Would he even stay in Benton or would the memories be so hard he'd take Benjamin to Atlanta to live? The sickness in her stomach grew acute. They couldn't go there; they just couldn't. Somehow they had to find Sharon.

The phone rang inside. Not willing to take another call from a reporter and find herself quoted on the news, she listened to it ring until the machine picked it up.

THIRTY-ONE

Luke shifted the skillet onto the heat. "Benjamin, how do you want your eggs?"

"Scrambled."

Luke cracked four eggs into the hot skillet, dumped in a bit of milk, and stirred hard. "Put in more toast for me, and find the grape jelly. Caroline prefers just toast and coffee for breakfast."

Mark came into the kitchen walking slowly. Luke recognized the signs of intense pain. "Rough night?"

Mark just grimaced. "I want to go with you today."

"So do I," Benjamin added.

"Then you'll both need a good breakfast." Luke held up two eggs to Mark and got a nod. There was no way to talk his cousin out of going along, and Luke didn't bother to even try. "You both want orange juice?"

"Just milk for me," Benjamin said.

Luke shoveled eggs onto plates and pointed a spatula to the glass jar of chili peppers as Benjamin passed by him doing the toast. "You want to join me for some hot help this morning?"

Benjamin laughed. "No way."

Luke tugged out two of the peppers to add to his plate. "Jackie, come grab a plate. You need to eat."

"I am." His partner appeared from the dining room, carrying a carrot stick and half a bran muffin. "I brought mine along, remembering your cooking." She poured herself a coffee refill. "The morning briefing got moved to the Benton sheriff's office in forty minutes. Where's Caroline?"

"Sleeping in, hopefully. Her toast will keep." Luke pulled out a chair for himself.

"I hope Mom is getting a good breakfast."

Mark leaned over to his son, spoke quietly, and Benjamin nodded and dug into his eggs. "I'm taking Pop-Tarts along with me for Mom."

"Good idea," Jackie concurred.

Luke looked over at his partner and hoped for everyone's sake they had a lead on Sharon's location by nightfall.

Luke refilled his coffee and carried the mug into the dining room where Jackie was gathering up the area maps.

"I'll take Benjamin and Caroline with me this morning to do more flyer distributions, if you and Mark want to spend a few hours with the task force to brief them on what you found so far from Gary's files," Jackie offered.

"I'll take you up on that." Luke looked at his watch. "I hate to wake Caroline up, but leaving without her isn't worth the fireworks that would happen later."

"Call her."

He sighed. "Yeah." If she was too tired and failed to set the alarm or had turned it off and was sleeping again — waking her with a phone call only to tell her he had no news wasn't something he wanted to do. The day was going to be long and hard enough without starting it off with disappointment.

"You loaned her your car last night. Walk over to her place. You can see how she's really doing before she has to put on a steady face for Mark and Benjamin's sake."

"Would you go ahead and take Mark and Benjamin in with you? We may be a few minutes behind you."

"Sure." Jackie paused beside him and set her hand on his arm. "Are you doing okay?"

Luke half smiled. "Remember that weekend when you shot me in the foot?"

Jackie smiled. "I'm not likely to forget given you never will."

"True." Luke's smile faded. "I feel like I'm walking around with a gut wound right now. Are we missing something, Jackie?"

"I spent the night wondering about that too. But what? I don't know. Henry James doesn't miss much. He's got the task force exploring every idea folks have had."

"I know. I'll go get Caroline and we'll meet you shortly."

Luke retrieved Caroline's newspaper from the box at the foot of her driveway. He tucked it under his arm and walked toward the house.

Luke saw his car parked off to one side; Caroline had parked so that she could still get to her own car in the garage. Officers had brought it back from Atlanta for her. Luke stepped up onto the porch. The wind had blown leaves into a pile before the front door. He shifted them aside with his foot and rang the doorbell. "Caroline, it's Luke."

He slid off the rubber band from the newspaper. As he had expected, Sharon's photo was prominent on the front page.

Luke knocked a couple times on the door, then folded the paper and walked around the house. If she was up, the coffee would be started and she would have already spent some time out on the back patio. If he just woke her up, it would be a minute.

He found the patio door unlocked. He slid it open and wiped his feet of wet leaves before stepping inside. The lights were off and the kitchen cool. "Caroline, you awake yet, darlin? It's Luke. You want me to start the coffee for you?"

He tugged over the filters and the coffee can. There was an open aspirin bottle and a half-eaten microwaved dish of pasta on the counter. His car keys were on the counter next to her tin of after-dinner mints.

Caroline didn't answer his call. He didn't hear the shower. He walked down the hall to the bottom of the stairs. "Caroline?"

Luke took the stairs two at a time.

He looked toward Benjamin's room since Caroline had slept there last time. Empty. He walked on. Her bedroom door was open, and one glance showed a made bed. "Caroline, answer me if you're here."

His words echoed in the hall, unanswered.

He pushed open doors to the bedrooms, the bathroom, and headed back downstairs. The alarm system had been off, the back patio door unlocked. His car was in the driveway. He scanned rooms on the main level and saw nothing out of place.

Luke grabbed his keys and headed outside to the garage to check on her car. Caroline had been here last night, she'd eaten a bit, but either that bed was recently made or it had never been slept in.

Luke pushed open her garage door.

Caroline's car was gone.

THIRTY-TWO

Luke shifted the phone in his hand so he could push in the alarm code sequence to get the time when the system had been shut off. The numbers flashed up in blue, and Luke searched his memory of last night to figure out when Caroline had called to tell him she was home. It had been before Jackie's last update of the night. The time looked roughly the same. Caroline had shut off the alarm system a few minutes before she had called him last night. She hadn't re-armed it as she normally did before she went to bed.

"Caroline's not at the community center," Jackie relayed.

Luke pushed buttons on the alarm system to reactivate it after a two-minute time delay. "I'm heading back to Mark's house. How she could have passed us when you were heading out and I was walking over here —"

"Luke, what's going on?"

"Nothing."

"Luke —"

"Her purse is gone, her car is gone, and other than an unlocked back patio door and a deactivated alarm system, everything here is normal. She's going to be at Mark's right now, wondering where we are."

"Do you want me to alert the — ?"

"There's no new problem, Jackie. Caroline and I just missed each other. I'll call you back in a couple minutes." Luke ended the call and hurried through the house.

He headed toward his own car. His palms were sweaty as he turned the key in the ignition and put his car into reverse. There was something wrong. Something terribly, terribly wrong.

Mark pushed open the back door of his home so hard it hit the wall with a thud. "Still no word from Caroline?"

Luke held up his hand, holding his cousin off. "I need to know where that number originates, and I need to know it now." He covered the phone. "After she called me last night, Caroline got a call that she returned. That's all I know so far. Sometime between then and this morning

Caroline left her house, got in her car, and headed somewhere without any note or message indicating where she was going."

"I thought they had her phone line tapped." Mark knelt to help Benjamin with his backpack.

"They do, but she must have returned the call on the cell phone she had borrowed from Amy when the batteries went dead on hers."

"Were you able to get the number?"

"Her home phone showed the last dozen incoming numbers." He turned his attention back to his call. "Repeat that?" He scrawled down a location, and his hand shook as he wrote the final part of the message. "Thanks." He closed the phone. "She got a call from a pay phone at a rest stop off I-20."

"Sharon?" Mark asked.

Luke stared at the paper and then turned to share a quick look with Jackie even as he shook his head. "Caroline would have been over here in a heartbeat to get you. And she's not one to go off on her own."

"She would," Jackie corrected softly, "if she thought it necessary."

Luke forced himself not to ball the piece of paper in his fist as he too thought of the possibilities. "Or if she thought the call was a false lead, but one she had to check out for her peace of mind. Regardless, there's no way she intended to be gone this long."

Caroline, I didn't need you being brave today, not this way. He steadied himself and looked at his watch. "I'm heading out there."

"I want to go with you," Mark said.

Luke shook his head. "She's not missing; she's AWOL. There's a difference. That call could have sent her anywhere, but I'll start with checking out where it originated. I need you two to head back to the sheriff's office and see what the task force has on phoned-in tips last night. See if any of the calls originated from this rest-stop location. Someone was able to get Caroline's home phone number; they may have been calling the tip line too. Caroline and I will join you at the sheriff's office just as soon as we can."

Caroline should have trusted him.

Luke disregarded the speed limit and passed a trucker by using the right lane. Heavy traffic made him regret not requesting an air flight. The depth of fear he felt was different than anything he'd ever felt before. What was he going to say when he found her? If he reacted as he feared, his emotions would roil out, and he'd regret for years whatever came out of his mouth. *You've scared me, Caroline — bad. And I don't do scared very well.*

He hit the turn signal to pull into the rest stop. It looked nearly full with several trucks lined up before the restrooms and soda area. Luke chose not to park, but instead cruised through the rest stop slowly. He hoped to find Caroline sitting at one of the picnic tables or in her car, having chased a lead and come up with a bunch of nothing. He could deal with tears and the awful question of why someone would call her with false information, build up her hopes and then kill them. Luke could deal with her disappointment, but he couldn't deal with her not being at this rest stop.

He circled the parking lot twice, but there was no sign of Caroline's car.

Had she turned back for home? Gone on with her quest? He should have insisted she stay at the house last night rather than let her return home. What had been said on the call? What had she come out here to find? Or had the call sent her somewhere else?

There was nothing here to find.

He left the rest stop and reentered traffic to take him back to Benton. Once she reappeared Caroline would be as apologetic as she could be for causing them to go through this. Two sisters — both missing. Luke wanted to pull to the side of the road and throw up.

THIRTY-THREE

The Benton sheriff had cleared two conference rooms and several desks for the task force. Luke paced in front of the timeline on the display boards, past the flyers and photos and leads that had been followed. So much work, and so little to go on. "She's not down at the volunteer center, the hospital, or with any of her friends we've been able to find." He was coming up empty.

Luke ran his hand through his hair. "He got to Caroline; that's the only thing that makes sense. He has Sharon and he came back for Caroline. Who knows why, who knows what's going on in this guy's head. But at this point, if he's still in the area, he won't be for much longer. We find her car, we find where they met up, and maybe we figure out which interstate he's using to get out of this area."

"Why didn't Caroline leave a note or get

word to us?" the sheriff asked.

"I don't know." Luke looked over at Mark, wishing he had something to offer his cousin.

Mark just shook his head. "This isn't like Caroline."

Henry James hung up the phone. "The officers have finished their canvass around Caroline's property. Her home, the surrounding grounds — they show no signs of foul play. The only tire tracks there appear to be your car and hers."

"I agree; I saw nothing at the house to indicate trouble," Luke said. "She apparently left on her own. Show me again where the road blocks are set up."

Jackie shifted the county map around for him to see the latest updates. Luke sat down to study the map.

Henry ripped a fax off the machine. "Listen up, people." The officers and FBI agents around the room quieted down and turned at his call. "Forensics just matched the bullets. Our three men dead in the camper — they were shot with a gun that traces back to Frank Hardin. So are we looking for Frank Hardin?"

"If Frank shot those men, then why did he leave the money? That makes no sense," Jackie said.

"Maybe someone also killed Frank and took his gun?" one of the task force officers suggested.

Luke shook his head. "We wouldn't get that lucky." He got up from the table to pace again. This was becoming impossible to sort out. Was he dealing with a kidnapping ring, a stalker, or both? "We suspect Frank was in this area to do a job. He was seen at the gas station Friday night after the snatch." Luke looked at Jackie. "The one credible sighting after that put him heading west out of the state. But check me on this, the trail went cold within hours, correct?"

"There were no more confirmed sightings."

"So Frank holed up and came back into this area, possibly to get paid? There's a falling out among the kidnappers, and Frank shoots his compatriots. Only that doesn't explain the left behind cash or why Frank would take Sharon with him, let alone why he would want to get to Caroline . . ."

"All we have so far on the three guys found shot is that Ronald Parks had the longest criminal record. The other two were support players in the past for car thefts and burglaries and probably had similar support jobs this time — drive the van, arrange the campsite. None of the three was the type to plan a kidnapping," Henry added.

"Frank isn't the kind to plan such a crime either; he's the guy who gets hired by someone to execute it." Luke turned to look at the sheriff. "Has anyone else turned up murdered in the last two days around here? Did Frank shoot the guy who hired him too?"

"We've had a couple shootings that look drug related over near Sandy Hill, and a domestic homicide south of Benton," the sheriff offered. "No homicides that seem to match this."

"I could see Frank leaving the money behind if he thought it was marked and too hot to dispose of," Jackie offered. "Someone set up this kidnapping and hired Frank, who then hired Ronald and a support crew. Once it all started to come apart, Frank could be cutting his losses and killing the people who knew he was involved."

"But why take Sharon out of the trunk?" Mark asked.

Luke looked over at his cousin. "Insurance maybe? A hostage to guarantee he could get out of the area?"

"And Caroline?" Mark asked. "He's trying to get to you, Luke, trying to make this even more personal."

Luke looked at Mark, a sense of dread building inside. Frank having Caroline was too terrifying a reality to consider. "Frank might want a fight with me, but to risk this? He would want to get out of this area, lay low, and make it a fight for another day." *If Frank had made this personal, Sharon and Caroline were likely already dead.* The impact of that thought had him recoiling inside and searching for anything else that explained this.

Luke shook his head. "Gary Gibson is involved. He's been watching them, photographing them, and he's been missing since this began. He's the only person in this who has an immediate need to involve Caroline. I still think this is more than a kidnapping gone bad. Sharon is only a substitute for what Gary most wants. He would feel compelled to contact Caroline."

Luke's phone rang, interrupting the discussion. He pulled it from his jacket pocket to answer the call. "Falcon."

"Luke."

"Sharon!" His exclamation froze the group. He forgot how to breathe as he met her husband's gaze. "Where are you?"

"I don't know. Somewhere on Dryer Road at a bait shop closed for the holiday. I can hear interstate traffic. I can't walk much farther."

Luke pressed the phone tighter to his ear and covered it with his hand to hear her.

"I only had two quarters, and I didn't know if Mark would be back at the hospital, or if I called the house . . ."

"It's okay, Sharon." Luke turned quickly and saw Jackie's confirming nod as she spoke on another phone. "We're tracing this call now."

"She swapped for me, Luke. Caroline swapped for me. And you've got to get her back."

He closed his eyes. "I will, Sharon."

"Is Mark with you?" Her voice broke.

"Right here, honey. Hold on."

He passed the phone to her husband.

"She swapped for me." Oh, Caroline, what have you stepped into? He put his hand on the back of a chair to keep himself upright.

His vision cleared and he saw a swirling room of officers in a rush to seize the moment. Henry stood in the midst of it, calling out rapid orders to officers both present and out on patrol. They had to get to Sharon, but they also had to close every road in the area to try and seize the man who had held her. Minutes were precious.

Luke watched it as he took a second deep breath and knew relief that he was not in charge of this task force. As badly as he wanted to run it, at this critical moment all he could think of was the fact that Caroline was now in intense danger.

"Jackie, you and Luke — get in the air and get to Sharon. Joe is landing on the pad to pick you up now. Call in as much backup as you need to search the location once you know what the area looks like. Mark, the hospital or your home? We can prepare to receive Sharon at either place."

Mark straightened, stronger now in a way he'd not been since the release from the hospital. "Our home. She'll need to see Benjamin. Sharon's on her feet and talking; the hospital stop can come second."

"Done."

When seen from the air, the bait shop stood out alongside a gravel road, the parking lot and winter storage areas for boats confirming they had the right site. The helicopter pilot circled the property. Luke could see no movement below.

"Joe, how long before the media helicopters track us down?" Jackie asked the pilot.

"You can bet someone at the task force has said something to the wrong person by now. I give you five minutes or less before we have unwanted company and are live on the air." Joe pointed to the east. "I'm going to set down on that frontage road over there."

Luke put his hands on the buckle of his harness. "What's the time from here to the nearest hospital in case we need to divert?"

"Four minutes."

The helicopter flared and set down. Luke shoved open the side door. He ducked low as he stepped out fighting the wind gusts then turned back to give Jackie a hand.

"I'm good. Go."

Luke ran down the rock road toward the bait shop, scanning for the pay phone Sharon had used.

"Over here."

Luke heard the faint call over the sounds of the decelerating helicopter blades and turned to his right. Sharon moved to stand up, one hand braced against a tree trunk to keep her balance. Luke scrambled around the stored boats.

"I need a jacket. I don't want Benjamin to see me like this." Her face was tear streaked and dirty, her hands bruised, her face too gaunt, the circles below her eyes dark — but she was standing if on wobbly legs and her voice was clear.

"Right here." Luke wrapped his own jacket around her. Her hands were icy cold, and her fingers curled much like a lady with severe arthritis. He eased her hands into the pockets of the jacket.

"She went with him," Sharon whispered, leaning against his shoulder. "Over two hours ago."

"Was it Gary Gibson?"

Sharon shook her head. "I've never seen this guy before."

Luke felt part of himself die. *Not Gary* . . . "Okay."

"I got the plate numbers of the car he's driving, and I can try to help you with a sketch."

"Both will help." He pushed buttons together and then tugged out Kleenex to wipe her face. She had never looked so precious to him as she did now. "Let's get you home," he said, his voice ragged against the emotions he felt. "Your family is waiting for you." He carefully picked her up.

"Luke?"

He watched every step he took, trying not to jar her. "Hmm."

"I'm sorry about Caroline not telling you. She would have never had the courage if she had told someone what she was going to do."

Luke hugged her tighter to him. "She loves you. She got you out alive."

"It isn't fair."

"Life isn't fair," he whispered back. He nodded to Jackie who stood ready to help at the rear helicopter door. He eased Sharon into the seat and saw the moment all of it became overwhelming for her. He let her lean against him as the tears became sobs, rubbing her back and taking the worst of the blow so Mark and Benjamin would not have to a few minutes from now, his own silent tears joining Sharon's.

Home had never, ever, looked so good. Sharon squeezed Luke's hands in thanks, trying to put a thousand emotions into the one gesture.

"You're welcome, Sharon."

She looked over at Jackie. "Thanks for the gift of the makeup."

"My pleasure."

Sharon turned toward the house. The front door flew open and the screen crashed back. She knelt and took the collision with Benjamin at full speed, wrapping her arms around her son and holding him so tight he giggled. "Benjamin, I hear you ran like a rabbit."

"I tried." He wrapped his arms tight around her neck and leaned back to see her face. His small hands touched her cheeks and traced the bruise, a frown on his face. "Dad crashed his car into a pond."

"I heard about that." She settled her hands over his, reassuring him, as she checked out every freckle on his face. Her son looked so tired, and so afraid. She kissed the back of his wrist and turned it to show him the lipstick. As his eyes widened, she smothered his face in kisses from ear to ear. "Aren't you glad I'm home?"

"Mom! I'm going to have lipstick in my hair," he protested with a laugh.

She paused to look up at her husband coming to join them. "Do you think your dad can save you?"

"You can go lipstick him."

"You sure?"

"I'm going to be scrubbing for an hour. You got my nose; I can see it."

She laughed with him, added one more perfect kiss to his neck, then released him. "Go start scrubbing. And then come join me in the kitchen. I'm hungry. I want some of your Pop-Tarts to start with."

She stood. She wanted to run and wrap her arms around Mark and bawl for a few hours, but she instead took a deep breath, smiled at her husband, and simply waited as he closed the last few feet. Her emotions would overwhelm her soon. At the moment she just wanted to appreciate the fact that her husband and son were alive.

He rested his arms across her shoulders and blinked away tears as he searched her face. "Hi."

Her own tears started regardless of what she planned, sliding down her cheeks. "Hi . . . she traded for me."

"I know," he whispered.

"I saw what was happening and there was nothing I could do to stop her, stop him."

"She loves you, Sharon. We all do. We'll get her back."

She straightened the collar of his shirt, one from his collection of golf shirts with a hospital logo, and rested her arms around his waist, her head against his shoulder. "I hear you missed me."

"A bit."

She leaned back to look at him.

He smiled, the emotion so tender she sniffed back more tears. He dropped a light kiss on her nose and struggled to lighten his voice. "I missed your soft snore that interrupts Letterman's monologue."

She choked back a laugh.

"Your pillow mashing me in the head when I try to see the alarm clock," he went on. "My shaving cream brush wandering away, socks that are not mine showing up in my drawer . . ." He let out a deep sigh and cupped her face in his hands. "I missed you."

She went up on her tiptoes to kiss him, holding back a wince as she stretched the ankle she had twisted during her long walk to freedom. "How many ribs did you break?"

"Two. It feels like more." He leaned his forehead against hers. "You need to go to the hospital to get checked out."

"Not now. Not while Caroline is out there somewhere."

"We will find her." Mark brushed her hair back from her face. "What do you need most right now?"

"Let me get the police sketch done, then have a shower. I'll spend a few minutes with Benjamin while I eat, then I need a chance to talk it through from the beginning while it's fresh in my mind."

"Done."

"Would you chase the dreams away for me tonight?"

"We'll do it for each other."

She kissed him a final time and unwound her arms. She turned with her husband toward the house. The helicopter lifted off again, with Luke and Jackie aboard. "I wish I could have told them more. I'm afraid I know so little that will help them find her."

"Luke will find her; he won't stop until he does."

"Caroline's in love with him."

"He's in love with her too." Mark hugged her. "Welcome home."

"Sharon said the swap happened near a vista pulloff," Jackie said, flipping through the notes of their brief conversation during the flight.

Luke shoved the map back up on the police car dashboard. "There are too many of them around here." He slowed the car and took another park back road. He could hear the three helicopters crisscrossing the area, but so far they had been unable to locate the place Sharon described.

"Sharon was walking for quite a while, mostly downhill, to reach the bait shop. The road turned both right and left several times and was paved with white gravel."

"A fact that matches just about every back road in this area. Did she say something about a hunter's sign?"

"Quail."

"Okay. This road looks promising. It's closed to public traffic, which would fit this guy's purpose."

Luke slowed as the road began to climb. If they didn't locate the site Sharon described where she had been released soon, this would become a nearly impossible search at night. After two minutes he began to wonder if he should keep on this road or turn around.

"Stop! There it is."

Luke stepped on the brakes as the trunk of the car caught his attention too. Caroline's car was under the limbs of an old oak tree, rolled off the road until the hood nearly touched the tree trunk. Luke stopped in the middle of the road and put on the high beams. "No wonder it couldn't be seen from the air."

Jackie called in their coordinates to the circling helicopters.

"It's going to take the crime scene technicians a good hour to get here and set up, and the light isn't going to last that long."

Luke got out of the car, retrieving his torch flashlight.

"Sharon said they drove off from here in a gray Plymouth. The plate numbers she gave us matched a car stolen in Florida two months ago."

"That car has likely been dumped by now too."

Luke stood on the road and shone his light across the ground beside the vehicle, not wanting to disturb any evidence that might be present. The ground was too hard to give them footprints.

"Getting Caroline out here without telling us . . . all he had to do was ask Caroline the question: *'What will you do to save your sister's life?'* Caroline would have done whatever it took to free Sharon."

Luke walked down the incline to Caroline's driver side door and shone his flashlight around the interior. "Her purse is still here."

"Maybe he left us prints when he rolled the car under the trees, or maybe up at the picnic table. Sharon said she was left at the picnic table while Caroline and the guy drove away."

Luke saw nothing in the car that immediately looked helpful. He walked back to the gravel road and looked toward the picnic tables Jackie pointed out. "Sharon's hands were bound with duct tape, and he left a pocketknife for her to cut herself free. Let's see how many pieces of that tape can be found before the wind blows it away. For capturing fingerprints, duct tape is excellent."

"We're close to her, Luke. They're only hours ahead of us now."

"We need a break, Jackie. Once this goes past midnight . . ." He shook his head rather than finish the thought.

The passing of time was like a boulder resting on his chest. Luke looked at his watch again and then up at the darkening night sky. If they didn't find Caroline in the next three hours, they were in trouble.

He pushed through more underbrush. The wind blew in almost a circular pattern around this vista, and nothing was staying close to where he expected it to rest. "What's that?" Luke paused, shining his torchlight on the item that had caught his attention.

The crime scene technician knelt to check it out, moving aside leaves. "Cigarette butts," he confirmed, reaching for another evidence bag from his pocket to recover them.

"I think they waited here for quite a while for Caroline to arrive."

"Even with good directions, trying to find this place in the middle of the night would be tough. They could have been here until almost dawn."

"So what else did our guy leave us?"

"Where would you take a leak if you were out here, drinking beers, waiting?"

"I'm not even going to go there," Luke replied, pushing on through the underbrush, looking for more of the blown tape fragments. From the pieces they had been able to locate and reconstruct, there was still roughly a three-inch piece to be found.

"Luke."

He turned at Jackie's call and saw her flashlight waving over near where he had parked their car.

"The car Sharon gave us plate numbers on — they found it abandoned behind a closed restaurant about five miles from here, off I-85. You want to check it out?"

Luke looked at the technician.

"I'll find that last piece of tape," he promised.

"Thanks." Luke paused. "This evidence goes back to the lab by air, and someone walks it through processing. There is no higher priority case tonight."

"You'll have answers as fast as they can be found."

The restaurant had once been a Burger Palace, but from the condition of the weathered signs and peeling paint, it must have been closed for over a year. Luke saw the blue van from the crime lab parked to one side of the building, along with three patrol cars, their headlights being used to light the scene. He showed ID to the officer keeping the parking lot off limits and parked behind a state patrol officer.

"Taylor Marsh is here," Jackie noted, closing her door.

Luke pocketed his keys. "It was likely his guys who spotted the car." They walked over to join the group.

"A patrol officer spotted the vehicle at the end of his rounds," Taylor said. "From the depth of the leaves blown in around it, the car looks like it's been here a few hours. There are fresh tire tracks that cross the tire tracks of this car, suggesting they transferred to a new vehicle. Based on the tread size, my guys think it's a sports van or truck of some kind."

Luke looked around, hating what he saw: a lot of uninhabited area and more dense woods. He feared Caroline could have been dumped along with the car. "You're canvassing the area?"

"I've got officers in the woods, both behind this restaurant and walking both directions of the frontage road. So far we've come up empty."

Luke spotted the flashlights moving around along the tree lines. "Sharon said this guy was on his own. Are there any signs he was joined by someone else?"

"It looks like only two sets of footprints," Taylor said. "I'm assuming Caroline is about a size six shoe?"

"That sounds about right," Jackie said.

"Then our guy is wearing boots, big ones, about a size eleven. We'll get casts of them to see if anything appears unique."

"He changed vehicles here and he's got Caroline with him, so I'm betting his plan is to drive through the night and be hundreds of miles away from here by morning," Jackie offered.

"Let's hope the roadblocks get lucky," Taylor agreed.

"Are there any fingerprints we can work with?" Luke asked.

"The crime guys were just getting started with the inside of the car."

Luke nodded. He left Jackie with Taylor and walked across the parking lot to the abandoned vehicle. "Tell me we have something in that car that is going to help us."

"Multiple prints on the glass and the door," the technician kneeling by the driver's door replied.

The crime scene technician working on the passenger side of the car shook open a large paper bag and transferred a folded-up jacket left tossed on the passenger seat into the bag. Luke heard him softly curse. "What?" He walked around the back of the car.

The technician clicked off his high-powered torchlight. He wiped his face before he leaned back and turned with a sigh. "We've got blood on the passenger seat. A lot of it."

THIRTY-FOUR

Luke heard the door behind him open as someone came out of Mark's house to join him on the back porch. He didn't bother to turn. It was almost midnight, and nothing an agent said would improve the situation.

She was dead. He had found Mark and Benjamin, recovered Sharon, and lost Caroline. Someone should just shoot him and put him out of his misery. Caroline was the best thing in his life, and she was dead out there somewhere, probably dumped by the side of the road.

"It isn't going to help to get drunk," Sharon said.

Luke looked at the can in his hand. "Nonalcoholic, unfortunately. Your husband doesn't keep the real stuff in the house. I could use a stiff drink right now." He set the can aside anyway. "You couldn't sleep? It's very late."

"Benjamin needed a late-night snack and reassurance that I was really home. I was inclined to indulge him." Sharon sat on the porch step beside him. "She's still alive."

He shook his head. "There was a lot of blood, Sharon. And four times lucky in one case — it doesn't happen."

"Don't give up hope on my sister. I won't let you."

He reached over and squeezed her hand. "She will have everything in me to find her, that's a promise. I'm not leaving her out there." His voice broke. "She loved you, Sharon, so very much."

She leaned against him and wrapped an arm around his waist. "I love her too, so do you."

It felt so awful, to be the one sitting here. He closed his eyes; he saw the blood. During the years of his job, he had been in too many situations like this to have faith that Caroline was still alive. He lived in a grim reality where faith and hope didn't have much room to flourish. He wanted so badly to believe Caroline was still alive, but he couldn't keep that hope alive.

"I went chasing some guy who took pictures he shouldn't have, who had a crush on Caroline, and I managed to miss the guy who took her." He took a deep breath and let it out, using it to stop his tears. "I don't know where to look for her."

"I can't explain the hope I feel, the confidence that she's still alive, but I know it's going to be okay. God knows where she is. Caroline's going to come back alive and well."

Behind Sharon's back, Luke lifted his hand to acknowledge Mark. His cousin had stepped to the door to check on his wife. In the days to come, it would be hard on Mark to breathe easy when Sharon was out of his sight. His cousin nodded and disappeared toward the kitchen.

Sharon leaned back and tugged a piece of paper from her pocket. "I wish I could have done a better job describing him to the police sketch artist."

"You did fine; they faxed a copy of the sketch to Jackie as soon as you thought the drawing was close." Luke took the sketch from her and smoothed out the folds. "It's Frank Hardin. Or close enough to be his twin. Mark was right. This switch for Caroline was all about Frank making this case very personal to me."

"You've been chasing this man a long time."

Luke nodded. "Murder, extortion, the

most likely suspect in the disappearance of an agent from Florida. Television reporters have shown me on the news with Caroline holding her hand. The local newscasters have repeatedly mentioned the fact that we're dating. Frank would have thought it was a good payback, to take the one person closest to me. He knows Jackie and I are hunting for him; he's taunted us before after we just missed capturing him in Louisiana. The agents trying to find him are like trophies in a game of cat and mouse for him."

Sharon was silent for a while, lost in thought. "Frank Hardin let me go; he left me alive, just so I could draw that sketch."

Luke sighed, wishing she hadn't made the connection that would haunt her over time. "Frank took Caroline as a way to strike at me. But unless I knew for certain he had her, it was a wasted action. Killing you was not as productive as letting you go."

"He's cruel."

"Yes he is."

"He'll want to get out of this area to live another day; you've told us he's driven by a desire for money. Killing Caroline doesn't help him with either. You'll find her, Luke, and she'll be fine. My sister is a survivor."

Luke reached over and wrapped his arm around Sharon, hugging her. Frank had a habit of cutting his losses early and moving on. Shooting his friends at the campsite was just the latest demonstration of that fact. Caroline was likely already another casualty. "I'll let you believe that for me tonight. There have been too many twists since Friday to keep my perspective."

She sat beside him in silence, and he studied her bruised face. "How are the memories tonight?"

"I'm jumping at boards creaking, people moving around in adjoining rooms, the phone."

"Time will help."

"I know." She drew up her knees and wrapped her arms around them. "If they had been able to grab Benjamin as they first intended . . . I don't know how to handle that thought, that fear. What if someone tries it again?"

He gently rubbed her back. "Bravery comes when you know the risks might happen, and you still go on with life. For the next while, let Mark hire you a driver and arrange more security here. You can be smart about the fear."

"Benjamin needs life to return to normal as soon as possible."

Luke nodded. "I'll help you out, Sharon. You won't have to live with the fear."

She smiled. "I'll look forward to that." She rubbed her cheek against her knee. "I wonder why Gary ran, if he didn't have anything to do with any of this."

"He got scared that he would be suspected, that his photos would be uncovered," Luke guessed. "Reasonable worries on his part as both happened."

"Mark showed me some of the photos. It's sad that Gary felt he had to try to become part of our family." She sighed. "Maybe if the task force can find where I was held, that might help answer the question of who hired this done. Whoever arranged this has to be stopped before he does it to some other family."

"We'll find him," Luke promised. "Are you ready for the media?"

"No, but I'm getting there. Henry James wants to give it till morning, while they leak enough of what has happened to generate a lot of public interest in my story. They think they can get even the national networks to carry the press conference live."

"If we didn't need the coverage so badly, I would never ask you to face this so soon. But Frank will likely be out of the state before morning. National news is the only card we've got left to play that has a good chance of generating more solid leads. He's been running a long time, and he's good at it. Once his trail goes cold — it may be a long time before we get another lead on his location."

"For Caroline's sake, I'll take every question they ask. At least the sketch of Frank and his last police mug shot are all over the news right now."

Benjamin called for Sharon. She hesitated, but Luke squeezed her hand. "Go, your son needs you."

"Can I at least get you something to eat that would qualify as a meal?"

"Maybe later." Something substantial to eat right now would just make him ill.

He watched her walk back inside.

Where was Frank heading? *I need ideas, Lord. What I really need is for Frank to keel over from a heart attack and end this.*

Luke wiped his eyes. He finished the drink and got to his feet. The task force had suspended the foot search so they could bring in the tracking dogs. Searching the woods from where Caroline's car had been left to where Frank's car had been abandoned would take the trackers most of the night.

He looked at his watch and made the decision to go join them. If they recovered a body tonight, he would be the one doing the identification.

THIRTY-FIVE

A cold front had moved in with the Friday dawn, making the damp morning all the more bitter. Luke pushed his way through intertwined vines to get to the small ridge that cut through the forest, a slab of rock marking where this area had once sheered away in a landslide. The area was covered with such rock slides, making the footing through this stretch of woods unreliable. Even with heavy boots he was finding it hard to maneuver.

Luke stopped long enough to shift his jacket collar where a tree limb had torn the fabric. The walking stick Benjamin had insisted he take along was proving its worth. Luke resumed his hike. Frank had the habit of dumping bodies where they would not be easily recovered.

To the east of him, Luke could hear the next searcher but not see him. They were spread too thin in this area to do an in-depth search. Until someone recovered torn fabric, found drag marks, something clearly showing that people had been out here recently, they had to hope a general canvass would be enough. At least with the dawn they had a chance to spot whatever might be here.

Caroline's smart. If she's being taken somewhere, she would do what she could to mark the route — dropped items, scuffed steps, something.

No matter how many positive thoughts he tried to hold for the sake of her family, for himself, it didn't change what he suspected had happened. Caroline had saved her sister's life only to give her own within the same hour. This wasn't a search and rescue; it was now simply a search and recovery.

He knew the task force members were also on the downside of the hope curve, doing their jobs thoroughly and well but with grimness now and knowledge that the odds had turned against them. Finding the dead was a hard burden to bear. As much as everyone wanted this case to be over, no one wanted to be the one to find the body.

Luke pushed the walking stick into another mound of leaves and kept walking.

Frank would have been carrying the body from where he parked the car, so he wouldn't choose the densest route into these woods, even if he did hike in for quite a distance before leaving the body. It would be like him to roll the body down an incline or into a rock crevice. Luke stopped and listened. He searched the air. Birds would know, forest animals. The smell of blood attracted so many creatures. Nothing sounded particularly helpful.

"Luke."

"Over here, Taylor."

The state homicide detective joined him. "Mind if I walk with you a bit?"

"Feel free. I'm heading to that old oak by the bridge."

Taylor had come better prepared, dressed in layers of hunting clothes and a backpack of supplies slung over his shoulder. "I've got coffee if you're interested."

"I'm okay for now."

Taylor fell into line ten feet to Luke's left to broaden the coverage. "They were loading up the tracking dogs when I left the road."

"I know." The search of the roads between the vista where her car was recovered and the restaurant where Frank abandoned his hadn't turned up any hits. The dogs had been in near-constant use since Saturday. They and their handlers needed a break.

"We don't know yet if that blood was hers."

Luke looked over at Taylor, appreciating the reason for the comment, even as he shook his head. "It's going to be hers," he replied, resigned to that reality. "It's possible Frank transferred her to the other vehicle and took her with him, but if so, it's likely he just wanted to make it that much harder for us to find her. He's not been in touch with another ransom demand. The roadblocks overnight didn't spot him. He's either already a state away, or he's sitting somewhere waiting us out."

Luke paused as another helicopter came in low over the trees, following the highway. The odds they would spot something from the air were slim, but even if they couldn't locate the body, the white van was still out there somewhere. It would take every bit of evidence they could find to generate a lucky break at this point.

Where are you, Caroline? I need to find you now, before the weight of this tears even more into Sharon and Benjamin and Mark. I need to find you, love. If only to tell you when it's too late just how much I love you.

The helicopter moved off to the south. "He may be holed up wherever they were holding Sharon originally," Taylor said.

"It's possible. Sharon was certain there was carpet under her feet when they pulled her out of that room and took her to the garage to put her in the car trunk. She remembers a full flight of stairs, suggesting it's somewhere inside a two-story house. But other than the fact it's somewhere near Benton, do we know much about where to even look?"

"Not enough."

Luke looked at his watch, wondering if Sharon had been able to get any sleep in the remaining hours of the morning. "Sharon's offered to go with us for a drive, to see if she recognizes the sounds of a bridge she crossed, railroad tracks, anything that will give us a sense of direction and distance she was driven, but it's a long shot. We need to find that white van. Maybe if we can figure out where they dumped it, or who originally bought it, we can get a lead on this guy who had enough money to set up this kidnapping. He's the one person who would know where that room is located."

"Jackie is with Sharon this morning?"

"Yes. She's remembered a number of useful details beyond the sketch. We haven't done a full debriefing yet. Henry wanted Sharon rested enough to get through the press conference this morning first."

"That's smart. The public will sympathize with Sharon a lot more than a police briefing. Luke, do you mind if I tag along for that drive around?"

"I'd appreciate it. You know this area like the back of your hand. You might be able to put together the small details Sharon can remember."

The trees began to thin out and the field came into view. The old oak Luke had been using as his guide to stay on a straight search line towered above them, decades of living having aged and thickened the bark and branches.

Vehicles lined up along the road on either side of a communications van being used as the field command post. "I'm going to go into town for the press conference. I'm guessing we won't head out to drive around with Sharon until midafternoon. I'll find you before then."

"I'll be around," Taylor promised.

THIRTY-SIX

The news at the top of the hour came on. Highlights of the press conference began to replay. Luke shut off the small television mounted under Mark and Sharon's kitchen cabinets. He opened the refrigerator and poured himself a tall glass of juice and carried it with him into the living room. Sharon had sought refuge on the couch, curling up under an old quilt.

"You did a good job." Luke shifted the ice bag she held against her face and looked at the bruise. "And that is getting better."

"I looked like an abuse victim on TV."

"The cameras are never kind," he commiserated. "You handled the questions like a pro."

"They say the tip line at the task force has been busy."

"Are you sure you're up to this?" he

asked gently, loath to push right now. He was exhausted just having been a spectator in the crowd; he knew she had to be running on nervous energy right now.

"Ask your questions, Luke. I'm up to this. It will help to have it over with."

"Relax, Sharon. Let's just talk a bit now, and plan to talk again later today and over the next couple days. Memories tend to have layers. You'll remember some details now and others will come to mind on their own. There's no pass or fail in an interview like this."

Mark joined them, shifting Sharon's feet so he could sit on the couch with her. Luke was relieved to see from his cousin's movements that his chest pain appeared to be abating.

Luke took a seat across from Sharon and opened his notebook. She had already gone over the timeline of events with Jackie that morning, and Luke didn't want to re-open any memories he didn't have to. "Why don't you start by telling me more about the room you were in. Describe it for me."

"It's not high enough to stand up in. The entry was up high on the wall, about three feet square. About the only thing I'm certain of is that it's got good soundproofing. I could hear nothing through the walls or the floor."

"Was anything unique that might be traceable? A particular video he purchased or an unusual food item?"

Sharon shook her head. "I'm sorry."

"What about when they hauled you out of the room? Do you remember what kind of place you entered?"

"They had shoved a pillowcase over my head. I remember getting pushed up and out of the room. When I cleared that entryway, I was on my hands and knees and it was carpeted. They pulled me to my feet and I lost my balance. I grabbed something that I thought was a coat or maybe one of those heavy fabric storage bags. My hands were taped, and it was more the feel of the rough fabric than anything else about how it was cut."

"The fabric wasn't on a piece of furniture?"

"It gave under my hands, and it was high — you know it could have been a drape. It had that same heavy feel to it."

"What happened next?"

"I distinctly remember being pulled down a lot of stairs that felt like they were at a steep angle." She bit her lip. "We made at least one right turn, and it seemed like a very long walk before I was pushed through a door into what must have been a garage. It was cold, and the floor was concrete. After they shoved me into the trunk, it was almost an hour before the car was moved. I remember thinking as I lay there that I was hearing a deep freezer run."

"Could you hear traffic? Other garage doors opening and closing? School buses? Conversations? Anything that suggested this place was near other buildings?"

"No."

"Do you have a sense of the time of day? Early or late?"

"I thought it was in the evening, around eight or nine maybe."

"This all helps, Sharon. When they pulled away from the house, do you remember which way they turned?"

"No, I couldn't keep the directions sorted out. I was lying pretty awkwardly and my head hurt pretty bad."

"Were there stops along the way? Or did they drive directly to what we now know was the campsite?"

"They didn't park and shut off the car, but I do remember several stops and starts, like they were at four-way intersections with traffic lights. Twice we passed over railroad tracks, and at least once we passed what might have been a hog farm. The smell was strong."

"Could you judge how long you were driven around?"

"An hour maybe. It wasn't a short trip."

Luke looked over to the doorway behind Sharon where Henry James had joined them to quietly listen in. Henry held up two fingers and lifted an eyebrow.

Luke opened his folder. "When you were taken from the trunk at the campsite, was only the one person present?" Luke offered the sketch she had drawn. "Was it only Frank?"

"After the gunshots, I thought I heard people yelling at each other, but I don't know. The voices could have been on top of the shooting. That gunfire really echoed around. Everything had gone quiet before I was hauled out of the trunk and taken away by just one person — Frank. I didn't see his face until after he had made that call to Caroline and we drove up to near the vista, but no one else joined us."

"Back to the campsite for a moment — did you hear another car start and leave the area around the time you were pulled from the trunk?"

"Maybe. There were a lot of vehicles

coming and going that day. One sounded like a diesel engine, and there was another — it almost sounded like a race car, very fast revving."

Luke closed his notebook. "When you were stopped at the vista waiting for Caroline to join you, how did Frank seem when he let you see his face?"

"He never showed much emotion during any of this. He left me sitting at the picnic table for quite a while before Caroline came while he walked around the area. He was smoking a cigarette, waiting. About the only thing that seemed to make him nervous at all was the sound of helicopters that occasionally flew over." She sighed. "Will any of that help?"

Luke smiled. "It will all help, Sharon. With the information you gave Jackie this morning, and what the task force has been able to discover about the guys who were killed — the picture is filling in quickly. Will you be up to riding around with us later today? Say about three o'clock?"

"Yes."

"Then let me get out of here so you can get some rest. I'll have an update for you on the search then."

"Thank you, Luke."

He paused by the couch to touch her

hand. "Hang in there, Sharon. This day isn't over yet."

"Find her, please."

"We're going to," he promised.

Luke followed Henry outside so they could talk in private.

"She's a strong lady," Henry observed.

"It runs in the family."

"I've intensified the search to find the place Sharon was held, given what she was able to tell Jackie about the timeline this morning. We've been over the times again, and the last sightings of the white van." Henry paused as one of the search helicopters departed from the county road. To keep media out, the road remained closed, and that made it a convenient place for pilots and search teams to meet up.

The noise abated and Henry continued. "I think the place we're looking for has to be east of Benton, and there are not a lot of homes out that way. Some very pricey homes and neighborhoods, as well as a number of very old farmhouses."

"What she described was a two-story house with an attached garage. That rules out a lot of places," Luke noted.

"Agreed. That room had to be built, and it sounds like enough effort was involved that there is no way it could be entirely concealed. I want to start a door-to-door canvass, ask neighbors who's been doing construction recently, if they've seen lumber being moved around, drywall, any deliveries being made."

"It's a good idea. We have enough volunteers to organize a flyer drop in that area as well."

Luke saw Benjamin disappear around the back of the garage, following one of the kittens. "Give me a couple hours, Henry, and I'll join you when Sharon is ready to go out."

"Sure."

Luke followed Benjamin.

The boy was lying on the ground, looking beneath a large burning bush. Luke watched him for a few moments before kneeling down. "How are you doing, buddy?"

"This kitten is the most skittish. He's the older one, and he keeps running away."

"Have you tried bacon?"

Benjamin looked over at him.

"Fried bacon smells wonderful to skittish kittens. And food is good for attracting even the most skittish of males."

"You'll keep an eye on him while I go see what's in the refrigerator?"

Luke sat on the ground and leaned

down. The kitten had backed himself up against the center of the bush, his small amount of fur raised along his back, his ears twitching. He didn't look afraid, as much as he seemed certain he didn't want to return inside. "Sure."

Benjamin went back to the house.

Luke waited a bit and extended his hand. "Are you interested in the smell of coffee?"

He tried to back up farther and couldn't. "There's a blanket-lined box for your mom and your siblings just waiting for you to join them. It's nice and warm and cozy, and you would be safe there. Not to mention you would be well petted."

He wasn't particularly a cat person, but he admired the independence in the animal. There wasn't enough consistency in his travel schedule to allow him a dog or cat at home. He'd missed something not having a pet depending on him.

Benjamin sat down beside him and held out a piece of ham. "Has he moved?"

"He's waiting for you."

"Caroline said we would take care of the cat and kittens until Gary returned and could care for them."

"Yes."

"I haven't named them, because they are

going to go back home soon. But I like this one a lot."

Luke rested his hands back on the grass. "Why?"

"He's stubborn." Benjamin lowered his hand. "He doesn't like the ham."

"He looks tired of running. We could catch him if you like."

"It would just scare him more." Benjamin set down the piece of ham on the ground partway to the kitten. "Can we go over to Caroline's?"

"Sure. Why?"

"I left my notebook over there."

Luke had seen Benjamin coloring in it at Caroline's suggestion, drawing what it was like to be in the woods overnight. Luke got up and offered his hand to help Benjamin up. "Let's walk over there. The kitten may be ready to come inside when we get back."

Luke lifted a hand to Sharon at the back patio door, confirming he had Benjamin with him for a while. She nodded.

Luke didn't try to start a conversation as they walked to Caroline's. Benjamin's attention shifted from fallen limbs he picked up to berries he could swing at and hit. The boy was recovering. Luke wished adults could recover as swiftly.

"When is Caroline going to be home?" Benjamin asked as they walked up the driveway to her house.

"It may be a few days. Do you understand what happened?"

"She took Mom's place."

"Something like that," Luke replied.

"So she'll come home too, like Mom did? He'll let her go?"

"That's what I'm working on now."

"Mom said I can hand out more flyers tomorrow, the ones they're creating for Caroline."

"I'd appreciate the help. Are you okay watching the cat and kittens for her on your own?"

"Yeah."

Luke deactivated the alarm system and held the door for Benjamin.

The house felt abandoned. The officers who had searched it and dusted for prints had left evidence they had been here. The fact no one had been here to wipe the patio door glass and straighten the chairs just added to the fact Caroline was missing.

"I think I left it upstairs." Benjamin didn't linger in the kitchen checking out the candy sticks as he often did. He moved down the hall to go upstairs.

Luke opened the cabinet beneath the sink and got out the spray bottle of ammonia and lemon Caroline favored. He tore off paper towels and sprayed the counter. Someone would need to vacuum the carpet to pick up the crushed leaves that had been tracked in, and the garbage cans would need to be carried down to the roadside tomorrow. A couple days after that, the milk would need to be poured out and the bread thrown away. Luke scrubbed a stubborn spot on the stovetop. He didn't want to think about what would happen if Caroline was not home in a week, a month.

"I found it."

"Good." Luke gestured to the candy sticks. "Why don't you pick out one to take back to your mom?"

Benjamin studied the jars and eventually pulled out two cinnamon sticks.

"Find me a trash bag, would you?"

Benjamin opened the pantry as Luke pulled out and tied the bag in the kitchen trash can. Benjamin shook open the new bag and put it in the can.

"Where does she keep her trash cans?"

"Behind the garage."

Luke carried the bag outside.

"Can I walk home on my own?"

Luke waved at Mark. "Your dad came over to meet you halfway. Tell him I'll be over in a few minutes after I lock up."

"Okay."

Luke waited until Benjamin joined his father before turning back to Caroline's house. He finished wiping down the kitchen counters and table, and then stored away the supplies. He turned off the lights and reset the alarm system.

The quietness of the day felt strange, given what was happening elsewhere.

Luke walked out the back door and took a seat on Caroline's patio, not ready yet to rejoin the search. He pulled out his billfold and retrieved the note Caroline had written him the night they had recovered Benjamin, before the ransom request for Sharon had arrived.

Luke — an easy life is fit for easy tasks; a hard life is fit for hard tasks . . . God knew every case you'd see, how hard it would be, and yet He set you on this course for a reason. He created a man who can keep going in the face of tremendous discouragement, in the face of emotional people and chaos and only scraps of information to work with. He made a man I needed . . . You are as ready for this task as God can make a man.

Luke read the words and sighed. *I wish I were that man, Caroline. I wish I were able to work a miracle and find you alive today.*

He resisted the emotions that wanted to flow. This hurt too bad for just tears.

"If a day comes when you have to tell me Sharon is dead, it will be okay to just say it. I already know your heart."

"Who breaks the news to me that you're dead, Caroline? Jackie? Mark? It's going to rip apart what's left of my heart."

Luke refolded the letter. The last year had been wasted. Rather than let Caroline into his life while he'd had the chance, he tried to put a buffer around his job to protect her from it. In doing so he missed out on the one relationship that mattered. If he got a second chance, he wouldn't make that mistake again.

They could distribute flyers, do another press conference, try to get the national cable news stations to pick up the case. By this weekend, they would need that extra interest to sustain the search into a second week. Public interest and volunteer help would begin to fade after ten days as people had to return to their lives.

Who would take Caroline's fifth grade class? Her kids mattered to her so much. Maybe he could stop by and talk with her class tomorrow. He wanted some way to connect with Caroline and didn't know how to do it.

"Luke." Jackie jogged up the driveway to join him. "Taylor needs us at the county landfill."

"What is it?"

"A bulldozer operator thinks he saw a body."

THIRTY-SEVEN

Luke pushed garbage out of his way and waded farther into the landfill. Red flags on long metal poles shoved among the punctured garbage bags was not how he wanted to find his crime scene.

Taylor Marsh rose from his crouch near a towering mound of garbage that didn't look stable. "It's not Caroline," he called over.

Luke felt a surge of relief that caused him to pause by a torn-open sofa cushion. "Who?"

"It's rough to get a solid ID, but it looks like Gary Gibson."

Luke reached Marsh's side and looked down at the body, partially visible through the piled garbage. The odor of human decay overpowered that of decomposing garbage. He swallowed back the bile that rose in his throat. "I agree that's Gary."

Marsh used a handle from a broken broom to push back more of the trash around the body. "I don't see a gunshot wound. It looks to me like a knife wound to the chest, hard and deep, was the killing blow. He's pretty much out of rigor, so time of death maybe twenty-four to forty-eight hours ago." Marsh stepped back and wiped the back of his sleeve across his nose.

Luke studied the shirt and jacket on the body. The dried blood highlighted the tears in the fabric; the knife had sliced through with neat precision. "Four stab wounds, maybe five. The work of a man in a rage?"

"A reasonable guess." Marsh poked around with the broom handle. "We've got industrial trash around him, not residential. There's no foodstuff or household trash; I'm seeing collapsed cardboard boxes, a lot of shredded paper, packing materials, tie wraps, several smashed lightbulbs, some glass tubing, and a lot of what, plastic molds?"

"A lighting repair shop maybe?" Luke asked.

"We might get lucky with a shipping label on one of these boxes."

"It would help," Luke agreed. "Okay.

Gary gets killed and his body dumped into an industrial dumpster. A two a.m. garbage pickup lifts the dumpster and drops him into the garbage trunk. A few hours later, he gets spilled out here and buried by the next load. Without the sharp eyes of that dozer operator, it would have been months before this area was turned and the body was spotted. That makes this a throwaway dump; there was no desire to have the crime discovered."

"I don't think it's a coincidence that the man who was watching Sharon and Caroline in the months before the kidnapping occurred is now dead," Marsh said. "Was he involved?"

"That's the thousand-dollar question. If I'm right, that he saw the snatch and what happened afterward, then his death suggests he got too close to the people who did it."

"Killing with a knife — it's a close and personal kill. He saw Gary watching them, so he grabbed and killed him?" Marsh speculated.

"I'm leaning that way. Does it look like any of his personal effects were dumped with the body?"

"What are you thinking might be out here?"

"His camera," Luke replied, looking around at the debris. "He apparently has two pretty expensive ones, and neither one was recovered at his house. I think he also took several photos with him when he abandoned his house and ran." Wind pushed the pungent odor into eye-watering intensity. Luke walked around to be up-wind of the body. "Have you checked his pockets?"

"No."

Luke crouched down. The fabric of the jacket had caked to the body with dried blood, and the way the body had been pushed around, the jacket was shoved up and twisted. Careful of the grime, Luke tugged the jacket free enough to get to the left pocket. The man was a hoarder. Luke set the first handful of items he pulled out onto a piece of newspaper: toothpicks still in individual wrappers, cough drops, fast-food receipts.

Luke checked the right pocket and had to tug to get items crammed into it to come free. He retrieved a spiral notebook, blue cover, and well worn, and three folded photos, the edges sharp and stiff. Luke pried one of the folded photos open and stilled. "This is the campsite where Sharon was held." He handed the photo up to

Marsh and worked to get the other two folded photos opened. "This one looks like a photo of Ronald at what? A gas station food mart?"

"I think so."

"He was definitely watching them," Luke said. "Tracking them. Who knows, maybe hoping to be a hero." He opened the third photo and turned it in his hand, trying to decide orientation. It looked like an accidental shot, a photograph of the ground.

"Why didn't Gary call us? Or at least call in an anonymous tip?"

"Maybe he did, Taylor. You know how many calls deemed less than credible are still being reviewed." Luke stood and moved away from the body. "Gary drives an old pickup truck. If this is Frank's handiwork, that truck may be what Frank is driving now."

"I'll get the information out to the patrols."

Luke straightened bent corners and opened the notebook. The page had two words scrawled in pencil, nearly undecipherable. Luke turned pages. They were all that way. "He must have been jotting notes while he was driving; the text is bouncing all over the page. I'll take this back to the task force to see if they can figure it out. If Gary followed them to the campsite, maybe he also located the house they used. See if the crime scene guys can find any more of these photos or those cameras. I'm willing to bet Frank could care less whether they were found or not, he may have tossed them into the same dumpster. If we get lucky, there may be enough here to lead us back to the guy who started this."

"Will do. I'll call with whatever is found."

Luke rolled down the squad car window, hoping to dissipate some of the smell hovering like a cloud around him.

"I think it's on your boots," Jackie said.

"And clinging to my shirt and jeans and jacket," Luke added. "I'm heading to Mark and Sharon's to change before we go to the sheriff's office." He nodded to the notebook she held. "Anything in Gary's scribbles that looks promising?"

"I either can't read the page or it doesn't make sense. Some of this looks like bird-watching notes."

"Let's hope someone on the task force can read it."

"Do you plan to tell Sharon Gary is dead?"

"She'll hear about it in the next few days even if we don't tell her. Gary is apparently the stalker who was bothering Caroline last fall, and if we're right that he was also the one to send that bouquet of roses to Sharon's office — knowing he's dead just closes several nagging worries. What do you think about me showing Sharon those folded-up photos?"

"I wouldn't. Gary knew where she was at and didn't get her help, at least indirectly that makes him responsible for Caroline being missing now. Hating a dead man is an ugly emotion to have to wrestle with." Jackie opened the photos. "The campsite photo confirms what we already know. The one of Ronald — it might help to know if Sharon recognizes him, but we could get that information with a formal photo lineup."

"When asked, we'll tell her that the state police found Gary's body, but that it appears he was killed before Caroline was called and the switch was made."

"I could live with that." Jackie watched the countryside along the highway, studying the houses. "Sharon was held near here. Everything points back to Benton. And that makes me think the guy who hired Frank is a local."

"Someone who wants money, who would have the contacts that could give him Frank's name . . . it's got to be a small universe of people." Luke turned on the radio. "It's time I had a long talk with Mark. His family wasn't chosen at random, and they aren't close to being the wealthiest people around here. Someone selected them for a reason."

"Luke, I've racked my brain for names," Mark said, pacing his study. "I've had my secretary pulling client lists, searching for anyone disgruntled, anyone who makes me uneasy, or who has come back into our lives recently out of the blue. I'm hitting a blank wall."

"Five million, then ten million, with incredibly short delivery deadlines — the ransom request itself suggests an awareness of how much cash you could make liquid quickly. Why not ask for twenty million?"

Mark shook his head. "I would have paid any amount, somehow."

"Do you remember anything more about the first ransom call?"

"I was driving back to Benton; the setting sun was in my eyes, and I had just reached up to move the visor. I picked up the phone, and a garbled voice said, 'I have your wife. I will kill her.' And then he told me where to take the money at midnight."

"Why the old church?"

"I don't know."

A tap on the door interrupted them. "Can I come in?"

Luke turned and smiled at Sharon. "Sure." He hugged her because she looked so tired, so stressed. The nap she'd taken didn't look like it helped much.

"There's no word on Caroline?" she asked softly.

He simply shook his head.

"They found Gary Gibson," Mark said, coming around the desk. "He was killed sometime in the last couple days."

Sharon winced. "His death is somehow related to what has been happening?"

"We'll work the case assuming that it does. I don't like coincidences."

She sank onto the couch and wrapped her arms around one of the big pillows. "I liked him, Luke. Despite everything you've told me about his watching us, calling and frightening Caroline — it's hard to put together with the man I knew. That man was nice. He'd bring fudge to my head nurse when he came by the clinic to have his blood work done. Caroline worked at the clinic part-time that summer, and I know she and Gary got to be friends while he waited for all the tests to be run. He cared about her students and would ask about them; he would bring cartoons from the newspaper he thought she'd like. I think he even asked Caroline out to lunch a couple times."

"That interest turned into an obsession. I doubt he ever thought this was what his life would become."

"Benjamin has been playing with the kittens you rescued, wanting to know how come Gary left them behind. What do you tell a child that makes sense of that? How do you tell him the man is now dead?"

"Let it go a few days," Mark replied. "Benjamin has enough hard things to absorb."

Jackie tapped on the doorjamb. "Sorry to interrupt. Luke, Marsh just called. They've found a camera bag at the landfill and a half-shot roll of film still in the camera. All of it is on its way to the task force to get developed. Do you want to come along?"

"I'll be right there, Jackie." Luke looked at his cousin. "Keep pressing on names. For that matter, write down every person you've ever done business with or met socially, from the insurance salesman to the PTA president at Benjamin's school. We'll eliminate them all if we have to in order to find that one name we need."

"I'll work on it."

Luke nodded and headed out to join Jackie.

THIRTY-EIGHT

The press had taken over most of the street in front of the sheriff's office. Luke ignored the shouted questions as he went in a side door with Jackie.

"Who's got the latest on the recovered trash?"

One of the agents waved him over. "He was killed in a business district east of Sandy Hill. If the boxes around him match up to the right dumpster, somewhere around Jefferson Brilliant Lighting, Inc. It's a custom sign business."

"It's being canvassed now?"

"Guys are walking the area looking for any sign of blood. A body in that condition — it's going to leave a messy trail."

"This is the rest of it." Luke gestured to the table. From the less-than-pleasant odor, he guessed the trash had come in with the recovered camera bag.

"Yes."

An agent sorting through the stack tacked another receipt to the board timeline. "He was buying a lot of film recently."

"Cash or credit?"

"Cash. We've run his credit cards and found nothing since Friday. The bank hasn't received any checks to clear yet against his accounts, but it may take five days before they start to show up."

Henry James walked over to join them. He passed Luke a stack of faxes. "You're getting popular."

Luke scanned the top sheets. They were numerous media appearance requests. "Jackie can handle them." He passed on the stack and his partner just grimaced at him.

"Photos are developed!" An agent pushed through the back door, holding up a manila folder. "I think we've got something."

The trash on the table was pushed back into a box to clear room. They spread out the photos as the task force and the sheriff's deputies clustered around. The lab had enlarged the prints to ten-by-ten.

"Interesting." Jackie picked one of them up. "Sharon and Benjamin together — that puts it before the snatch occurred."

"Isn't that the same outfit Benjamin was wearing when we found him?"

"Get me a photo from Saturday for comparison, that one of Benjamin getting his scraped knee checked out at the scene by the paramedic."

The sheriff lifted the tack and retrieved the photo from the board. "The same clothes," he agreed. "This photo of Sharon and Benjamin had to be taken Friday afternoon, after they had returned to the house and Benjamin had changed, but before the snatch occurred."

"So Gary was definitely at their house. What else is here?"

Henry picked one of the photos. "Do we have the place Sharon was held? This house fits the general information Sharon gave us."

"What about this one?" Luke found another photo of a home. "Or this one. What was Gary doing? There are at least eight houses here. Architecturally interesting, expensive homes."

"Did the lab send a print of the negative strip, so we can see the photo order?" Henry asked.

Jackie picked up the envelope to shake. "Yes." She pulled it from the protective sleeve.

Luke looked at the strip and shook his head. "The photo of Sharon and Benjamin together is the last one taken on this roll of film. This entire roll was taken before the snatch happened on Friday. It's a dead end."

"If this film was still in the camera, and Gary was killed days after the snatch occurred, why didn't he ever finish taking this roll of film? He didn't use the camera after Friday afternoon, yet it was found at the scene where his body was dumped?" Jackie asked.

"Two cameras. Maybe he shoved this camera back into the camera bag Friday, tossed the bag into his trunk, and never reached for it again?"

"Remember those photos in his darkroom?" the sheriff asked. "One of his cameras has a good zoom lens on it. He was photographing even hummingbirds up close."

Luke stepped back from the table. "We recovered the one camera that can't help us."

"It's proof Gary was there. I'd say that makes it relevant," Henry corrected. "We need to find that second camera."

The sheriff's secretary held up a phone. "Luke, there's a call for you. Line three."

He reached over for the phone on the nearest desk. "Luke Falcon."

"Do you want her back?"

Luke had heard Frank Hardin's voice only on wiretaps, but he knew it when he heard it. Luke spun around to look at Henry James. Henry immediately picked up another phone and started a trace. A fine sweat began along Luke's back even as he cooled his voice to a business calm. "Of course I want her back."

"For the right price, I'll give you back your precious Caroline and the guy who hired me to snatch the doctor. He double-crossed me. I'd kill him, but he's a man better suited to the *joy* of prison time."

Luke didn't care why the men were at odds with each other; he only cared that there was a slice of opportunity to exploit. "What's your price?"

"Ten million, in diamonds this time, no more bills you can mark. And you don't have much time to deliver them, if you want the guy who hired me to still be in the country when you learn his name."

"I have to talk with Caroline first."

"No. You've got two hours. Call me when you have the stones." Luke scrawled down the number Frank gave him. Then the line went dead.

396

Luke looked over at Henry. He shook his head as he listened in on the attempt to trace the call. "The trace came up short, Luke. He dropped off the line too quickly."

"Ten million in diamonds, and I need them now."

"Any particular size or color?"

Luke shook his head.

"There's a standing arrangement with Whitman's. With the cash already in hand, the Atlanta office should be able to fly them out here in twenty minutes."

"Tell me we got a tape of this call."

"On that line we'll have a tape of it."

"Is she alive?" Jackie asked softly.

Luke forced himself to take a deep breath and unclench frozen muscles. "He's not offering any proof. He's staying around to get paid, so let's accommodate him. Bug the package, Henry. Get creative and plant a tracking device among those diamonds."

"Luke?"

He shook his head as he headed to the side door. "Caroline's dead, Jackie. And I'm not going to let the guy who killed her walk away from this." He had to talk with Sharon.

By the end of the day, this would be over and his worst fears would be confirmed.

THIRTY-NINE

Luke watched Sharon pace across the living room and finally stop by the bay window. "You understand the risks of planting the bug, Sharon?"

"I understand them." She sighed as she turned to look at him. "You think she's already dead." Sharon was crying, and it hurt him to see those tears, knowing he had been the cause.

"I don't know whether Caroline is alive or dead," he replied carefully, "but I do know Frank Hardin has to be stopped. In the last few days he killed his girlfriend and shot three men. He may have killed Gary. We may not get another chance this good to stop him."

"Do you really think you can track these diamonds without his knowledge?"

"We can." Henry joined the conversation for the first time. He opened a small case and offered it to Sharon. "One is the bug; the other two are real diamonds for comparison. Which one is it?"

She accepted the case. "They look the same." She picked up the stones and weighed them in her hand. "Under magnification you could tell."

"Yes," Luke conceded. "But Frank's going to be in a rush, and with that bug buried in a pile of real diamonds, I don't think he'll have time to check every stone with an eyepiece. It's a reasonable risk, Sharon. If Frank has left Caroline somewhere, the only way to guarantee we can find her before she bleeds to death is to grab Frank. I don't trust him to tell us the truth about where she is. We have to grab him."

Sharon turned away and stared out at the lawn. She sighed and turned. "Make the call."

Luke looked over at his cousin. "Mark?"

He nodded. "Catch the guy, Luke."

"Henry?"

"We're ready."

Jackie handed Luke the slip of paper he had jotted the phone number on. He picked up the phone on the desk and dialed. "I've got your diamonds, Hardin."

Jason Fromm stuffed the papers critical

to accessing his private accounts into his briefcase. Everything he loved in this home office — the collectibles, the artwork, the sense of presence in the cherry wood and leather furniture — he was having to walk away from. Frank would pay for this.

At least Frank had done him one favor — shot everyone who knew of his role in the kidnapping. Frank himself would be facing a death sentence, so he'd never let himself be taken alive. But tying up the final points of the failed kidnapping didn't solve his original problem. Without an infusion of cash, in a matter of weeks it would be known that his financial world was collapsing, and he was basically broke. The bank would collapse.

It was best that he just disappear and start over again somewhere else. One stop by the bank for a special withdrawal, an equally short stop at the guest house to collect a few personal items and turn on the pilot lights of the stove and let a gas explosion destroy the house and safe room, and he would be on his way to the airport. It would be next week before they figured out he was not in Atlanta as his staff thought, and by then he would be in the remotest stretches of Europe with a new name, back in his home country.

Jason carried his bags to the car. Benton had been a source of trouble for long enough; he wouldn't miss the town.

FORTY

The small bag of diamonds didn't look like ten million dollars. Luke stuffed the pouch into the inside pocket of his jacket, then picked up the small items Jackie had set on the kitchen table: a pocketknife, keys to police cuffs, a roll of medical tape. "A whistle?"

"Benjamin thought you might need to call one of his favorite dogs or something."

Luke smiled and pocketed it. He wouldn't need any of these items, but it couldn't hurt to have something in his pockets that might help if he found Caroline bound and gagged but still breathing.

"Are you sure you don't want me along, Falcon?"

"I need you here with Sharon and Mark. You know what the odds are now."

"I know."

Luke nodded toward the road where a police helicopter was now coming in to land. "This is going to be another one of Frank's dances from place to place before he tells me where to leave the diamonds."

"Caroline — I'm so sorry this happened, Luke. That we didn't know in time to stop her from going out on her own."

"Benjamin has his mom back. Caroline would have thought that to be worth any price." He reached out a hand and squeezed his partner's. "Stay with them, Jackie. I'll be in touch."

He zipped up his jacket, picked up the briefcase carrying one of the many tracking units for the package he carried, and headed outside to meet his ride. It was some reassurance to see no media helicopters hovering, recording this. The restricted airspace seemed to be holding. He knew Sharon and Benjamin and Mark were watching from the living room window, but he didn't turn to wave goodbye. This was hard enough as it was.

Luke took the copilot seat, slipping on the headphones Joe handed him. "The first stop is a bridge five miles east of here."

Joe nodded and lifted off. "I'm carrying enough fuel we can stay in the air four hours, and two other pilots will be ready to join us once that package starts moving.

Do we know how many people might be with Frank?"

"Except for the guy who hired him, I think he's probably the last one left."

"So the fact this bird is carrying enough firepower to stop a tank could be considered overkill."

Luke smiled. "At this point, I will use whatever's available. There are enough flares aboard if we end up searching the woods into the night?"

"Flares, the spotlight, and cases of bottled water for the guys on the ground. None of us plan to come back empty-handed today."

Joe keyed the radio to confirm a clear flight path over the area hospital.

Joe circled the bridge while Luke scanned with high-powered binoculars. "Frank could be under it, but I don't see any sign of life."

"Agreed. Set it down."

Joe set down in a field east of the road, away from the power lines. Luke pulled on gloves and opened the door. As soon as he stepped out of the helicopter, Joe lifted off again to hover and provide security.

Luke walked to the bridge, scanning the area, searching for movement.

There was a white post beside the bridge as advertised. Luke shoved a thorny bush away from the base and saw the taped envelope on the post. He tugged it free.

A map was stuffed inside, a red felt marker having bled through the paper. A glance confirmed he was expected to continue on by air. He signaled Joe to set down again.

It didn't make sense, these hop-around delivery routes.

Luke took the copilot seat again. "Take a look, Joe." He offered the map.

"This is annoying."

"Tell me about it. Does the quarry sound familiar?"

"I've flown over it a few times in the last few days."

Luke buckled himself in and slipped back on his sunglasses. "He's sending us away from Benton and where I think Caroline might have been left."

"Let's hope he runs out of interest in this game." Joe handed him back the map, then lifted off and turned them north.

Luke pulled the binoculars out of their case again.

After two minutes of flight time, the quarry appeared beneath them, a sudden change from heavy foliage to sheer cleared rock. "He likes abandoned areas."

"The lawsuit shut down this quarry more than two years ago, leaving it all in limbo. Unfinished, the land unrecovered. What a waste."

"Down there." Luke pointed to the red flag planted alongside the quarry road, flapping in the wind right where it had been noted on the map.

Joe circled the area twice and then set down. There were too many places for a shooter to hide in this forsaken area. Luke ran. The red flag had been tied to a short shepherd's hook. At the base of the pole was a small orange metal box. Luke ripped open the envelope taped to it.

Put the diamonds in the box and lock it. Fly due south for exactly one minute and drop the box out into the woods. Keep flying south. I'll call your office when it's delivered.

Luke tossed the flag away, picked up the box, and jogged back to Joe. Frank must have planted some kind of tracking device in the box, and it made him sweat — the thought that two tracking devices might jam each other or both signals might be visible to Frank. Luke considered for a moment not putting in the marked diamond, but he didn't have time to sort it out and the loss of their tracking device was unacceptable. The risk had to be taken.

"Head due south, Joe." Luke handed over the note for him to read and saw one eyebrow lift. Joe nodded. Luke started the timer on his watch as they lifted off.

Luke grabbed the map. The box would drop in an area of thick woods, steep hills, and several hunting roads crossing the area. There was even a small river, giving Frank the option of leaving the area by boat. It was the kind of place Frank would trust.

Luke tugged the pouch of diamonds from his jacket and stored them in the box. It was a hunter's case, the thick walls designed to survive a shotgun blast. There were no obvious signs of how Frank was tracking the package. Luke turned the key. "At least he bought something that would survive the fall."

"That diamond bug has a range of three miles; we'll keep track of that package."

"When the call comes in, you and I divert to get Caroline. The other two units in the air can keep a distant watch on this package. After we have Caroline, we'll deal with wherever this package has gone," Luke replied.

"Agreed."

"Get ready to get buffeted."

Luke braced one hand on the side of the seat and with the other shoved open the small window. His watch clicked sixty seconds. Luke tossed the package out of the helicopter.

FORTY-ONE

"He's taking his sweet time about recovering that package." Joe shifted his hands to flex his fingers and work out the stiffness. Hovering two miles south of the drop site for an extended period of time took its toll.

Luke locked his gaze onto the tracking display, determined not to blink at the wrong time, wanting to see the very first hint of movement. "It's probably lost down some ravine." If it had burst open on impact, then they were about to have one of the most difficult ransom recoveries in a long time. Finding and accounting for every stone would take an archaeological-level search of the area.

"If he intended to recover that package today, Frank has to already be near that drop site. Do you think Caroline is as well?"

"I don't know. It's not what I would expect." Luke glanced at his watch. Too much time was going by. "Come on, find the package."

"It may be best that we set down and save some gas. We can track that package from the ground without a problem."

"Another five minutes," Luke replied.

Joe changed the secondary radio channel to another local news feed. "It sounds like news of the ransom demand has leaked to the media. They don't have that the delivery is in progress yet, but there's a reporter broadcasting from the end of the road to Mark and Sharon's home who believes you're meeting with Sharon and Mark right now about that ransom call."

"That puts them what, four hours behind what's happening? Someone is going to break the news the diamonds have already been flown to Benton."

"An hour, and they will know the ransom is being delivered."

Luke opened another bottle of water. "There! The package has begun to move."

Joe leaned over to watch the beacon. "It's slow enough he's definitely on foot. Frank's going to call once the diamonds are recovered?"

"That's what he said."

"And if he doesn't?"

"Then we go get him now." Luke watched the coordinates begin to change. "Head toward Benton. I think Caroline would have been left south of here, not farther north."

Joe brought the helicopter around to circle toward Benton.

Luke watched the second hand sweep by, and then the minutes. "What is taking him so long?" Frank was going to stiff them and not call.

"Do you think he's checking the stones?"

"The package has kept moving. He's just taking his time about calling. From the speed, I'd say he's no longer on foot." Luke picked up the high-powered binoculars and focused on the road to their left. "It's too bad you can't read license plates from up here."

"The angles are bad." Joe opened a second bottle of water. "He may be selling the diamonds within the hour for all we know. The stones may change hands on us in exchange for a wire transfer to the Cayman Islands."

"We'll take the risk. No matter how far he runs, I'm going to find him."

"Luke."

He reached for the radio, relieved. "Go ahead, Henry."

"8754 Logan Road. Caroline's in the back of a white van."

Luke started at the simplicity of the message. He looked at Joe, even as Joe sent the helicopter diving toward the tree line and turning southwest. "We're diverting now, Henry."

"Don't rush in without backup. I've got everything here rolling. We're expediting details on the address now."

Luke traced the map. "Logan Road, that's almost to Sandy Hill," he realized, surprised at the number of interstates Frank had been willing to cross with Caroline in his car.

"Three minutes by air," Joe reassured him.

Henry came back on the radio. "Luke, 8754 Logan Road is one of three homes in this area owned by the president of the Benton Bank. This is trouble."

The fury that swept over Luke made him tremble. "I just met him. Jason Fromm was intimately involved in assembling the initial ten million, and he was in a position to know how we planned to mark and track the cash. No wonder Frank knew to leave the money behind. And Fromm would know exactly how much cash Mark could raise late on a Friday night."

"It's the guy who plans a crime from the inside who hurts us the most."

"Jason arranged a kidnapping and is a coconspirator for several deaths. Tell me we can locate him."

"The sheriff should be literally walking into his bank office now to detain him. I'm heading to Logan Road. Wait for backup, Luke, that's an order. This is listed as a vacation home, not his principal residence, but if he's not at the office and is still on this property —"

Luke cut Henry off. "How many places can a white van be hidden? You've got about sixty seconds after we land before I storm at least the garage."

"I hear you. Patience, Luke. We'll be moments behind you. We've got to hit all three properties at the same time to avoid tipping him off."

"And if he's already fled?"

"A flash alert is going to every airport to check outgoing flights. The sheriff saw Fromm in town this morning. We'll find him."

"We'll meet you at Logan Road." Luke closed the radio channel. "Joe, I need options."

"If we fly too close, we advertise our interest in the property. But with those binoculars I'll get you a good look at the property before we set down and move in."

"The white van, the safe room — was the guy so arrogant as to hide the evidence on his own property?"

"How many people are going to suspect a banker?"

Luke checked the batteries in his flashlight, knowing they would soon be dealing with a setting sun and gathering darkness. He would prefer to double-check his weapon but deferred that while they were in the air.

If they ended up having to stake out the house, SWAT would want to wait until dark to move in. Luke couldn't afford to risk such a delay. If Caroline was indeed in a white van on that property, they had to find her fast.

Caroline lifted tape-bound hands an agonizing few inches to dislodge a beetle moving across her sleeve. The insects came and haunted her in real life, then invaded her dreams as she fought the pain only to fade in and out of consciousness. *Don't dream anymore; just don't dream.*

The gag prevented her from moistening cracked lips. She would never take cold water to drink for granted again. Tears ran from the corners of her eyes. *Jesus, I'm going to be seeing You sooner than I expected.*

If she died here, Sharon and Benjamin would grieve but go on. Luke would spend the rest of his life blaming himself. If only she had left him a note to say she loved him one last time.

She tried to turn her head on the rough carpet but didn't have the energy. The sudden storms of life . . . she hadn't been ready for this weekend. But the bedrock foundation of her faith had held through the storm. She would be going to see Jesus. It was so silent outside now. This van was going to be her coffin and grave.

Are you okay, Sharon? Did you make it out okay? The doubts ate at her hope. She had been so foolish thinking she could get her sister out alive. If Sharon hadn't been able to get out of the woods, if she wasn't home now safe and sound, then all this willfully independent action had accomplished was to add an unbearable burden to Benjamin, Mark, and Luke with both of them being missing.

Caroline coughed. The pain tore through her chest like a sharp knife.

She hoped she'd killed the man. She hoped she had hit an artery in Frank's leg with that pocketknife, and he was bleeding to death somewhere. The odds she had succeeded — it was a day of failures.

She could feel the blood still flowing from the compound fracture of her left arm she'd received in return for her attempt to stop him. Bone had broken the skin, and the pain radiated from her shoulder to her wrist. The swelling just kept building.

Hurry, Luke. She was dying. And there was no way to stop it.

FORTY-TWO

"This isn't a guesthouse; it's a three-car garage, probably six-bedroom monstrosity. It's impossible to tell if someone is home." Luke lowered the binoculars. "I've seen enough. Where is the best place to set down?"

"Neighbors aren't close, but we're a loud and novel thing to see come land. I'd suggest the parking lot of that business park. We can cut through that landscaped berm and come up on the back of the property."

Luke nodded. "Get us on the ground." He shed anything he was carrying that wasn't needed in order to eliminate any extra weight. "I'll need you along for the hike."

"Until cop cars begin to roll in, just try to get me away from your side. I doubt anyone in this neighborhood knows how to hotwire a helicopter." Joe set down the helicopter and flipped switches to shut it down. "Let's move."

A few cars were slowing to see what was happening, but luckily no one out walking a dog or jogging along the roadside. Luke led the way from the county road into the neighborhood. The landscaped berm provided a sound break from the road. Luke stayed parallel to Logan Road until he reached the cluster of elm trees he'd noted at the end of the property, and then he cut south into the grounds so that they'd come out near the garage. Joe stayed with him step for step.

He stopped within sight of the roofline and crouched near the fountain.

"I don't see any windows on that garage," Joe whispered.

"All brick. It's too early for lights to be on inside and too late to expect housekeeping might be around to tell us if he's home or that the van is here." Luke wanted to break into that garage, but they risked triggering the alarm system, the fact she might not be in that van, or that it might not even be here.

"We'll have to go in that front door with force and spread out fast inside," Joe counseled.

"Let's cover the back of the house to make sure no one sees the cops arriving and tries to bolt out the back way."

"I'll get Henry on the radio and give him a heads-up on the layout of this place."

Jason saw the cars approaching his guest home and knew they were police cars, even though they had on neither lights nor sirens. They came in both directions on a one-way road, a dozen vehicles moving fast. The man in the lead would no doubt have a warrant to search the house and grounds.

Jason considered for a moment meeting them at the front door and playing the surprised owner more than willing to cooperate with their search. There wasn't anything here they could find, but cooperating would lead to endless hours of questions. There wasn't time for that kind of delay.

He pushed the last personal papers he had come to retrieve into his briefcase and then retreated from the office and headed upstairs. Let them search. He could hide in the safe room. They would look around his property, not find the room, and he would be in the clear.

There wasn't a scrap of paper or piece of trash left to suggest what had occurred here. His car was two blocks away, getting cleaned by one of the best detail businesses in the area. There wouldn't be so much as an unwanted fingerprint left in the vehicle when they were done. He just needed to hide for a few hours.

Jason reached the master bedroom and walked into the closet. Moving to one side the shelves for the shoes, he found the seam in the paneling for the first hidden door and opened it. He tugged out the soundproofing. He lifted the metal plate upward and stuck it in the wooden jambs that held it up. The entry way was too small. He swore softly as he worked his way into the room.

The doorbell rang and someone knocked hard on the front door. His hands slippery with sweat, he turned and leaned back out into the closet, pulling over the outer door and reaching under it to grasp the shelves and rock them back over in place. He yanked his hands in as the outer door closed. Okay. He was okay. The entrance to the room was covered. Unless the shoes had all tumbled off at the movement, he was fine.

"Jason Fromm! This is the police. We have a warrant to search this house!"

He heard the shouts as he frantically pushed in place the soundproofing tiles and then grabbed the wooden jambs to re-move them and bring the metal plate down. The weight of the metal plate caught him by surprise, and he just got his fingers out of the way before it slid down and buried itself in the framing. Jason stumbled back into the mess of the room and fell back to sit on the short bed.

He was in. He was fine. If they realized the closet shelves could be moved, if they tapped on the wall, or for that matter kicked at it, all they would hear was solid wall. The steel plate and soundproofing would do their jobs.

He listened to his heart rate slow down and eventually looked around the small room and let out a long breath. What a mess. When Frank had broken in to get the lady out, he hadn't been neat about it. Jason tossed a smashed box of cereal off the bed so he didn't have to share the perch with crushed Cheerios.

He leaned against the wall and looked at his watch. Three hours. He would give them three hours to do their searching, and then he was going to get out of here and vanish for good.

Luke was a step behind Henry James as they entered the house. The entry way opened onto a great room with vaulted ceilings, moonlight streaming in through tall windows casting shadows across bookcases and plush chairs.

"Search it, basement to attic and every crevice in between." At Henry's order, officers spread out.

Luke headed toward the garage, Taylor Marsh and Joe right beside him. Luke shoved open the door and found the lights.

The garage was cold and empty.

"Frank was jerking us around," Marsh said.

"She's here somewhere." Luke turned to Joe. "I need you back in the air. Circle the area and drop flares, look for where else a white van might be hidden. If Frank abandoned the vehicle around here in a storage building or garage —"

"I'm on it." Joe headed out.

Marsh looked down the long hallway. "If this is the location of the safe room —"

"Sharon was brought down a flight of carpeted stairs." Luke headed back down the hall and took the stairs going to the second floor two at a time, Marsh on his heels.

Marsh went down the rooms on the right, his sidearm drawn. "Expensive little place for a banker's guest house."

"I'd check your account in the morning to see if it has any cash left in it." Luke walked to the window of a guest room to see what options a guy would have going out of a window. One glance ended that idea. They'd be scraping him off the pavement.

The rooms on this floor were huge but odd shaped — walk-in closets and bathrooms and angled storage spaces and even a laundry drop to the floor below. Luke hit walls as he walked around, listening for an echo. A six-by-eight room with a small restroom. That meant plumbing and power. "Sharon described a three-by-three entrance to the room."

"It's got to be visible if only by walls that don't make sense."

"This place is an architectural nightmare. What was he doing, trying to avoid a straight line?" If there was missing floor space taken from the rooms, Luke didn't spot it as he tried to calculate angles. "Where's the attic entrance?"

"I'll find it," Marsh said.

Caroline was here somewhere, probably bleeding to death, and he couldn't find her. Luke headed for the stairs and leaned over the railing. "Henry, what about the other homes this guy owns?"

"Teams are sweeping them now. First reports are like this place — no one home and no sign of a white van. His staff says he left for a meeting in Atlanta."

"I'll buy that when someone locates him. We need to find that van, Henry."

"Frank could have been lying."

"We finish this search, then we grab Frank and those diamonds, and you let me have first crack at talking with him."

"We'll talk about it."

"The attic entrance is down here," Marsh called.

Luke headed back down the hall to meet him. "Someone get me another flashlight!" He'd handed his to the sharpshooter searching the grounds.

Where are you, Caroline?

Luke crawled on his belly to yet another point along the joining of the rafters and wall, shoving back insulation. Plumbing could not be hidden nor electric and cable wiring. The warrants didn't allow them to break into walls without at least a suspicion they had found the room location, but they could follow the trail of building arteries leading to that room. Luke peered down with the light.

"Anything?" Marsh called.

424

"No. If they didn't make the easy-to-reach tap-ins up here and drop wires down the existing walls, they had to splice in the wiring somewhere."

"Henry wants to trip breakers and isolate the wiring to the safe room that way."

"It would take an electrician hours to prove there's another outlet on the line. It would be faster to prove the cable wiring has been sliced into to add in another TV," Luke guessed. Both would take time they didn't have. He crawled backwards until he rose to a crouch and walked back to the attic entrance. He walked down the folding stairs.

"Sharon said second floor, but I don't see how they built a room in the attic given the floor plan of this place. It would be crazy for him to keep her at his own home," Marsh said.

"It's crazy to try and kidnap someone." Luke used a towel from the guest bathroom to wipe insulation fibers off his arms, the fibers sticking to his sweaty skin driving him crazy with the itch.

"I'm not done with that basement. It's all concrete walls and floor, and they could have built a second false wall down there," Henry said, joining them. "We can try and chase plumbing from down there."

"Unless someone can find the entry door, this search will take too long." Luke could hear the officers working to find it, moving furniture and tapping on the walls. "Where are Frank and the diamonds?"

"Heading east on I-16 and staying below the speed limit they tell me. The units tracking it by air are hanging two miles back."

"Let's go get him. He knows where that room is. He knows where Caroline is. He might not want to talk, but I'm willing to bet we can make him talk."

"Frank isn't going down without a fight. And the tactical units will want to take him down in as remote an area as possible."

"I'd settle for driving up behind him and slamming into his back bumper."

"We only get one shot at him, Luke. It would be better to watch him, make sure Caroline is not with him, let him lower his guard and think he got away. The odds improve if we try to take him after he stops to sleep."

"We don't have that luxury of time. He's our only link to Caroline, and she's been out there too long." Luke looked at his watch. "Another twenty minutes?"

Henry nodded. "The dogs are searching the grounds now; that will give them enough time to walk the house."

"I'm going up with Joe to get another look at the area from the air."

FORTY-THREE

Luke closed his eyes as another flare burst in the air, turning the night brighter than the day for a brief moment. He raised the binoculars again. "Joe, what are we missing?"

"If there is a white van in this area, then it's parked inside a garage or warehouse, or so deeply buried in the woods it's going to turn up when they clear this land to turn it into another subdivision. The officers canvassing the neighbors have so far come up with nothing helpful."

"This is a dead end."

"I'm afraid so."

"Frank spun us a line. Ten million dollars for a lie." Only Luke would have gladly paid the price to have Caroline back.

"I disagree."

Luke glanced over, surprised.

"Frank probably told the literal truth," Joe said. "The guy who hired him owns

8754 Logan Road, and Caroline is in the back of a white van. Only Frank left the white van somewhere else."

Luke bit back a curse, thinking about Frank's games. "You're probably right."

"We need to go get him."

"Set us down. It's time I had a heart-to-heart with Henry on how to proceed."

"While you caucus, I'll get this bird refueled. Let him know I can take three with me." Joe set down on the road east of the house on Logan Road. Luke unclipped restraints and stepped out. He waved Joe on and headed toward the house.

He found Henry in the driveway. "Anything?"

He shook his head. "Dogs are still working the rooms, but they haven't alerted for Caroline, and by this point they should have."

"Let's go get him, Henry."

He walked over to his car and retrieved his map. "He's still traveling on I-16. The strike team wants to take Frank here, where traffic narrows to two lanes to cross this bridge. They propose causing a traffic jam at the bridge just before he arrives to slow him down and to eliminate the passing traffic. When his car comes to a rolling crawl in the line of cars, they'll come in on both sides of the vehicle to yank him from the car before he realizes they're even there."

"If Caroline is in the car with him . . ."

"They'll move fast, Luke. Do you want to be there? Joe can get you there with a few minutes to spare."

What he wanted and what was best were two different things. "Just take him alive. He dumped Caroline somewhere around here, Henry, I'm convinced of that. I'm staying in this area. We just have to know where to search."

"We'll take him alive."

Luke picked up the headset and settled into the copilot seat of the police helicopter. "Joe, head back toward the drop site where Frank picked up the diamonds."

"You don't want to be at the takedown?"

"What I want is to be on top of where Caroline is when they radio in with where Frank actually left that white van. Henry is sealing this place until tomorrow morning and sending the dog teams on to search the other properties Fromm owns. This area is covered. I think the van is somewhere near that quarry where that red flag was planted. How else would Frank know about that deserted area unless he'd been out there recently?"

Joe nodded. "The drop site it is."

Jason couldn't stand to pace in the small room. Hitting his head again on the low ceiling, he punched it with his fist. He shoved back a spilled stack of videos and sat on the short bed again, pulling the nearest plastic tote over and reaching in for the first food item he saw.

The potato chips were stale. He tossed the bag aside and looked at his watch. 2:12 a.m. They had to have left by now. He hadn't heard anything since coming into this room, but surely he could risk opening the door. He couldn't stand to be in here any longer.

He climbed over to the door out of this room and slid his hands across the smooth steel plate to get traction and push it up. He couldn't budge it. The steel plate had dropped into place and wedged itself into the frame.

Jason stepped back and looked at the door, considering the problem. He had to get that metal plate to move, the direction didn't matter, just enough movement to force it up again. He looked around the room for something to pry with and found what would work as a hammer and chisel.

He went to work on the corner of the framing.

He scraped his knuckles and drew blood. The wood refused to move. He felt a shiver of dread. Forget the door. He'd get out another way. What had Sharon been doing as she tried to escape? He looked around the small room, stepped into the small bathroom, and realized she'd been chipping away at the tiles beneath the sink, following the pipes. "Great. This is going to be doable in the next decade."

If he couldn't get the door to open, then he had to get into the walls. He turned and kicked the tiles and the wall, shaking the pipes and getting pieces of the wall to break away. With the fourth kick, the pipe broke, and cold water began to spray across the room.

No one could hear him as he cursed the mess. The water would run through the floor and soak through the ceiling and destroy his art collection in the room below him. If the cops had already left the home, it would be hours until his housekeeper came. They'd find him after the damage was irreversible.

Ignoring the water, he set to break into the wall to get himself out.

FORTY-FOUR

Luke tried to search while they flew over the land. The helicopter spotlight illuminated the tops of trees and the open fields momentarily as it passed over them, but outside the circle of light the area was near black. Homes in this stretch of ground were few and far between. "How many flares are left?"

"Twenty-three. I brought along extras."

"Why don't you head north toward the river."

Joe nodded and changed directions.

"Thank you for not saying we're flying randomly with no hope of spotting a white van this way."

"Hey, when you don't know where to look, looking anywhere is progress," Joe replied. "It would take two hundred search teams to cover these woods with any level of decent coverage."

"Luke."

He picked up the radio. "Go ahead, Jackie."

"Sharon is getting . . . I'm worried about her. Is there anything we can safely do that would be helpful?"

"They are going in now to apprehend Frank."

"She knows."

"Put her on, Jackie," Luke requested.

"Hold on."

"Luke, it's Sharon."

"Hey, lady." Luke didn't have adequate words to convey the emotions he felt. "I'm sorry, Sharon. We don't know where Caroline is. The leads have gone nowhere . . ."

"Luke, where are you now?"

"Flying up near where the diamonds were delivered."

"Come home."

"Sharon —"

"They'll grab Frank, the task force will put him in a room for the next day trying to get him to admit where he left the van, and you'll stay out there slowly dying without knowing where to look for Caroline. Come home. Wait for news with us here, with family."

The reality of what she said compelled him to agree. "I love you, lady. I'll stay out here looking a while longer, until Joe needs to refuel, then I'll be home."

"Thank you."

Luke set down the radio and lifted his hand from it slowly. "Send up another flare, Joe. Let's search the riverbanks."

The water reflected back the light but gave away none of its secrets. The banks of the river were crowded with trees and the occasional fishing dock where a flat boat was tied up, marking a nearby farmhouse.

Luke rubbed his straining eyes and lifted the binoculars again. The moving ground and the motion of the helicopter left a disorienting sense of vertigo whenever he paused to think about it. The waiting ate at him. He wished Jackie were along, her occasional comments breaking the silence and keeping alive his hope.

"Luke."

He snatched up the radio. "Go ahead, Henry."

"We just got word from the strike team." The pause lasted a beat too long. "I'm sorry, Luke. Frank's dead."

His breath stopped. "Repeat that."

"He put a .22 to his chest and pulled the trigger before they could get the car door open. He must have had the handgun resting in his lap as he drove."

Luke absorbed the news, and with a hand grown stiff depressed the button. "Caroline?"

"Nothing, Luke. The car was empty. The diamonds are in Frank's jacket pocket, and the vehicle has temporary plates. It looks like a new purchase. They didn't find so much as a gas receipt inside. We're at a dead end."

"Okay, Henry."

Luke set down the radio, feeling like a very old man.

"Luke?"

"Take me back to Sharon and Mark's home. It's over, Joe."

"You don't want to search at least while we have flares and fuel?"

To say no would be giving up. To say yes would be futile. There wasn't anything else to have faith over. When Caroline was finally found, it would be by accident years from now, long after a broken heart had killed him and put him in the grave.

The thought of facing Benjamin's tears was too much to bear. "We'll search until the flares and fuel are gone." He strained for breath for the words. "Let's retrace the path of the diamond drop."

Joe changed course.

FORTY-FIVE

Caroline wished she had been able to write her essay for the kids. She found herself oddly awake again, not aware she had been sleeping, just suddenly awake and looking at the roof of the van. What were they going to think when their teacher died only a few weeks into the school year? Who would they bring in to teach her class? Who would help them understand how to still have hope when life suddenly turned dark?

The discomfort had faded to a distant pain, and her thoughts felt clear. Had her life mattered? It was ending in an odd way, at such an early time. She'd touched a few years of students' lives, helped Sharon, loved on Benjamin. It wasn't such a bad life; it just stopped without much to show for it. She wished she had folded and put away her laundry. Someone would be opening her dryer to find her most personal clothing.

Caroline smiled as she thought of all the bits and pieces of her life that would embarrass her to now have someone see. The letters on her desk, the bills, the mementos she had found worth keeping that someone else would hardly understand.

Luke, I sincerely hope you're the one to find the pot-sticker sticks. I don't think Sharon would understand why they are beside the few cards you sent me.

It wasn't so bad, loving Luke. She closed her eyes content to let herself drift through the memories of their time together. Her only regret that there weren't more of them to hold on to tonight.

Did life come with second chances? The pain pulled Caroline from the memory of Luke's first kiss back to the present and the headache growing in intensity. It would be so nice to have the last months to live over again, to be more patient with herself and kinder to Luke. Relationships took so many turns through high moments and low. If she had it to live over again, she wouldn't mind nearly as much about his shift-to-work modes.

More candy sticks, Christmas presents, movies, and kisses for no reason whatsoever . . . She smiled at the thought. She was dating Luke, for as long as it lasted, as many turns as the relationship took. She'd chosen a long time ago, that night walking around the carnival. He was her choice. If God gave her a second chance, she was going to tell him so.

The desire to rub her nose was intense, as was the knowledge that to lift her bound hands that high was beyond her. She tried to shift the gag enough to get a breath around the cloth but couldn't do it. The headache came as much from where the knot on the gag pressed against the back of her head as it did from the physical assault to her system in the last hours. There wasn't a good way to move. She lifted one foot and eased an inch to the left to take a bit more pressure off her back. Flies would come with the morning, and this misery would be more than she could bear.

She refused to go there. Tomorrow's troubles would take care of themselves. She was no longer with Frank, and she was certain he would not return. That left the van to be found by searchers or accidentally by a local resident. It was a big vehicle to be left abandoned. She tried to think about Benjamin and Sharon. The doubts crowded in. She'd risked everything to give

Benjamin his mom back, and she didn't know for certain that Sharon had made it. Would her sister even understand why she had done it?

Her vision clouded and she took a painful breath, struggling not to cough. Surely Sharon would understand.

Come on, Luke. I need you here.

FORTY-SIX

"Luke!" Joe pointed south as another flare burned white and bright, turning the area briefly into day. "I think we've got something."

Silent tears had been clouding his vision for the last forty minutes. Luke blinked them away to clear the image in the binoculars. The trees repeatedly blocked and then cleared from his view, leaving him with only an impression of what he was seeing. "That's a vehicle," he confirmed.

Joe brought them to a hover at the treetops, holding at as much of an angle as he could so the helicopter didn't block the view. Luke's heart jumped. "That may be a van, and it definitely used to be white. Can you get me down there?"

"The trees are too dense. We'll need a third person aboard if you want to try and be lowered down."

"I don't want to lose it now that we've found it." Luke reached for the radio. "Patch me through to Jackie."

The dispatcher connected them.

"I'm here, Luke."

"Bring Mark's jeep and meet me at the Hickory Point Bridge."

"You have something?"

He didn't want to raise false hopes, not with Jackie standing beside Sharon and Mark. "Joe's spotted a vehicle farther off the road than we would expect, and it's worth checking out. Only we're in too rough a terrain to set down."

"Sharon and Mark want to come along."

Luke hesitated and then said. "Let them."

"We're on our way," Jackie confirmed. "See you soon."

Luke listened to her drop off the call. "Henry, did you get that?"

"I've been listening in. What are the co-ordinates?"

Luke read them off the GPS. "It's a van, it's white, and if it's campers using the van as a place to sleep, we've been hovering over it with the spotlight going on several minutes without movement below. Send in officers to check it out; I'm going to wait and come with Sharon and Mark."

"The sheriff has two units out your way. You'll be seeing lights of their cars soon, coming from the west."

"Tell them to trust Joe's spotlight for the location. It looks like the van left the road, drove along a streambed and then up into the trees. It's not going to be easy to see until they're on top of it."

"Will do."

Luke took a seat on the bridge railing, keeping his balance with one foot around the lower rail, while he waited for Sharon and Mark and Jackie to arrive. Watching Joe, he saw the helicopter return to a hover, once again marking the location point of the van. It would be a twenty minute hard walk in the dark from the road to that van. The officers already heading in should reach it anytime.

He wanted to race past the officers to the van and get there first, but he forced himself to let the others make that journey instead. He would go in just as soon as Sharon and Mark arrived. He was determined to do tonight what he knew Caroline would most want — protect and care for Sharon.

Luke looked up and studied the stars above him. *You've been very quiet during this storm, Lord. Letting me deal with the emotions and roll with events as they came. I would love having Your mercy and kindness give me back Caroline alive. But this storm is in Your hands, and only You decide its end. I won't let Caroline's courage to save her sister be forgotten. She loves people without reservation or limitation. And the sheer breadth of that action — it helps me understand more what You did on the cross, Your sacrifice.*

Luke pulled himself together enough to look at his bare left hand and wish he'd been smart enough to bind them together with a ring a year ago. *I love Caroline, Lord. Please give me a chance to tell her that.*

The quiet of the night answered him.

He knew the odds of it being the right van were slim. Frank wouldn't make it that easy. Luke had walked out on a limb to believe this would be something less than a severe disappointment. But it was the last hope of the day.

If this was a hunter's vehicle or one abandoned years before rather than be scrapped . . . He stopped the thought and chose to hope. This storm in their lives had thrown enough at them. It was time for a rainbow. And until he heard otherwise from the officers checking out the van, he was going to believe that good news was possible. From his perch on the rail, he tugged free a sliver of wood and systematically broke it into small bits.

He heard the vehicles and turned his head to see the lights coming his way. Mark's jeep came fourth in the procession of cars. The roadside became a parking lot as they stopped.

Henry stepped out of the first car. Jackie, farther back with Sharon and Mark, moved forward to join Henry, and they walked toward him together. "Is she in there?"

"We don't know yet," Luke replied. "The first officers should just be reaching the van."

He stepped down from the rail and walked down the road to meet Sharon and Mark. He hugged Sharon gently and then leaned back to study her face, grateful to see her looking steady on her feet even at the end of this excruciating day.

"I guess the diamonds didn't work," she whispered.

"Not sparkling enough for him I suppose." Luke rubbed her back. "Frank only knew how to be cruel."

"I know." She pulled together her composure to smile at him. "I think it's time we took a hike."

"It's going to be a difficult walk to make in the dark. It might be better if you both wait here until there's word one way or another. I'll stay with you."

She squeezed his hand. "I understand what disappointment is. I would rather walk than wait. I've done too much waiting lately."

"Okay." Luke offered her a flashlight. "The odds are good it's not the vehicle we need to find."

"I know. But the bad news will be the same whether we're walking or waiting here." Sharon buttoned up her jacket and tugged gloves out of her pocket. The night would only grow colder, and it was already damp.

Luke offered Mark a flashlight, and when he accepted it, Luke didn't release it right away. He shared a long look with his cousin. Mark nodded. If this was bad news, it wasn't going to be so confident a walk back.

Luke led the way from the roadside into the woods, following the path the other officers had already selected, letting Jackie walk with Sharon and Mark. Henry joined them and moved to the front of the group beside Luke.

"The first officer nearing the scene reports a strong smell of gasoline," Henry whispered. "That van may have hit a rock and punctured the gas tank on the way in."

"Or it's been booby-trapped," Luke cautioned.

"They've been warned not to walk up to it and open a door without searching for trouble first. If it is this van, and Caroline is inside . . ." Henry nodded back to the others. "Are you sure this is a good idea?"

"If she's there, we'll know it long before we reach the site," Luke replied. "It's been a brutal few days. As bad as this could be, closure matters more. I understand Sharon's need to be here."

Luke watched the overhead spotlight marking their destination. "Joe spotted the van. Without him, I would have given up the search when word came about Frank. Did we lose any of our own, when Frank acted as he did?"

"Minor injuries from the shattered glass. But losing the last link to Caroline — the team took what happened very hard and very personally."

"Frank would have likely strung us along and never told us the truth," Luke said, thinking of the wild goose chases Frank could have dreamed up to send them all over the county looking for Caroline's body. It would have been so stressful it would create visions of killing Frank for the mental anguish he was causing. They walked on in silence.

A flashlight appeared ahead of them on the path, an officer coming back toward them at too fast a pace for the condition of the path. Luke and Henry moved ahead to meet him.

"Sir."

The patrolman was young, breathing hard, and stressed, his acknowledgement to Henry quick.

"Tell us," Henry said.

"There are suspicious wires inside on the front doors, and no windows in the back to let us see in. The side door panel locks have been damaged. Even if we could risk trying to open them, the threat of more wires would caution against it. We can't cut our way in with the hand torch because of the lingering gas fumes. I'm going back for another crowbar. They're trying to peel back enough of the side panel around a spot of rust to get a look inside."

"Any sound at all from inside?" Henry asked.

"It's quiet, sir. We've been calling trying to get a response, but there's nothing."

"Go get that crowbar."

The patrol officer nodded and hurried down the trail.

Luke watched him pass by Sharon, Mark, and Jackie. No one tried to ask him for information; they just stepped aside to let him pass.

"Frank wouldn't wire the vehicle if there wasn't something inside he didn't want us to see," Henry said.

"Quiet isn't good," Luke replied. "Take the lead? I'm going to walk with Sharon and Mark for a bit."

"Sure."

Henry took the lead, lighting the best path.

Luke walked back to join Sharon and Mark. "How are you doing?" He could see they were both breathing hard, and Mark was sweating now. Neither were in the physical shape after what had happened to be taking a mile walk, let alone through rough terrain.

"Getting a workout," Sharon replied with a brief smile.

"We're almost there."

His partner sent him an inquiring look.

"It's a white panel van. They don't know if it's the right one or if Caroline is inside. The patrol officer is going back for more

449

equipment to help them with the locks. Jackie, Henry needs you for a minute."

She nodded and moved up the trail.

"This is the van?" Mark asked.

"Maybe. Someone went to a lot of trouble to make it hard to open." Luke didn't ask if they wanted to stop and rest for a moment, but he shortened his stride and slowed them down a bit. He wanted to know more about what they would find before they arrived at the scene.

They walked in silence, pausing only when the patrol officer returned and passed them, risking jogging on the path to make the trip quickly.

As they approached the area, the helicopter spotlight above made it seem nearly day. Joe held at a hover high above, but the noise still made it difficult to be heard. "We're almost there," Luke observed, stating the obvious. Henry and Jackie had disappeared ahead a few minutes earlier.

"Is that gas I smell?" Sharon asked.

"Yes. It's dissipating with this downdraft."

The sounds were reaching them now, men's clipped words and shouts of direction. They followed another turn in the creek bed and the van appeared.

It faced up into the woods at an angle,

driven up an embankment and into a cluster of young birch trees, branches rubbing against the top of the van and the tires mired in torn-up foliage and fallen logs. The van leaned heavily to the right, suggesting flat tires or a broken axle.

Four officers were working at the side of the van. Heavy gloves protecting their hands, they were pulling at an opening they created, peeling back the metal by force. "That's good enough. Let me look."

The group stepped back a step as one officer tried to angle his light inside and still see through the opening.

"She's in there!"

Sharon stiffened and Luke tightened his grip.

"Is she alive?" Henry asked quietly.

"I can't tell. I need more light, a better angle." The officer stepped back. "Try to force it down with that crowbar, two more inches, and I can see past the backseat."

They resumed work on the metal, forcing it to give. The officer pressed in tight to the van's side trying to stabilize the light. "She's breathing. She's definitely breathing. We need cutters in here."

Sharon hugged Luke and he felt her shoulders began to shake. He hugged her briefly and hard and then gently passed her to Mark.

"Jackie, arrange for an ambulance at the road, and a medevac flight in as close as they can get to that bridge," Henry ordered. He turned to officers around him. "Blankets, a stretcher, and lights for the trail. Call in help. I want a mile cordon around this area to keep reporters out of this crime scene." Officers took the orders with brisk nods and quickly moved to comply.

Luke joined the officers at the van. "Let's get her out of there."

"There's a lot of dried blood," the officer whispered.

"We'll deal with it. Just get this wide enough so we can get inside."

"I need a thicker piece of wood to use as a fulcrum for the crowbar. It's got to handle more pressure than the metal. We're running out of rust-weakened metal to work with and coming up against rivets."

"Whoa guys, stop!"

Luke turned to the officer close to the front of the van.

"Those wires are wrapped around a block of something that I don't want to guess what it is. We can't rock the van like this. Those wires are swinging like strands of Christmas lights in the wind."

"We can't wait for a bomb squad to get here."

"Find more wood. We can wedge it under the van to stabilize it. If we brace it right, the van isn't going to move even when we get inside."

Luke listened to the debate among the officers and nodded. "It will work."

They hurried to get enough wood under the van to steady it. "Good, that will do it. Let's get inside and get this done."

Luke put his muscle into pulling back the metal panel. It began to give as a seam was reached. "More, that's it!"

The opening widened so that Luke could see through to the officer at the front. Caroline lay in the front where the first bench seat had been removed, her head resting against the side of the captain's seat. Her left arm was broken. He could see the bad angle where the bone penetrated her skin and the blood saturating her sleeve. The gag tight around her mouth looked like it had drawn blood too. As hard as he watched, he saw no movement that indicated she was gaining consciousness.

"Any wires to contend with back here?" Luke asked.

The officer was able to get his head inside the van to better follow the light. "We're clear." He pulled back and they resumed work. It reached the point where they could use rocks to hammer the metal back.

"I can get in there," Luke finally said, stopping the work. "Get me above it so I can lower myself in through the opening." He stepped up on the wood braces and grabbed the cargo rack railing on the top of the van to lift himself up, relieved the wood bracing did its job and held the van steady. He heard his coat tear as the metal grabbed it.

Where to put his feet was a problem. He held himself suspended until he was certain he was coming down on the seat and it wouldn't give and send him crashing onto Caroline. "I need more light!"

He braced himself inside, one foot on a seat and the other on the floor.

They passed him three flashlights and he positioned them around himself.

She was breathing; he could see the faint movement of her chest. Luke didn't let himself linger on how much pain showed on her face. "I need a knife."

The pocketknife the officers had to offer was no larger than the one in his pocket.

Luke carefully cut away the gag and removed the fabric from her mouth. He ran a finger gently across the cut edge of her mouth. He turned his attention to the tape binding her hands. His hand shook as he eased her once-bound hands to her sides. He was almost glad she was unconscious; that broken arm looked bad. He gently turned her head to see if he was also dealing with a head wound causing the unconsciousness. "I need Sharon."

"I'm right here, Luke."

He turned. Sharon looked away from Caroline to meet his gaze only briefly before her attention returned to her sister.

"Her hands are icy; she's not responsive. Can she be moved, Sharon?"

"Your priorities have to be breathing, blood, then bones. That injury is going to rip open and bleed again when she's moved. We don't have medics here yet with the supplies I would need to deal with it, so for now, let's wait."

Luke nodded. Unzipping his coat, he tugged it off and spread it over Caroline, hoping the warmth would hold long enough to help her. He picked up one of the flashlights and turned his attention to the seats.

"See if one of the officers has tools — a

screwdriver, a wrench. Getting the seats out will help."

Luke could hear work going on outside and knew Henry would be looking at options to widen that opening even further. Lifting Caroline up and out without causing undue pressure or movement on her shoulder or arm — they needed options.

Henry appeared with the tools Luke needed to free the seat. "The gas tank is being drained, and we're working on a way to use a hand torch to widen this opening if we can figure out how to control the sparks."

"I'd rather figure out that option then deal with those wires up front and whatever else Frank left as his surprise. The downdraft should help us with the fumes. Still, I'd rather move Caroline as soon as we can, even if we have to lift her through this hole. How long on the medical help?"

"Firemen and paramedics are bringing supplies and a stretcher down the trail now."

"We move her one way or another as soon as they arrive." Luke forced the seat up from the floor. "Let's get this out of here."

The seat was awkward and almost larger

than a person. Two-thirds of the way through it jammed. Luke put his shoulder into it but couldn't get the leverage to turn it.

"Hold on, Luke."

The seat rocked as officers outside tugged at it. Luke felt the metal suddenly give. "Okay. That should do it."

They yanked the seat out.

Breathing hard, Luke stepped back. Without the seat as an obstacle, he had more options. If he turned Caroline and lifted her so her face looked to the sky — her shoulders would clear without a problem. Once her torso cleared, her legs would be no problem. He shone the flashlights around and reached for the floor mats. He used the heavy fabric to cover the worst of the sharp metal.

"The medics are here."

"I need something to keep her arms immobile."

"This will do the job." They passed him a mesh sock that stretched to become a cocoon around her torso, holding still her shoulder and arm. Luke tried not to look at Caroline's face as he worked, knowing that would slow him down and cloud his vision with more tears. "Hang on, honey. We're almost out of here."

He set the flashlights out of his way. "Are you ready?"

"We're ready."

"Don't pull her; let me lift her from below." He slid his hands behind her back and lifted her.

Hands reached in to steady her through the opening.

"Her arm —" Luke gasped.

"I've got her," Henry said, his hands under her head and sliding past the injury to make certain her arm stayed immobile. Her tennis shoe rubbed on the metal and then she was out.

Luke pulled himself out of the van as they laid Caroline down.

They were almost free of this nightmare.

Caroline disappeared from his sight as Sharon and the paramedics took over.

Luke ran the back of his hand across his face, wiping away sweat, tears, worry. She was out of that death trap — and alive. *Thank You, God.*

Mark joined him. "You okay?"

His smile felt real. "Fine."

He watched them work as paramedics reached for IV bags and Sharon ripped open pressure bandage packets to stop the renewed bleeding. *Not quite fine.*

Luke took a seat on the nearest fallen

log. If they had abandoned the search until morning, Caroline would not have been found alive. It was that close. His hands quivered.

God, I'm sorry I doubted a good outcome was possible. I forgot that nothing is impossible with You.

Mark sat beside him and offered a candy stick. "They work well for stress."

Luke accepted it. "This wasn't how I thought it would end."

"She survived; that's enough."

"It's a very bad break."

"Sharon and her colleagues are very good doctors."

Luke let his hands rest across his knees, exhaustion taking hold. "One week of this stress is enough to kill you."

"When this is over, we're all taking a long vacation somewhere with a beach, good food, and no press."

"I like your thinking, Mark."

"If the medical crews have room, I'll let Sharon go to the hospital with Caroline while I swing home to pick up Benjamin. I think he'd rather spend some time at the hospital with us than be home without us."

"I think that's wise. It will be good for him to see everyone together again, to see for himself that Caroline is okay."

"What about you?"

"If they tell me Caroline is stable, then I've still got work to do tonight. Frank is no longer a factor, but the man who hired him — he's still out there."

"You really think it was Jason Fromm?"

"Frank could have chosen that name as a diversion, but if he did, you would figure we could locate Fromm. He's not in Atlanta where he told his staff he was heading."

"Luke!" Sharon turned and waved for him to join them.

He surged to his feet and hurried over. "Right here."

She moved aside to let him in beside the stretcher. Caroline already looked better. Her broken arm sported a bright splint, and white pressure bandages were controlling the bleeding. They had washed her face of the blood traces and two IVs were going. The pain had eased; Luke could see the change in her face. The silver thermal blanket tucked around her looked cozy.

"Someone would like to say hi," Sharon said simply.

Luke started and looked back at Caroline. He suddenly realized her eyes were flickering.

"Caroline?"

Her eyes opened. "Hi."

He tried to keep his hand steady as he touched the side of her face. "You look beautiful."

She tried to smile. "Liar." She took a deep breath. "Thirsty."

Sharon pushed a straw into a water bottle and handed it to Luke.

"Right here." Luke lifted her head and helped her drink. She nodded her thanks and set aside the bottle.

"I love you," she said softly.

"I love you too," he replied calmly. "We need to get you to the hospital."

"Yeah. Sharon?"

"I'm here, sis."

"Frank broke my arm."

Sharon tugged a strand of Caroline's bangs as she smiled. "We'll fix it."

Luke looked at the paramedics. "Are we ready to go?"

"Yes. In preparation for the trip she's been given as much painkiller as we can risk."

Luke looked back down at her. "Caroline."

She looked up at him.

"Why don't you go back to sleep for a while? You're not going to miss anything on this walk."

"I'm tired. See you later?"

"Count on it."

Four firemen and paramedics lifted the stretcher from the ground. They held it steady as another thermal blanket was put beneath the stretcher and up over it, creating another layer to keep her warm.

Luke followed with Mark and Jackie on the slow walk to the road.

He watched as they loaded the stretcher into the ambulance.

Sharon came over to join him. "She's stable, Luke, and her vitals are strong. There will likely be a brief surgery tonight to clean the break, and then they'll give it some time for the swelling to subside before a second surgery sets her arm."

"Okay. I'll be a call away if anything changes, and I'll join you and Mark at the hospital later tonight. There's unfinished work to deal with."

She searched his face and then squeezed his hand. "Be careful."

"I will."

Sharon joined Caroline in the back of the ambulance.

"The medevac flight was able to land near the road junction. She'll be on the way to the hospital within a few minutes," Henry told him.

Luke nodded. "I'm going to find a radio and thank Joe." He looked at his partner. "Then I want the man who did this."

FORTY-SEVEN

Luke picked up a soda from the cooler and walked over to study the task force fact board at the sheriff's office. The timeline of events and discoveries since Friday's snatch were documented in a neat sequence of notes and photographs. The mood in the room was so different from the last time he had stood here. Men and women were relaxed, and occasional laughter was heard amidst the conversation.

"It's good to have Caroline back," the sheriff said, joining him.

"Wonderful," Luke replied with a smile. "Caroline was feeling well enough to tease her sister." Luke gestured to the board. "Talk to me about Jason Fromm."

"The only thing certain is the fact we can't find him. We've got Frank's word that Fromm was involved, but so far none of the independent evidence we've discovered confirms that."

"When was he last seen?"

"Around noon, when he left the bank, telling his staff he was going to Atlanta for a meeting tomorrow."

"Before the diamond ransom demand came in."

"Yes."

"Anything troubling in his finances? The man owns three homes, and from the one I saw, he is living very wealthy."

"He also owns a home in Atlanta. The Benton Bank is privately owned, and he's been president five years. I'd say those homes and his lifestyle are well beyond what the job pays, but I always heard he came from family money. It will take a federal auditor to tell us if fraud is going on at the bank." The sheriff sighed. "I'm beginning to wonder if he's dead."

"If he double-crossed Hardin as he said in his call, I would almost bet he was," Luke agreed. "Joe said something interesting. He said Frank was probably being literally correct — the man who hired him does live at 8754 Logan Road and Caroline was in the back of the white van; it was just abandoned somewhere other than that address."

"Half of Joe's statement has proven true."

"I want to search that address again. There's a safe room somewhere, and I'm still willing to bet we missed it in that sprawling home."

Jackie joined them and Luke offered her one of the French fries from his dinner. Luke finished the soda. "Think about the planning that was done for this kidnapping. It's elaborate. A safe room. Vehicles. A secondary place at the campsite. The details in the first ransom demand, the photos that showed they had been watching Sharon and Benjamin before the snatch."

"The man who planned this spent months preparing," Jackie guessed.

Luke nodded. "It sounds like a banker's personality — trying to control everything and yet stay a step removed from what's being done."

"Do you want to go out to the house tonight, or wait until the morning?"

Luke looked at his watch. "I'm not ready to sleep yet, not before this is done. Let's head out there now. If we come up empty handed again, then we'll regroup in the morning."

Luke shoved the initial paperwork of the day's events into a folder and leaned around to set it on the backseat of Jackie's car. "I'm going to owe you a few years' worth of doing your paperwork to make up for the weight you carried for me these last few days."

Jackie smiled. "You're welcome. We'll wrap up the details, Luke, then we can both take a vacation and put this far behind us."

"How many times did I step on Henry's toes?"

She laughed. "Not enough for him to mind. He said he'd be joining us once he's comfortable that van has been rendered safe for the crime scene technicians." She turned on the radio briefly, heard the news was on, and shut it off again. "The press has been clamoring to talk with you. You won't be able to avoid them for much longer."

"The media can wait another couple days until Caroline and Sharon decide how much they want to make public." Luke's smile faded. "Do you know a good psychologist? Sharon and Caroline are both going to need some time to decompress from this."

"So will you."

"There are days I wonder if I'm getting way too old for this."

"You were made for this job, Luke. How many other agents could handle what went down here this weekend? Not many."

"I appreciate the vote of confidence."

Jackie pulled into the driveway of Jason Fromm's guest home. "Where do you want to start?"

"With a measuring tape and a sketch pad."

"You know, it's possible the rooms were intentionally built in those odd angles, to hide a large walk-in safe or a private closet."

"I'm a bit suspicious about the height Sharon described for the room. This place might be built with a height difference between the floors, an intentional void built to let them hide things like one of those safes, to expand the heating and cooling vents for greater distances so they don't have to put in as many between floor casings." Luke changed the batteries in his flashlight while he waited for the sheriff to join them. "When did they seal the house?"

"Shortly after the dogs completed their search."

Luke used his pocketknife to slice the police tape on the front door. The sheriff let them in, two of his deputies joining them.

"We'll start in the basement and see what can be traced regarding the plumbing," the sheriff offered.

"Jackie and I will start on the second floor." Luke found the lights and led the way upstairs.

"Did you hear something?" Jackie asked, pausing at the landing.

Luke stopped to listen. "It sounds like a faucet dripping."

She shook her head. "It sounds more like rain." She reversed directions and returned to the main level. Luke followed her.

She turned on lights in the study. A drop of water splashed on the desk, a small puddle now forming on the polished wood. "Where is that water coming from?"

Luke studied the light fixture above the desk. "There, off that decorative leaf. It's coming through around the base of the light."

Luke moved the wingback chair over and stepped up on it to tap the ceiling. He reached over and removed the ceiling hook for a planter. Water poured down in a thin stream. "Where does this study put us relative to the second floor?"

"We're somewhere under the master bedroom suite."

"I suggest we follow the water. I have a feeling it's a neon sign to what we seek."

"A leaking pipe — water might be running all the way along the pipe until it reaches a bend before it drips down. The leak could be anywhere."

"True. But this leak looks new, or at least it's gotten worst very recently. The officers would have noticed this."

Jackie led the way back upstairs and to the master bedroom suite.

Luke stood in the doorway and listened. "It's quiet."

"I don't see signs of wet carpet. The source of the leak must be under this flooring." Jackie turned on lights in the master bathroom and knelt to open the cabinet below the sink and pulled out items. "It's dry here."

"And it's dry around the stool."

After a moment's thought, Luke walked back into the bedroom and shoved back the bedspread. "It's not a full or partial waterbed mattress."

He paced away from the window until he was about the same distance into the room as the desk was in the office below them. "It's pooling somewhere about here."

"If we're wrong, we pay for either carpet or for ceiling plaster."

"Carpet is a lot less messy and a whole lot cheaper. Tell the sheriff to shut off the water and then bring up a camera. We'd better document what I'm about to do." Luke studied the furniture, trying to decide what to move in order to roll the carpet up and give him access to the flooring.

"Move the bookshelf. We can pull the carpet back in the closet to see if its been tacked or glued down, and then keep rolling it back out into the room."

"Okay."

"I'll be right back." Jackie headed downstairs.

Luke unloaded the bookcase and moved it into the hallway.

He turned his attention to the closet. "Jason does love suits." He pushed them aside to move the items on the floor. He'd need a hammer or a screwdriver and a couple pairs of pliers to lift the carpet.

The guy loved shoes like he did suits. Luke moved the shoes and pulled out the elaborate shelves. He picked up the top half and carried it into the hall. He knelt to lift the lower half of the shelf and froze. The seam in the paneling looked split.

He set aside the shelf unit and turned his attention to the wall. There was a split, a subtle one, but a break. He started looking for a horizontal break and found it, right along the edge of the floorboard. It appeared as part of the wall.

He couldn't find any mechanism to open the panel.

"What is it?"

Luke started as Jackie stopped behind him. "I found the room. I just can't figure out how to get into it." He traced the seams for her.

He began tapping the wall. The panel moved. "Got it!"

It swung to the left, and behind it he found waffled foam. "There's the soundproofing." He tugged out the soundproofing panels. An angry voice cursing the water echoed through what looked like a solid piece of metal.

"Well whaddya, know. That voice sounds very much like Jason Fromm." Luke picked up the hammer Jackie had brought up with her and struck the metal plate, the impact ringing through the master bedroom and the concealed room. The words stopped.

He sat down and leaned against the closet wall across from where the suit jackets hung and rested his arms across his knees.

"You're not going to open it?" Jackie asked, surprised.

Luke looked at his watch. "Give him another twenty minutes to think about the fact we know where he is. You and I both know what a killer it is to wait and wonder what's going to happen or when."

Jackie sat in the doorway. "I could order in a pizza for us."

Luke laughed. "Now that has a definite appeal." He tugged out his phone and dialed. "Henry, come join us."

FORTY-EIGHT

Luke parked in the upper level of the hospital parking garage and shut off the car. He leaned his head back against the headrest, feeling a week's worth of exhaustion overwhelming him. There were so many things he wanted to enjoy with Caroline in the years ahead. God had to give second chances.

Would she be able to set aside the trauma enough to keep her confidence about life? Would it leave her fearful and scared every time he took a page from work? The uncertainties of what was ahead were too much to face this morning.

He picked up the roses from the passenger seat and locked his car. The reporters were being kept away by security. Luke lifted a hand to the officer on duty and headed up to the surgical floor. Sharon was already pulling strings among friends so the doctors coming to Caroline's aid were some of the best in the state. They were confident she'd regain nearly full use of her broken arm with time. He joined Mark and Benjamin in the waiting room.

The boy had his toy cars out. "Nice track, Benjamin."

"Thanks."

"It's done?" Mark whispered.

Luke took a seat beside his cousin. "Henry said Jason Fromm gave a full confession and is looking for a deal on the bank fraud and kidnapping to avoid accomplice to murder charges."

"When do I get to land a fist in his face?"

"Stand in line. Sharon's in with her?"

Mark nodded. "They're just moving Caroline to recovery now. The initial surgery went well."

"Sharon still figures she'll be sedated for the day?"

"They want to keep her under, give her about four hours of IVs, then set the arm."

Luke winced at the image.

"You're welcome to return to the condo with us and get some sleep. We'll be back for the surgery this afternoon."

"Thanks, but I think I'll hang out here. She might not be able to remember what I say, but I'll take the time I get with her anyway."

Mark smiled. "I wouldn't let her out of your sight for a while. Luke, for everything — thanks."

"Anytime, Mark. We're family." Luke held his cousin's gaze, and the man nodded. Whatever life threw at them, it was going to be faced together.

"Mom."

Benjamin got up as Sharon joined them. "Dad said I could maybe keep one of the kittens."

She smiled at Mark over Benjamin's head and knelt to straighten the boy's shirt. "One or all of them?"

"All of them if you said it was okay."

"Yes, it's okay." She rose and took a seat beside Mark. "Caroline's doing fine, Luke. They'll be ready for us to come back and see her in a few minutes." She turned her attention back to her son.

Luke listened to Sharon and Benjamin, watched Mark, and thought again what a good family photo they made. He folded his hands across his chest and glanced at the clock. One more long day ahead. They couldn't keep Caroline in the hospital forever. He'd catch up on his sleep once she was finally home.

★ ★ ★

Caroline stirred and her eyes flickered as she woke. Luke leaned against the side rails of the hospital bed, watching her every move. The pain lines were finally banished from her face. She looked so peaceful sleeping, he almost hated to see her waken. He waited until she opened her eyes and turned her head toward him. "Hi, beautiful."

"Hi, yourself. You look tired."

He smiled at her simple words. "Probably. I don't remember when I last slept."

He brushed hair back from her face, spreading the fine blond strands across the pillow. They had washed her hair and it was beginning to curl.

"Having you rescue me was . . . really nice."

"You took a few years off my life," he replied, finding her hand and making sure the covers were tucked in around her to keep her warm.

She looked around at the flowers and cards. "It appears as if I've slept through most of my company. What time is it?"

He looked at his watch. "About ten. It's Saturday night," he added, anticipating the next question. Two surgeries and more doctors than he cared to remember had made it a very long day for her.

"How are Sharon and Benjamin?"

"Mark said they both slept without nightmares last night. Sharon's strong; she seems to be recovering quickly. Would you like to talk with her? I can get her on the phone for you."

"In a bit." She took a deep breath and let it out as a sigh. "I understand better how heavy your job can be on you. This week was brutal."

"Silver linings, Caroline?"

She gave him a small smile. "Between those brief moments of terror were long stretches of agonizing uncertainty and boredom. It was eye-opening. I think I'll stick to being a teacher."

He squeezed her hand.

She studied his face for the longest of times, and he didn't break the silence.

"I'm sorry I didn't leave you a note," she whispered.

"I understood why."

She shook her head. "When I didn't know how it would all end, that ripped me up more than anything else. That I hadn't left a note to say good-bye, to say again I love you."

Luke stilled as she reached up to wipe away the tears on his face. He turned his head and kissed her fingers. "I love you too, honey. And the hours that passed after we found the car and the blood on the seat until we found you . . ." He couldn't finish the thought.

"I know."

"It's okay, what you did. I know the choice you faced with Sharon's life allegedly in your hands. You did what you had to do."

"You're a generous man." She lowered her hand and smiled. "How long are they going to keep me here?"

"A few days."

She settled back against the pillows. "I think when I get out of here, we should plan another weekend for the family. A baseball game, a movie, a nice dinner out . . ."

"You've got a deal."

Her eyes drifted closed and she was silent for a long stretch. Luke eased back, knowing she'd be drifting in and out of sleep for the rest of the night.

"What did Frank want as ransom for me?" she asked, startling him.

"Ten million in diamonds."

She opened her eyes just enough to see him. "Why are you smiling?"

"Since we got the package back, I figured I might keep a few of the stones rather than return them all. They would make a nice ring."

"If that's your way of asking if I like diamonds, I love them. But your timing could use a little work. Did you notice which hand is in plaster?"

He stilled her words with his hand. "I'll work on the timing; you go back to sleep. I'll still be here in the morning."

She smiled as she closed her eyes. "Thanks for the pleasant dreams."

"You're welcome." He leaned over and kissed her softly on the forehead, then sat back to resume his vigil. The storm was past. Life was good again. He enjoyed the stillness of the moment.

"Did you bring me roses? I seem to remember you saying you brought me roses," she murmured, not opening her eyes.

"I did."

"That's nice. I like roses."

She didn't say anything else. A brief time later he saw her drift fully back to sleep. "I like roses too," he whispered.

Luke watched Caroline sleep and let himself dream. It wouldn't be so hard blending their lives together, living in Benton near Mark and Sharon, and driving in to work at Sandy Hill for the day. When he needed to be gone overnight, Mark would be around to keep an unobtrusive eye on her and keep her safe. They would finish that tree house for Benjamin, and one day Caroline and his kids could join in the fun.

Life had been too serious lately. It was time to put work back to being a slice of life and not the whole pie. Caroline needed him and he needed her. He reached over to slide his hand around hers and stretched out to take a catnap.

A vacation sounded good. Mark's suggestion of a beach, sunny skies, and no reporters fit what they all needed. Somewhere romantic so he could propose, somewhere Caroline would consider a nice place to return to each year to renew the memories.

Luke thought about the photo in his pocket — Caroline in her bridesmaid finery at Sharon's wedding — and started mentally planning a wedding. She'd make a beautiful bride. Benjamin would want to carry the ring.

"What are you smiling about?"

He turned his head resting on the back of the chair. "You. And you're supposed to be sleeping."

"I'd rather just talk to you."

He shared a smile with her. "The roses got your attention."

"The confidence of the man delivering them. You forgot to kiss me properly."

"I didn't forget. I'm under orders not to take your breath away."

She laughed softly and tugged his hand. "Come here."

He leaned over to kiss her properly, letting the kiss linger. "Are you sure you're going to be okay?"

"I'm going to be fine. Promise."

He rested his head against hers for a moment, then leaned back. "You've got to sleep. I promise, no bad dreams are coming. I'll be right here to chase them away."

Her hand around his tightened, and she closed her eyes with a soft sigh. Luke kissed her fingers and tucked her hand back under the blanket. He settled back to watch her sleep.

For tonight, he had the most important job in the world.

Discussion Questions

1. At the beginning of the book, Mark reflects on how it has been worth it to move from Atlanta to Benton for the sake of his new family. Have you ever made similar sacrifices for your family? What difference has it made for them? Was it worth it?

2. Early in the book, Mark thinks Luke and Caroline won't have a long-term relationship because Luke so often cancels their plans because of work. What kind of balance do you find for work and family? How does that affect your relationships? Your work? Are you pleased with the result?

3. Sometimes Luke feels like a failure because he has to face Caroline or Mark or Benjamin or Sharon with bad news. How does he cope with that? If you've ever felt like a failure,

how did you cope with it?

4. We expect evil from obvious bad guys like Frank Hardin, but Caroline didn't think Gary could possibly be the stalker, and Mark never suspected that Jason Fromm, his banker, was behind the kidnapping attempt. Have you ever been betrayed by a friendly acquaintance? How did that affect you? How did it affect the way you view people?

5. Caroline trades places with Sharon, becoming a hostage. Do you think she was wise to do this? What would you have done in her place? Are there people in your life you would risk your life for? Who are they?

6. After Caroline swaps for Sharon, Luke's experience in law enforcement keeps him from hoping that Caroline will still be alive. Does your life experience ever blind you to hope? If so, how?

7. Luke was ready to quit searching for the white van when he learned that Frank was dead, but they decided to keep going as long as they had flares and fuel for the helicopter. If Luke had given in to despair and called off the search that night, Caroline prob-

ably would have died. Have you ever been tempted to despair? How did you handle it? What was the result?

8. When Caroline is in the van, she thinks about her relationship with Luke and that if she had it to do all over again, she'd be more patient with the ups and downs and canceled plans. Have you ever been impatient with relationships? What effect did that have?

9. The day her family disappears, Caroline reads the following Scripture: "Every one then who hears these words of mine and does them will be like a wise man who built his house upon the rock; and the rain fell, and the floods came, and the winds blew and beat upon that house, but it did not fall, because it had been founded on the rock. And every one who hears these words of mine and does not do them will be like a foolish man who built his house upon the sand; and the rain fell, and the floods came, and the winds blew and beat against that house, and it fell; and great was the fall of it" (Matthew 7:24–29).

• In light of these verses, which characters do you think built upon the rock? Upon sand? Why?

- Have you ever built your trust on things that were sand? What was the result? Have you found things to be different when you put your trust in the Word of God? How?
- These verses don't say "if the rain fell" but rather "the rain fell, and the floods came, and the winds blew." Storms come into every life. What storms have rocked your life lately?

10. Luke didn't weather the storm of the kidnapping as well as Caroline, because over time he allowed the demands of his work to draw him away from a close relationship with God. What areas in your life interfere with your relationship with the Lord?

11. The national news includes kidnappings of women and children quite regularly. How do you deal with this reality in our culture? How can a person hold tight to the Lord and trust Him in light of it?

12. Through Benjamin's and Sharon's reactions to the trauma, Luke knew what it felt like to receive grace. How

have you received grace from others in your life? How have you given grace to others? What is the importance of treating others with grace?